ONE OF US WILL BE DEAD BY MORNING

ONE OF US WILL BE DEAD BY MORNING

DAVID MOODY

ST. MARTIN'S PRESS NEW YORK

ONE OF US WILL BE DEAD BY MORNING. Copyright © 2017 by David Moody. All rights reserved. Printed in the United States of America. For information, address St. Martin's Press, 175 Fifth Avenue, New York, N.Y. 10010.

www.stmartins.com

The Library of Congress Cataloging-in-Publication Data is available upon request.

ISBN 978-1-250-10841-8 (hardcover)
ISBN 978-1-250-10842-5 (ebook)

Our books may be purchased in bulk for promotional, educational, or business use. Please contact your local bookseller or the Macmillan Corporate and Premium Sales Department at 1-800-221-7945, extension 5442, or by email at MacmillanSpecialMarkets@macmillan.com.

First Edition: December 2017

10 9 8 7 6 5 4 3 2 1

TO DAD, WHO TOOK ME TO PLACES LIKE SKEK,
BUT ALWAYS MADE SURE I GOT HOME SAFE

MONDAY

1

The air here is filled with noise. The low, belly-shaking, rough-roaring engine grind clashes with the crashing of the waves. The freshness of the seawater salt tang is offset by the stench of diesel fumes. Rolling and tipping, listing this way then that, climbing the surf then crashing back down. It feels nonstop. Chaotic. Barely controlled. All-consuming.

And yet, over all of this, most of the kids are oblivious. The adults charged with looking after them struggle to make themselves heard: angry yells compete with excited, high-pitched screams and lose out every time. They're desperately trying to find their sea legs while the kids they're supposed to be looking after run rings around them. The patience of the adults is limited, already wearing thin. The energy of the kids, on the other hand, seems to know no bounds.

It's too early for this, Joanne Hillman thinks. She never wanted to come on this stupid school trip anyway, but Dad had made her. It might have been bearable if Jackie hadn't backed out last week (like she always does). And Louise has been acting weird all morning, keeping herself to herself and barely saying anything to anyone like the whole world's against her. Dad said it would be good for Joanne to spend some time away from home, to force her out of her shell and make her mix with people, but she's quite happy in her shell on her own, thank you very much, Dad.

She sits on the bench on the wooden deck and watches the churning waves, swinging her feet and pulling her waterproof jacket tight around her to keep out the cold and the spray. She should still be in bed. Normally she wouldn't be up for hours yet. She'd just about got used to the idea of being away from home, but the colly-wobbles (as Mum calls them) set in last night, and right now she'd rather be anywhere but here. She feels sick: a combination of the constant rolling motion and her nervous belly. And this is just the beginning. She has a whole week to get through. *Grasp the opportunity,* Dad kept telling her yesterday. *Make the most of it. You'll be back before you know it.* Dad really does talk a lot of crap sometimes, Joanne thinks. Trouble is, when you're thirteen and a half, a week feels like forever.

She thinks about insignificant stuff to try to distract herself. If she wastes time thinking about nothing, she reckons, then the days should go by that much faster. She knows it's an illusion because time never speeds up or slows down, but right now that illusion is just about the only thing she's got left to hold on to. The week stretches out ahead of her like a prison sentence. Days and days away from home and her bedroom and the TV and the cat with no chance of early release. She's already marking time like a convict. About a hundred and seventy-five hours before she gets back, she's worked out. She puts in her headphones and cranks up the volume to drown everything out.

Too wrapped up in her music and her miserable, melancholy thoughts to care what's happening elsewhere, Joanne's blissfully oblivious of the chaos unfolding just meters away from where she's sitting. She doesn't hear the screams, she doesn't sense the panic, and she doesn't see the kid approaching. The kid who's about to kill her.

The first she knows of the attack is a vicious swipe around the left side of her head. The weapon is actually a length of chain taken from the safety railings, but when it hits, it feels rigid like a length of lead pipe, and it burns like nothing she's ever felt before. Joanne's on all fours with her ear split and blood running into her eyes and mouth before she knows what's happening. She gasps for breath, her mind in overload, struggling to work out what, who, how, and why and at the same time trying to cope with the most horrific pain imaginable. It fills her whole body, hurting so much it steals her breath from her lungs. Her arms give way and she hits the deck and rolls over onto her back, looking up into the rain and spray. She's numb and slow to move, and the chain lashes down again and again. She instinctively raises her hands to protect her face, but it does her no good. Busted fingers, split skin, broken teeth, more blood, and so much more pain that it almost stops hurting.

The last three things she thinks before she loses consciousness are *I'm really scared. I want Dad.* Then *I know you . . . why are you hurting me?* And then *Am I going to die now?*

Joanne passes out and her killer loses interest. Job done.

As a hastily improvised weapon, the coiled chain-whip is devastatingly effective. Simple and brutal. A single lash cuts down two more unwitting victims. Bones snap like dry twigs. Lesions and lacerations. Blood everywhere. Indiscriminate. Unchecked. Unstoppable.

A boy cowering way over to the killer's right tries to run for cover, but his way through is blocked by Joanne's fallen body, and all that his frantic, scrambling movement achieves is to draw attention to his being there. Might as well have painted a target on his back. The attack is fast and intense and he's dead in seconds.

Belowdecks the engine grind muffles the noise. A sudden

stampede from above is the first indication that something's wrong: a flood of kids running for cover, tripping and falling over one another down slippery wet metal steps to get out of the way.

When Roger Freeman goes up to investigate, his first reaction is utter disbelief. The disbelief is immediately replaced by panic. It takes a couple of seconds for him to fully comprehend what he's seeing because it's so unexpected and so wrong. It's a damn massacre. Death and violence everywhere. He forces himself to go out onto the deck—no plan, just a sense of duty and his instinct to protect driving him forward—but he's held up by the mass of terrified kids still trying to go the other way.

Roger's in clear space now, and as he walks out onto the deck, the killer strides toward him with a vicious intent way beyond her years. She's growing in confidence with every attack, beginning to understand what she's doing and why she's doing it. A small boy gets in the way at the exact wrong moment, and within range of her unforgiving chain weapon, he bears the brunt of the savage strike meant for Roger. All Roger wants is to run, but adrenaline keeps him focused. He does what he can to try to halt the inexplicable massacre, acting without thinking because he's responsible for these kids and he knows that every second he delays, more of them will die.

The weapon lashes down across another young face, spraying blood and spit and teeth. The end of it flails and wraps around a handrail, and Roger lunges and grabs it before she can uncoil it and whip it back. He grips even tighter as the chain is almost yanked from his grasp, then he uses it to reel in the killer.

Roger's acutely aware of the risk he's taking and the danger he's now facing. But it doesn't feel like danger. There's confusion more than anything else because he's struggling to understand how and why things have changed, and what the kid in front of him has become. Earlier this morning the two of them sat and chatted at the harbor while they waited to leave, talking in depth about nothing in particular as the sun rose over the town. Roger was reassuring and supportive as ever, offering whatever advice he could. The kids all like Roger. They trust him. *She* trusted him.

But now he can't understand the look in his soon-to-be-murderer's eyes. This morning an innocence was there, an unspoken vulnerability. Typical early teenage cockiness, the first inkling of maturity tempered with an undeniable childlike fragility bubbling just below the surface. She was telling him about the boy bands she likes, and he was teasing her about their pretty-boy looks and how all bands sound the same to him these days, and how music was real music when he was a lad with proper instruments and lyrics that meant something. She took it all in good spirits and they laughed and joked about the gulf between their likes and dislikes until it was time to get on the boat.

All gone now.

Nothing left but *the Hate*.

Roger tries to fight back as best he can, but it's difficult when you don't want to hurt the person who's trying to kill you. Holding the chain in one hand like a dog's leash, he swings a reluctant punch, which misses its mark. Off-balance now, he struggles to keep track of his assailant, who, lightning fast, driven by an intense ferocity he himself clearly lacks, slips around and behind him and reverses their positions. She climbs up onto a wooden bench, wraps the chain around his neck, then pulls harder and harder until Roger's eyes bulge wide. As he starts to choke, she bites down and takes a zombielike chunk out of the side of his neck. But there's no horror-movie flesh eating here, just unadulterated and uncontained aggression, an insatiable desire to kill. She yanks her head back, teeth still clamped down hard, and tears away a ragged ribbon of skin.

Utter mayhem is everywhere now. Hysteria. Bodies strewn across the deck. Everyone's aware of what's happening, but on the boat there's no possibility of escape and they all know it. The solitary lifeboat is ignored in the panic and confusion of the moment. Some kids jump overboard in desperation, figuring that even the slightest sliver of possible salvation in the ice-cold water is better than no chance at all. Others run from the diminutive killer en masse, doing whatever they can to put maximum distance between themselves and their inevitable deaths. They fight with one another to get away. Friendships are forgotten, relationships betrayed. In the blink of an eye, everything has been reset. All that matters now is self-preservation. Fuck everyone and everything else.

Following the lead of others they've seen, even more of them jump now, succeeding only in assuring themselves of a different kind of death, maybe even bringing the end of their lives forward by a few minutes. But then again, maybe that's not such a bad thing? Perhaps still having a choice counts for something as your final minutes and seconds tick away? When faced with almost certain annihilation, is there something to be said for going out on your own terms, or is it better just to resign yourself and let it happen? The quicker and more violent the end, perhaps, the less it will hurt overall.

Or maybe there's no thought to any of this, no reasoning. Just instinct. Panic and dread.

The killer is becoming increasingly assured, feeding off the cumulative fear of her victims. She had a few anxious seconds before her first kill (hard to believe it was just minutes ago) when the nerves were hard to handle and the deed was hard to do. But the longer she's been in the grip of the Hate, the easier it has become. It's not a case of wanting to kill, it's about *having* to do it. And like the few remaining Unchanged, who herd away like frightened sheep from a hungry wolf, the killer is equally concerned with self-preservation. The only way to ensure she stays alive is to eliminate the enemy. Every last fucking one of them.

The Unchanged are no match for the unbridled ferocity of a Hater. They cannot compete with the girl's instinctive aggression. There's an unspoken clarity and certainty to this Hater's blood-lust, and there's only one way this is going to end.

The Hate is here, and there is no escape.

2

There he is.

Paul O'Keefe climbs over the low rise and looks down toward the thin stretch of shingle shore. He's been sent out to find his colleague Matthew Dunne, and after walking half the length of the island, he's finally found him. Matt's standing at the water's edge looking out to sea, the low waves stopping just short of the toes of his boots. Frigging idiot.

Matt turns around when he hears Paul's heavy footsteps crunching through the shingle behind him.

"What the hell are you doing out here, Matt?"

"Enjoying the silence. Well, I was."

"You're supposed to be back at base. Ronan's having a fit."

Matt's face drops and he checks his watch. Panic. "Shit. I lost track of time. Is he annoyed?"

"He's not impressed. What are you doing out here, anyway? Playing at being the last man on Earth?"

"Nothing. I was just thinking."

"What about?"

"Just stuff."

Paul sighs. "Bloody hell, Matt, you're hard work, you know that?"

Matt just shrugs. "I just lost track of time."

"You certainly did, mate. You've been gone ages."

"What can I say, I like my own space."

"You mean you're antisocial?"

"No."

Paul stands next to Matt and admires the view. Immense yet undeniably unimpressive. Gray nothingness for as far as Paul can see. "Be pretty cool to be the only one left on the planet though, wouldn't it?"

"You think? No thanks."

"Why not? I'd have thought that was your ultimate fantasy. Imagine it, you could do what you like, when you like. Go anywhere, do anything, wouldn't have to talk to anyone else . . ."

"Well, that might be what it's like in the films, but I don't expect it'd be that easy. Imagine the responsibility you'd have."

"What responsibility? There'd be no one else to think about, no one else to answer to."

"I know, but you'd have to sort out your food and keep yourself warm and occupied."

"And that's an issue because . . . ?"

"Boredom would be a real problem, I expect. A real mental challenge."

"You're a mental challenge."

Matt ignores him. "It's not just a question of eating tinned food and living the life of Riley, you know. What if you got sick? What if you had an accident and hurt yourself?"

"Jesus, you're such a bloody killjoy. You suck the excitement out of everything."

"I don't."

"You do. You spend too much time thinking and not enough time doing, that's your problem."

"Didn't know I had a problem."

"Well, we both will have if we don't get back to base pronto. Ronan wants us all together."

"Why?"

Paul holds his hands up. "Don't ask me. I'm just the messenger. You know what he's like."

"Yeah, I know exactly what he's like."

The two of them start walking back. The breeze down here is bracing: it whips off the sea then blows back off the headland, seeming to come at them from all directions at once. Apart from the wooden jetty jutting out into the waves way over to their left and the overgrown remains of a concrete World War II gun turret perched on the top of the rise above them, nothing else man-made is visible from here.

"So what exactly were you thinking about out there on your own then?" Paul asks again, shouting over the wind and waves.

Matt knows Paul won't let up until he tells him. "Just what an interesting place Skek is."

"Interesting? Fuck me, Matt, it's a rock in the middle of the ocean. It's about as interesting as any other rock, just harder to get to than most."

"And harder to get off."

"Exactly."

"You'd be surprised, though. It's got quite a history. I did some research before we got here."

"See. What did I say? You think about things too much. You're such a nerd." They climb a couple of rough-hewn wooden steps, then approach the end of the jetty. It was only built a few months ago apparently, but it's so discolored and weatherworn it looks like it's been here for a hundred years.

"There's nothing wrong with taking a little interest in your surroundings. Did you know the Danes arrived here first in the late 1800s? That's where those fishing cottages are from."

"Fishing cottages? There's nothing left of them but a couple of piles of rocks. Barely even any walls. I wouldn't have even known they were there if Natalie hadn't pointed them out."

"You can't begin to imagine how harsh it must have been living here."

"It's still pretty harsh if you ask me. Maybe that's why the Danes saw sense and fucked off home."

"I think I read that they died out, actually."

"No surprise."

"They were here for about seventy years, I read, then the place stayed unoccupied until the army moved in, in the sixties."

"And moved out again pretty quickly, from what Stuart said. Do you have a direct line to Wikipedia? Ever thought of applying to be a tour guide?"

"No," Matt answers quickly, oblivious of the sarcasm. "Then there was a whole load of research scientists based here in the eighties. . . ."

"Who all disappeared mysteriously, didn't they? No known survivors, I heard."

"That's rubbish."

"I know it is. You've got to admit, though, it's the perfect setup for a movie."

"Is it? Depends on the kind of movies you watch, I suppose."

"Anyway, I heard about them too. They also disappeared after a few years once they'd discovered there was nothing here worth researching. Can you see a pattern emerging?"

"I guess," Matt admits.

"So by that logic I don't give Hazleton Adventure Experiences much longer before they see sense and pack up and move on too."

"I think you're wrong. I actually think Rod Hazleton's onto a winner here. It's a solid business model. He's got the transport sorted, a fairly reliable power source, and he's got the infrastructure left by the army and the scientists to build on. They've already done the hard work for him. Should net him a decent return in the long run."

"Fascinating. Are you this interesting at home, Matt?"

"Are you mocking me again?"

"A little. I just wonder how Jen puts up with you. You check out every little bloody detail before you do anything. It must drive her crazy."

"It's called due diligence."

"It's called being boring as hell. Are you like this about sex too?"

Matt ignores him. He's used to this. "I make no apologies for being rigorous, Paul. I'm an accountant, and Ronan hired me because I'm a safe pair of hands. Your problem is you struggle to tell the difference between being boring and being cautious."

"I reckon it's the same thing."

"It's absolutely not."

"I'll ask your missus when I see her. If I ever meet her, that is. If she even exists."

"What's that supposed to mean?"

"No one's ever met her, that's all."

"She's not been well."

"It's being with you that does that."

They're at the top of the climb now. They pause next to the abandoned army lookout: a squat, two-meter-square rough concrete cube that would be the ideal place to look out over the ocean if it weren't overgrown with weeds. A bunch of huge white-tipped tufts hang out of the front of the structure like hairs in an old man's ears. Matt can't resist peering inside, ever curious. It's damp and empty. A gun turret without a gun. Barely even a turret. He fumbles in his pocket for his inhaler before they continue on their way. The damp is really getting on his chest this morning. "So what does Ronan want?" he asks, wheezing.

"One more group task, apparently."

"Another one? Shit, I thought we were done."

"Not quite. And he wants to do a postcourse debrief afterwards."

"Didn't we do that after breakfast?"

"No, that was the course preclosure assessment and evaluation session. Come on, mate, keep up. You know what he's like. There'll probably be a post-postcourse debrief when we get back on the ferry, then a post-post-postcourse debrief when we're back at work on Wednesday."

"Ronan can be such a dick."

"Yes, but he's the dick who pays our wages."

It's a short walk back to base from here. It's a short walk to anywhere on Skek. The island is just over three miles long and two miles across at its widest point. The main buildings sit grouped together on grassland just left of center: almost smack-bang in the middle, but not quite. The angular, rough gray shapes look at once both out of place and completely at home here. The barnlike stores building is nearest. The office, dorms, bathrooms, and kitchen are housed in the largest building, another couple of hundred meters away. It's rectangular with a flat roof, like a cinder block with windows, weirdly monolithic. Close by is a small shed with room for the generator and not a lot else. A little way over to the east—far enough to give the illusion of privacy but still close enough to be in shouting distance—is the prefabricated bungalow that is home to Stuart and Ruth Phillips, the island's only true residents (for eight months of the year, at least).

Distances are deceptive here on Skek. It looks like Matt and Paul still have a fair way to go, but in a couple of minutes they're there. "Everyone else already here?" asks Matt.

"Everyone but you."

Paul opens the door and ushers Matt inside. There's no escape—the door opens straight into the mess hall—and he enters to a sarcastic round of applause.

The slow clap is led by Ronan, their diminutive boss, standing center stage, all togged up in his designer survival gear. "Finally, Matthew. Glad you could find time in your busy schedule to join us."

Matt finds himself an empty chair and sits down between call-center team leader Rachel and Natalie, one of the Hazleton Adventure staff. "Sorry, Ronan, I didn't realize how long I'd been gone. I was checking out the sights."

"Sights?" IT manager Gavin Taylor mumbles. "Did you find any? We've been here since Friday and I've seen nothing worth writing home about."

Rajesh, another of the island team, quickly counters, "To be fair, Gavin, you've done everything you can to avoid leaving this building since you got here. You're never gonna see much if you spend all your time indoors looking at the walls."

"Gavin doesn't get out much," Frank Hall, Ronan's business continuity manager, says. "Typical IT nerd. He likes being on his own in the dark. He gets up to all kinds of things."

"Give it a rest, Frank," says Gavin. "Blokes like you are all the same."

"Blokes like me? What's that supposed to mean?"

"Homophobic arseholes."

"I'm not homophobic. I don't care what you do, as long as you keep it to yourself and I don't have to get involved."

"Don't flatter yourself, love," Gavin says, cranking up the camp. "I wouldn't touch yours if it was the only one left."

"I just wouldn't touch his full stop." Rachel giggles.

Ronan clears his throat the way he always does when he's struggling to keep control and make himself heard. "All right, all right, that's enough," he shouts over the hubbub, attempting to bring the rabble to order. "You'll be pleased to hear that we've got one final activity planned before we head home."

Cue groans of protest.

"I thought we were through with all this," office admin queen Joy grumbles from the corner, making no attempt whatsoever to disguise her displeasure.

"Not quite. I want us to maximize the limited time we have left on Skek, so Rajesh and Nils have arranged one last team-building and communication exercise."

"Team building, that's a joke," Stephen Hughes, the other call-center team leader, mumbles to himself. He looks directly across the room as he speaks, glaring at his manager, Vanessa, with his piggy eyes. "Yeah, right."

Vanessa hears him, but she doesn't react. Natalie does. She tugs Matt's arm and pulls him closer. "What's his beef?" she whispers. "He's been goading her all weekend."

"She just got the promotion he reckoned he'd been promised."

"Ah, right. Say no more. I really do not miss office politics one bit."

"Tell me we ain't going outside again," Joy says. "I've only just got dry from last time."

"No one cares what you look like out here, Joy," Gavin says. "No need to worry about your public image."

"Public image? There's no public but us on this damn island. Let's just get out there and get this over with. I'm ready to go home." She crosses her arms defiantly and slumps back in her seat.

"You're a real ray of sunshine, Joy." Rajesh laughs. "I swear, I've never met anyone with a more ironic name than you."

"I just tell it how it is, is all. I ain't got time for bullshit and corporate mumbo jumbo." She doesn't take her eyes off the boss.

Ronan looks away, embarrassed. "Right then, I'm off to the

gents before we get under way. I'll leave you in Nils's capable hands and I'll see you all out front in a minute or two."

And with that Ronan's gone. His staff visibly relax.

Nils swigs his coffee, then gets up from his chair. "Right then, folks. Who wants to murder a workmate?"

Wrapped up in waterproofs, the group assemble outside as instructed. The wind's whipping up, but Nils is used to the weather here. He's a distinctive-looking bloke: sinewy and trim, with long silver hair tied in a ponytail and a neatly trimmed goatee. He has to shout to make himself heard. The louder his voice, the stronger his Danish accent. "Okay, we started the weekend looking at trust and communication, and I want to see how far you've come in the time you've been here. I'm going to split you into two teams. Outside the stores building we've marked out a base that one team needs to defend from the other team's attacks."

"I wanna be on Joy's side," Paul says quickly. "No offense, Joy, but you terrify me."

"The attacking team will be given an object to smuggle into the other side's base, okay?"

"What kind of object?" Vanessa asks.

"That would be telling."

"It all sounds a bit childish to me," Rachel says. "Can't you boys play and the rest of us watch?"

"All of you are involved, no exceptions. If you have a problem, I suggest you take it up with your boss on the ferry home later, okay?"

"Waste of bloody time," she grumbles, then she looks up as Rajesh ties a length of lime-green wool around her arm. He's working his way around the group doing the same to everyone else. "What's this?"

"Your life," he tells her. "This breaks in the game and you're out. Dead. Kaput."

"Can't I just rip it off now and commit suicide?"

"And how exactly is that going to help your team?"

Nils continues, "If you lose your life, you must head back to your base to get a new one, understand? We've already split you up so Paul, Rachel, Ronan, and Frank—you're in defense. Stephen, Vanessa, Matt, Gavin, and Joy—you're the attackers. You five go with Raj over to the old fishing cottages. He'll show you what it is you need to smuggle in. When you're ready, Raj will fire a flare to start the game. I'll fire a second flare once the game's over."

"How long's it last?" Stephen asks, clock-watching. "Until we get it in?"

"You've got to get past me and Frank, first," Paul says, sounding more enthusiastic and competitive than the rest of them combined. "No chance, eh, Frank?"

Frank just grunts. He's had enough of all this now. He just wants to go home. "I'm too old for this shit."

"No hiding in buildings, no physical contact, the game lasts half an hour maximum," Nils tells them. "Any questions?"

Silence.

"Come on then," Vanessa says, resigned. "The sooner we get started, the sooner we get home."

3

The flare races up toward the clouds; searing, incandescent orange-white against countless shades of muted gray.

This reminds Matt of when he was in the Scouts, way back when. He might well be playing games with his work colleagues, but something about the location and the setup of this exercise has given him a genuine adrenaline rush. He's not the only one. Gavin's feeling it too, Matt can tell, and when Rajesh just now told them what they needed to smuggle into the base, the entire team talked tactics with childish enthusiasm. Now that they're on the move, on the attack, Matt's pulse is pounding.

"I bet they're shitting themselves," Gavin says as the two of them jog down the west flank of Skek.

"You reckon?"

"Absolutely. Ronan'll be telling Paul what to do, he'll be telling Ronan what to do, Frank will be doing whatever he feels like doing . . . between them they won't have a frigging clue what's going on."

They approach the main buildings and pause parallel with the narrow archery range to catch their breath. The archery targets, perversely, provide them with some welcome cover. "Nils said no hiding *inside* buildings, he didn't say anything about hiding behind them," Gavin whispers as they edge closer to the generator shed. They both press themselves against the back wall of the building like they're caught in the middle of a shoot-out.

The chugging noise of the machinery makes Matt feel safe and vulnerable at the same time. "Bit mad all this, isn't it?"

"Totally. Andrew's never gonna believe me when I tell him what I spent the morning doing," Gavin says.

He's about to step out into the open and start running again, but Matt pulls him back. "Wait. We've got plenty of time. Give them a minute longer."

"You think?"

"Absolutely. Paul and Frank will expect us to go steaming straight for them, screaming and shouting, all hell-for-leather. The longer we keep them waiting, the more agitated they'll be when we make our move. Keep them dangling long enough and they'll tie themselves up in knots."

"Very devious," Gavin says. "I like it."

Way over to the east, Stephen and Vanessa can be seen edging down the length of the island too. They're matching Matt and Gavin's progress, their fluorescent cagoules making it all but impossible for them to hide even from this distance. Stephen's rotund belly makes him look comical, like an escaped life buoy. Regardless, Matt finds seeing his teammates moving into position strangely exhilarating. It gives him an undeniable buzz being part of a group making a coordinated attack. It makes him feel like he's part of a tribe.

"Right, let's do it," Gavin says.

As they'd planned, Gavin and Matt sprint in the direction of the stores. They start together but quickly diverge, and a distant yell from Vanessa indicates that she and Stephen are doing the same (although she's already left her portly colleague in the dust). Four of them are now coming at the stores building base from different angles.

The defenders have been waiting for this and are primed.

Rachel runs at Gavin. She tries to catch hold of him, but although not at all athletic, he's tall and willowy and he slips her easily. Her feeble attack is less than convincing. Off-balance, she stumbles in the wet grass and gives him a mouthful.

Paul's in hiding. He's dumped his cagoule in the grass to make it look like he's somewhere else. He's done well to stay out of sight because places to hide are few and far between on this barren rock. He spots Matt and leaps up, adjusting his trajectory to cut him off. Matt tries to accelerate and change direction, but it's hard and his chest is rattling. A shimmy and a mistimed side step and the two of them end up face-to-face, just a couple of meters apart. "Gotcha," Paul says.

Matt holds back. "This is weird. We share an office. Don't you think playing games like this is weird?"

Clearly not.

Paul dives forward and takes Matt's feet from under him. The two of them roll over and over.

"No physical contact, Nils said," Matt complains.

Paul holds him down then snatches at his woolen life and yanks it from his arm. "Tough luck. You're dead, mate," Paul says, panting with effort.

"So are you," Matt quickly counters, and when Paul looks down, he sees that he's lost his life too. He was so busy killing Matt that he didn't notice Matt killing him.

"Jammy bastard," Paul says, genuinely annoyed. He gets up and runs back toward the base he's supposed to be defending, desperate to be back in the game.

Matt climbs to his feet and brushes himself down. He sees that Gavin's lost Rachel and is still managing to avoid being caught, despite now being pursued by both Frank and Ronan. He changes direction repeatedly, zigzagging, slowing down, then speeding up, taunting his unfit pursuers.

"You dead, Matt?" Rachel shouts to him.

"Yeah."

"Me too. What are we supposed to do now?"

"Go back and get another life, I guess."

"We should take our time. I'm in no rush."

Gavin is still managing to dodge Ronan and Frank, and everyone else is momentarily out of view when the second flare is fired into the air unexpectedly. Matt and Rachel look at each other, confused. "What? Is that it?"

"Must be," she says, and the two of them walk back toward the stores building.

Paul gets there before anyone else. "What happened?" he asks Nils. "Why did you stop the game?"

"Because you lost," Nils tells him.

"Bullshit. We can't have."

Nils moves out of the way so Paul can get a better view. Joy's casually sitting in a deck chair in the middle of the cordoned-off base area, an enormous grin on her face instead of the usual scowl.

"That showed you," she shouts. "You boys are all mouth, no trousers."

"Nice one, Joy," Gavin says as the others congregate.

"How the hell did you manage that?" Paul demands. "You must have cheated. Where's the thing you were supposed to be smuggling in?"

She waves at him again. "Here."

"Where?"

"It's me, dummy."

"What were you expecting?" Nils asks. "A bomb? Something valuable?"

"That's what this exercise is all about," Natalie, who has been observing, explains. "Challenging assumptions. You all assumed you'd be looking for something, not someone."

"This is bullshit. That's cheating," Paul says.

"No, tying your life around your arm again after you've been killed is cheating." She pulls at the luminous yarn he's miraculously reattached.

"I'm a zombie," he grumbles. "Deal with it."

"Face it, the other team got you good and proper. You assumed they'd all be as aggressive as you. You defenders were so busy attacking that you didn't notice Joy stroll around the back, quiet as anything."

"Bullshit. It's a con."

"You're a sore loser, Paul. Like I said, you were supposed to defend, not attack."

"You lost sight of your goal, mate," Nils says, laughing.

"Why have we stopped?" Ronan, late to the party, breathlessly asks. He takes off his glasses and wipes them clear of mist.

"Because they cheated," Paul says.

"Because you lost," Natalie corrects him.

"But that's impossible. They hadn't even started to—"

His words are abruptly truncated by a yell for help. Noises can be strangely difficult to pinpoint on Skek—the swirling winds and the general flatness of the landscape combine to make sounds seem directionless and camouflage their source.

Another flare. Fired from over toward the cliffs to the east. Rajesh is on the horizon, waving his arms wildly to the others.

Natalie and Nils look at each other momentarily, then sprint across the island to their colleague.

Stephen's close to the edge of the rock-climbing cliff, sitting on the wet grass like a lost kid left behind. He looks up when he hears the others. His movements are sluggish, and his chubby face appears distressingly vague; empty, almost. Ronan pushes his way to the front of the group. "What happened?"

Stephen doesn't answer. He just lifts his hand and points toward the edge. Rajesh is already hooking himself up to one of the climbing ropes. His face is ashen.

"Fuck's sake," Nils shouts. "What did I tell you people about getting too close to the edge? There's a fucking safety line marked, for crying out loud."

Paul ignores the cordon and moves toward the top of the cliff and peers over. Ronan waits a couple of meters back, legs heavy. His stomach flips when Paul leans right out over the edge. "Careful, Paul," he shouts.

"Did you not hear what I just said, Paul?" Nils bellows at him. "Get back."

Natalie pushes Paul away and takes his place, looking right over and down. "Fuck, fuck, fuck," she says.

"What's happened?" Ronan asks again, getting frantic now.

"Get your staff back to base," Rajesh yells to him as he starts his descent. "Nils, get the stretcher and bring it down the footpath. One casualty to bring up. Let Ruth know what's happened."

"For crying out loud, will someone tell me what's going on?" Ronan demands for a third time, desperate now.

Stephen's still sitting in the long grass, staring into space. He looks up and answers his boss. "Vanessa . . ."

Ronan defies orders and creeps closer to the edge. Vanessa is lying on the rocks about thirty meters directly below. Her pelvis is shattered and her right leg is snapped so badly that the heel of her foot is wedged under the small of her back. The back of her head has popped like a balloon. Sea spray steadily washes away the red. The waves gently move her body, but there's no question she's dead. Gulls swoop and caw around the corpse; throngs of them dart away from the cliff face, then race back again, skimming the waves. The bravest few strut around the dead woman as if staking their claim. Fresh meat.

In the time the others have been dawdling, Natalie's already assessed the situation and has fetched Stuart and the first-aid kit (for what good it'll do). She follows Nils the long way down the footpath to the rocks below. Stuart roughly grabs Matt by the collar, then points at Stephen. "Get him inside and keep an eye on him," Stuart orders. "Don't leave him alone. Don't let him out of your sight, understand?"

"I understand. But what if—?"

"Ruth's trying to raise the mainland. She'll know what to do."

"I don't get it. . . . Did Vanessa slip or . . . ?"

"I don't have time for this. Just do it."

"But how did she . . . ?"

Stuart lowers his voice. "Get that bloke indoors and sit on him and don't let him move a fucking muscle. According to Rajesh, it looks like your friend here pushed Vanessa over the edge."

Matt's head is spinning. What Stuart just told him couldn't possibly be true, could it? With considerable effort he pulls Stephen to his feet and tries to get him to move, but Stephen doesn't want to leave the cliff top. Matt's pulling one way, he's pulling the other. "Come on, mate," Matt says. "We need to get inside."

After a violent tug on his wrist, Stephen finally starts moving in the right direction. His feet are leaden, like they're almost too heavy to pick up. Matt has to push him forward to keep him going.

They pass Joy and Rachel, and the two of them glare at Stephen in silence.

"Get him in here," says Ruth, waiting at the door of the base. She takes Stephen into the building and pushes him into the nearest chair. He slumps down heavily, then looks up and around the room, slowly as if he's on a time delay or drugged, only just realizing where he is. "It's shock," Ruth tells Matt. "I'll get a hot drink."

Matt doesn't know what to do or say. He goes to walk away, but Stephen grabs his hand and drags him down into the seat next to him. "It wasn't me," Stephen whispers, a hint of panic in his hushed voice. He's sweating, breathing hard. "I didn't do it, I swear."

"We'll talk about it later, Stephen."

"I thought she was going to kill me."

Matt's confused. He thinks he probably shouldn't ask, but he can't help himself. "What are you talking about?"

Stephen pulls him closer still and whispers like he doesn't want to be heard. "One minute I was talking about going home, next second she just turned on me. She was acting fucking crazy. I never did anything to her Matt, I swear. I thought she was going to push me over the cliff. She came at me and I managed to get out of the way, and she just lost her footing. I didn't know we were so close to the edge. . . ."

Stephen's getting more and more agitated now. It's making Matt nervous. "Calm down, Stephen. We'll get it sorted. Just wait until the others get back."

"I didn't want to hurt her." Tears are running down Stephen's face now. He's still holding on to Matt's hand and refusing to let go. "She was the one trying to attack me. You have to believe me."

Matt knows it's not what he believes that's important here.

It's a relief when the others start to return to the base in dribs and drabs. Rachel's in tears, Gavin comforting her. For once, even Joy is subdued. Matt happens to look out the window at the exact wrong moment. The driving rain out there now is streaking the glass, but he still sees more than he wants to. Nils, Stuart, Natalie, and Rajesh are carrying a stretcher. On it lies the distinctive shape of a tarpaulin-covered corpse.

Ronan's on Nils and Rajesh as soon as they get inside, berating them about safety standards and procedures. Ronan's panicking, not thinking straight. "Do you people not understand the seriousness of this? The reputation of my business is on the line here."

Rajesh stops and squares up to him. "For fuck's sake, man, one of your people is dead. Who gives a damn about your frigging business."

Ronan storms away to find Stuart and Ruth, and the noise goes with him.

Everyone's back now. All of them are sitting away from Stephen or in other rooms altogether. Even Matt makes his excuses to put a little distance between them. He's loitering by the kitchen serving hatch where he can hear Ruth talking. She's on the radio in the back room, trying to get through to the coast guard on the mainland.

Paul stops to talk to him. "Hope this doesn't slow things down too much," he says quietly.

"What?"

"They're bound to want to send people over to investigate. We'll be stuck here a while longer, I bet."

"What do you expect? Vanessa's dead, Paul."

"I know, but I've had enough. Don't know about you, but I can't wait to get off this bloody rock."

"So do I, but they need to find out what actually happened first."

Rachel's walking past and overhears them talking. She yells at

Matt, unfairly venting all her anger and emotion on him. "I'll tell you what happened. That bastard was fighting with Nessa like he always does. The fucker's twice her size. She didn't stand a chance." Rachel points accusingly at Stephen. "He killed her."

4

It's a quarter to one. The boat will be coming to take them home soon.

The atmosphere in the base is understandably tense. Hardly anyone speaks. No one knows what to say. What's happened feels impossible yet irrefutable. It's hard to accept that Vanessa is dead, even harder to accept how she died. Dagger looks and whispers come from Rachel and Joy. Ronan and Stuart keep Stephen in the corner of the mess hall, separate from the others. The lack of space on Skek feels like both a blessing and a curse right now. Stephen can't go anywhere because there's nowhere else to go. And while they all know he needs to be kept under a close watch, no one wants to be anywhere near him. Whatever happened to innocent until proven guilty? To his (and Vanessa's) work colleagues, the evidence (or lack of) is incontrovertible. Stuart's managing to keep a level head. He's been both a special constable and a volunteer on lifeboats before now. He knows how to handle situations like this. Not that there's ever been a situation like this on Skek before. Not on his and Ruth's watch, anyway.

Almost hometime, Matt thinks. Well, maybe not quite hometime in view of what's happened, but the start of the process that'll eventually get him away from here and back home to Jen. He can't wait to see her. It was hard enough being away from her before all this happened, but now it feels unbearable. It's been a long time since he's been away from Jen overnight, and that he hasn't even been able to talk to her makes matters worse. Mobile phones are useless here—only good for taking pictures, playing games, and checking the time, not communicating. Just a quick conversation would have been enough, but there isn't even a landline here. Hell, there's barely even any land. Jen gets nervous when they're apart. He worries about her worrying.

"You okay?" Natalie asks, disturbing his thoughts.

"What? Sorry . . . yeah, I'm okay."

"Sure?"

"I suppose. It's all gone a bit shit, hasn't it?"

She sits down next to him. "You're right about that. Horrible way to go. Paul was saying she could be difficult at times, but you wouldn't wish that on anyone."

"He shouldn't speak ill of the dead."

"What's she gonna do about it, put in a formal complaint? To be fair, being pushed over a cliff by a colleague seems like reasonable grounds for taking out a grievance though."

"Bloody hell, that's a bit off. Have some respect."

"I know. Sorry. I can't help it. It helps me deal with stuff."

He's gotten to like Natalie's humor over the last couple of days, though it often takes him a while to work out whether she's joking or being serious. Getting to know Natalie has been one of the highlights of the weekend. Late on Friday evening they sat in a corner together, disconnected from everyone else, and bonded over the dregs of a bottle of cheap wine and a mutual appreciation of trashy movies.

She digs him in the ribs. "She weighed a ton too," Natalie says, really sticking the boot in.

"That's sick."

"You didn't have to carry her."

He thinks about that, remembering watching the stretcher bearers. "Can't believe she's dead."

"I know. It's a fucking horrible way to go. Would have been quick, though, if that's any consolation."

"It's not. Paul was right, though, she could be difficult to work with. Well, difficult or good at her job—depends which side of the fence you're sitting on."

"And which side were you on?"

"I didn't have a lot to do with her, to be honest. Not my department."

"Not my department. That's such a corporate excuse."

"It's true."

"I don't doubt it. So what about him?" Natalie nods over at Stephen. "Did he have enough of a problem with her to do her in?"

"They definitely had their moments, but she'd have had to have done something pretty awful for him to have done what they're saying he did."

"You think it was an accident then?"

"I don't know what to think. He keeps saying she went for him."

"What's your gut saying? You know him better than I do. Did Vanessa fall or was she pushed?"

Matt thinks for a second. "Don't know how much I trusted Stephen or Vanessa, to be honest. How well do you really know anyone you work with?"

"Natalie, love," Ruth shouts from across the room, interrupting their whispered conversation. "The boat's due in and Stuart's stuck talking to Ronan. Do me a favor and go down to the jetty. We need to keep the kids away from base, just until everything's sorted."

"Sure thing," Natalie says, jumping up. "You coming?" she asks Matt.

"I should probably stay here."

"Why?"

"I dunno. I just reckon I should."

"Why?"

"Because of what happened, I guess."

"What difference does it make?"

"Ronan's going to want us to stick together."

"You're on an island, Matt. No one's going anywhere."

She grabs his arm and pulls him up, then clambers over the mountain of luggage the group has left assembled by the front door. Matt snatches his waterproof jacket from the back of his chair and puts it back on.

"Where are you going?" Frank asks, blocking his way.

"Down to the beach with Natalie, why?"

"That's not a good idea. We've already lost one of the team. We can't afford to—"

"What do you think's going to happen, Frank?" Natalie interrupts. "Christ, you people are as bad as each other. Vanessa's the first and only fatality we've ever had on Skek. Do you think I'm going to march Matt up to the top of the cliffs and push him over too?"

"I didn't say that, I just—"

"Or maybe you think he'll drown? What's he going to do, slip off the end of the jetty and forget how to swim?" She looks at Matt. "You can swim, can't you?"

"Of course I can swim."

"My job is business continuity and security, and I need to consider the risks," Frank continues, getting annoyed.

"Bit late for that."

"Don't trivialize what's happened here. A woman—a *colleague*—has died."

"I'm not trivializing anything, but Vanessa's death doesn't make it any more or less likely that anyone else is going to die, does it? Of course, if your man Stephen asked me out for a cliff-top walk just now, I might have to politely decline. . . ."

"I don't like your attitude."

"And I don't like your accent, but we just have to put up with these things, don't we?"

"What's my accent got to do with anything?"

"Nothing at all, and that's my point. Come on, Matt."

Matt's been standing between the two of them, following the conversation like a tennis umpire. Now he feels like he's got to make a line call.

Despite the way Frank's glaring at him, he chooses Natalie and follows her outside.

The mist being blown off the sea mixes with the low cloud that has smothered the island like a damp blanket. Matt and Natalie were wet through after they'd only been on the jetty for a few minutes. They've been outside almost an hour now, and they're soaked to the bone. "Even when the weather's this shitty and you can't see anything, I still prefer the view from your office window," Matt says.

"It's pretty special, isn't it? You like your job though?"

"Bits of it. The bits when I'm left alone to get on with it, mostly."

"So you're a poor little misunderstood introvert?"

"I work better on my own sometimes. Nothing wrong with that."

"Nothing at all. What about the rest of the time?"

"You know how it goes. We've all had jobs that have their moments."

"Too right. That's why I'm here, actually. I got halfway up the corporate ladder and realized I was climbing in the wrong direction. I had a nice flat, a pretty decent bloke . . . I just wasn't happy."

"Shame."

"Not really. Much happier here."

"Even on days like today?"

"Until now there haven't been any days like today. It's bloody horrible what happened, but it doesn't change anything, does it?"

"How can you say that?"

"Pretty easily. We might never know the full facts, but it's likely it was an accident, don't you think?"

"Yeah, but accidents like that are more likely to happen here, aren't they?"

"I suppose, but then you're more likely to be hit by a bus than I am."

"What's that supposed to mean?"

She shrugs. "Just making a point. Risks are relative."

"If you say so."

"I do. I have seen someone fall like that before, as it happens."

"Shit. Really? You said Vanessa was the first fatality you had here."

"Oh, it wasn't here. It was in Croydon. I was temping in an office block for some insurance company. There was a multistory car park on the other side of the road. Apparently a firm in the same block as we were in went belly-up after a market crash or something."

"What's that got to do with anything?"

"I was sitting looking out of the window one afternoon, counting the minutes till hometime, and I saw this guy on the top floor of the car park. He walked right up to the edge and chucked himself off. Turned out he was the CEO of the company that had gone under."

"Lovely story," Matt mumbles sarcastically.

"You can see my point though, can't you?" She can tell he's not entirely sure, so she spells it out for him. "The surroundings are largely irrelevant. It's people that are usually the problem."

"You're a proper ray of sunshine, aren't you?"

"I aim to please." She grins as she braces herself against a vicious gust of wind.

The conversation falters. Matt checks his watch. That he's still on Skek makes his stomach tighten with nerves. "You think something's up?"

"They'll get here when they get here."

"So why's the ship late?"

"Boat. I wouldn't call it a ship."

"Whatever. Why's it late?"

"It won't be long," Natalie assures him.

"But they should have been here by now, shouldn't they?"

"Like I said, they'll get here when they get here. George is never in much of a rush. You can't be too precise about timings with him, and the mist won't have helped. You have to remember, the sea's not as predictable as you might want it to be. It's not a motorway, you know."

"Suppose."

"Look, I know it's been a shitty morning, but you should loosen up, Matt. Stop clock-watching."

"I'm not."

"You *are*. I see it all the time when folks come here. It's because you're so used to having to count every minute and second back home. I used to be the same. You might as well chuck your watch in the ocean. Everything moves at its own pace on Skek, and there's nothing you or I can do to change it."

Natalie's words rattle around and around in Matt's head, but he's not convinced. After another half hour, even though the mist has begun to lift, there's still no sign of the boat.

5

"It's obvious something's not right," Paul says to Matt, keeping his voice low. "You watch their body language. I did a course on this last summer. See the way Stuart keeps disappearing to talk to his missus? And none of them are involving us, you notice that? They're just talking to each other, keeping us out of the loop, all turning their backs."

It doesn't take a genius, Matt thinks, but Paul does have a point. Rajesh, Nils, Natalie, Stuart, and Ruth are in the middle of an intense-looking confab in the kitchen. Matt can see them through the half-open serving hatch. What worries him more than anything else is the way they keep looking out at the rest of them in the mess hall, then look away again whenever they make eye contact with anyone who's *non-island*.

"I've had enough of this," Ronan announces, getting up and heading for the kitchen. He's been tapping away on his laptop for a while, trying to prep in his diary for a couple of meetings tomorrow, but getting frustrated because he can't access his emails. "I'm going to find out what's going on."

"Christ's sake, Ronan," Frank says. "Come back and sit down, will you?"

But Ronan won't. "I know it's a cliché, but time's money. I've got important meetings set up for this evening and tomorrow. I can't afford to spend an entire day sitting here twiddling my thumbs."

"For crying out loud, Ronan," Rachel protests, "don't you ever stop? Vanessa's dead. Doesn't that put things into some kind of perspective?"

"Of course it does," he answers angrily. "But the sooner I can get back and speak to the police and her family, the better. Like I said, I can't afford to just sit here doing nothing."

"And I want to get home to see my daughter, but getting angry with the staff here won't make it happen any faster."

"Don't look like you got any choice till the boat comes," Joy adds unhelpfully, but that's the last thing Ronan wants to hear. Frustrated, he marches into the kitchen and starts demanding answers from the Hazleton Adventure Experiences staff, who clearly don't have any. The sparse conversations in the main hall are silenced as everyone strains to listen to what's being said elsewhere.

"Ruth's already spoken to the coast guard, you know this," Stuart says, clearly agitated and annoyed by the interruption.

"When was that?"

"A couple of hours ago," Ruth replies.

"And what did they say?"

"That the ferry left port as planned. No reported problems."

"And the police?"

"They're aware of the situation. They know about Vanessa."

"So where are they? Isn't it time you tried again?" Has Ronan overstepped the mark? His voice is accusatory, borderline patronizing.

Ruth bites her lip, doing what she can to keep herself calm. Stuart picks up on his wife's frustration and tries to explain.

"Look, Ronan, we've got established procedures and we're following them. Rod's red-hot on safety. He has to be, otherwise we wouldn't have lasted five minutes. We've a number of protocols we use when there's an issue with—"

"Damn your bloody protocols," Ronan shouts, cutting across Stuart. "A member of my team is dead. You should have either got us back to shore or got someone out to the island by now. It's unacceptable that we're all still sitting here waiting and—"

"You think we want a situation like this, you silly little man?" Ruth yells. "I've been trying to get hold of the coast guard again for the last hour. I've been on to them constantly."

"So why haven't you got through? Is there a problem with your equipment?"

"There's nothing wrong with the equipment. The problem is no one's answering."

Ronan's mouth opens and closes like that of a fish out of water. Nils looks over his shoulder and sees frightened faces and wide eyes staring back at him from the mess hall. He nonchalantly slides the serving hatch shut, but all that does is increase the suspicion outside.

"This is crazy. What the hell's going on?" Gavin asks.

"I knew this trip was a bad idea," says Frank. "I said to him it's frigging madness sending your whole senior management team out to a place like this."

"And what did he say?"

"What do you think he said? He never listens to anyone. Ronan knows best, you know what he's like. I said it's all well and good telling me how good Hazleton Adventure's track record is, but what about contingency? What about disaster recovery if something happens?"

"What, like one of your team being pushed over the edge of a cliff?" Rachel says, voice full of accusation and animosity. She glares at Stephen.

He's still alone in the far corner of the room. He's barely moved all afternoon, but he slowly lifts his head and reacts. His voice is a dry croak from a broken man. "I never did it. It wasn't me."

"Bullshit," Rachel spits back. "We all know you had it in for her."

"What, and you thought I'd just been waiting for the right moment to bump her off? Give me a fucking break."

"You killed her, that's all I know."

"Then you know nothing, because *she* came for *me*!"

"And you threw her off the cliff in self-defense?"

"I didn't throw her off the cliff, you stupid bitch, she fell," Stephen screams at her.

That's enough. Rachel cracks. She gets up and launches herself at Stephen, who cowers back in his seat. His weight makes it difficult to move with any speed, and the legs of his chair scrape back along the floor, making an ugly, abrasive sound. Stuart's remarkably alert, and he's out of the kitchen before Rachel can get anywhere near. He blocks her as she lunges, talons lashing, and he holds her back as she fights to get past.

"Chill out," he orders, and he manhandles her away. He turns her around and pushes her toward Gavin. "Get her under control."

"Calm down, Rach . . . ," Gavin says, reaching out for her. Rachel storms straight past him and disappears out through the main entrance, filling the building with wind and noise. Natalie also tries to stop her, but Rachel's not having any of it.

"Leave me alone."

"Come on, Rachel . . . let me get you a cup of tea."

"I don't want a bloody cup of tea. I want to go home."

With that she's gone.

She leaves the door wide-open. They can still see her. "Is someone gonna go after her?" Joy asks, making it clear with her question that she herself has no intention of going.

"She won't get far," Frank says.

In the distance Rachel slips and almost falls. She angrily picks herself up and keeps walking, looking more determined than ever to get away.

"Bloody hell," Natalie says, "you're just going to leave her?"

"It's like Frank says," Gavin agrees. "Where's she gonna go? No sense us all getting cold and wet again."

"Looks like all that teamwork training really paid off, eh?" Natalie says as she looks around the room, disgusted.

Paul's the first to take the hint. "I'll go." He snatches up his waterproof jacket. But Natalie's beaten him to it and is already on her way outside.

By the time Natalie and Paul catch up with Rachel, she's almost reached the beach. She stops when Natalie calls out to her. "Come on, Rachel, come back inside. You'll catch your death out here."

"Probably not the best thing to say in the circumstances," Paul says. He immediately wishes he hadn't.

Rachel turns on him. "You can be such a prick, you know that?"

"All right, all right . . . there's no need to be like that."

"Vanessa is dead. Do you not understand?"

Rachel turns and storms away again, then stops and rocks back on her feet like she's hit some kind of invisible wall. Then she sprints down toward the water.

Paul looks at Natalie and shakes his head. "What the hell's the matter with her? She's fucking crazy."

But Natalie's not listening. She sidesteps Paul, then races down onto the sand after Rachel.

Rachel's up to her knees in the surf and is dragging something out of the water. Some*one*. The washing of the waves helps her get the body onto semidry land. It's a young boy. Unruly hair. Five foot nothing. She drags him farther up onto the sand. Her hands are numb with cold and the kid's clothes are heavy with water, and she drops him. He lands facedown with a painful-sounding slap. With Natalie's help Rachel flips him onto his back. Natalie drops to her knees and tries to resuscitate him, her emergency first-aid training immediately kicking in. She listens for any sounds of breathing—her ear pressed against his swollen lips—but all she can hear is the wind and the waves. She shoves her fingers into his mouth, then pulls out a long strand of slimy seaweed he's half swallowed. The greasy vegetation keeps coming like a gross magic trick, ribbons from a top hat.

The boy's face is ice white, skin like marble. His eyes are empty, pupils fully dilated. He's not responding.

Natalie does what she can, but it isn't much. She works flat out for several minutes, alternately breathing into his mouth, then pounding his chest, before giving up when Rachel pulls her away. "It's too late, Natalie," she says, shivering with the cold. "He's dead."

Truth is, he was gone long before they hauled him out of the water.

"What the hell's going on here?" Paul demands. He can't tear his eyes away from the dead kid's engorged face. "I hadn't seen a dead body before today. Now I've seen two."

"Make that three," Natalie says, and walks back toward the waves. Another body is out on the water, floating facedown. A little girl this time, wearing a purple fleece.

"What the fuck is this, Nat?" Paul asks. "Where the hell have they come from?"

"Where do you think?"

All three of them know the answer, but no one wants to say it out loud. If I say it, Rachel thinks, then I have to admit this is really happening, and if this is really happening, then how am I ever going to get home?

6

They find the wreck of the *Heavenly Vision* smashed against the rocks near where they found Vanessa dead this morning. The boat's blue-and-white hull is ruptured, wedged between two fierce-looking rocks that jut up out of the water like upside-down vampire fangs. For the second time today Rajesh rappels down the cliff face. Natalie and Nils are close behind. Paul follows too, while most of the others gather up top and watch nervously.

The boat looks bigger than Paul remembers. Considering the Hazleton Adventure operation is relatively small scale, the *Heavenly Vision* is a surprisingly substantial vessel. It was a salvaged passenger ferry, rescued and refurbished by a charity by all accounts. It wouldn't look out of place pootling down the Thames, though it's clear that no amount of renovation or restoration will save it this time.

By the time Paul's made it down, Rajesh, Natalie, and Nils are already approaching the wreck. The waves are crashing against the rocks and the wind continues to howl tirelessly, but the boat itself appears unnaturally still like a freeze-frame, like it's been abandoned. It should be teeming with movement. People should be scurrying to safety like half-drowned rats.

Nothing.

Natalie climbs up the beached hull by straddling the narrow gap between the side of the boat and one of the jagged rocks, then grabbing a dangling length of safety-rail chain and hauling herself up higher. The deck's seriously off-kilter, and the unexpected listing of the vessel catches her out at first. She gets her balance and looks up, and only then, once she has a higher vantage point, that she sees many more bodies are drifting out on the waves beyond the boat like spilled cargo. She counts seven of them. All different shapes and sizes, but mostly small.

She clears her throat and shouts, "Hello? Hello . . . is anyone here?"

Rajesh is right behind her. He startles her when he speaks. "What's gone on here, Nat?"

"Dunno." She's trying to catch her breath. "Some kind of panic?"

"Seriously? You think something panicked a load of kids enough for them to start throwing themselves overboard? Enough for them to jump rather than use the lifeboat?" Rajesh takes a few steps closer to the *Heavenly Vision's* sole lifeboat and sees that it's been crushed against the rocks. Ignored previously, useless now.

"A problem with the boat itself, then?"

"Maybe. But it hasn't sunk yet. If it had been going down, I might have understood."

"It must have been moving at some speed to end up on the rocks like this. Rules out engine failure or fire."

"Guess so. But again, why the panic?"

Natalie takes a couple of cautious steps forward, pausing only when a wave hits the side of the boat and showers her with icy spray. It's like the water's trying to push her back, trying to stop her from seeing any more. She reaches the bridge and turns the key on the control panel to kill the power.

The ferry's skipper, George Auden, is dead at the wheel. Natalie's legs threaten to buckle when she finds him. He's curled up on the floor, wedged into a gap that's too small. He was a big man, overweight and unfit, but he looks like he was snapped like a twig. His face has been smashed in, skin split and jaw broken, and he has unusual bruising on his upturned cheek. She realizes it was made by footprints.

"Some kind of stampede?" Rajesh suggests.

"Yeah, but what were they running from?"

Whatever has caused the carnage on the *Heavenly Vision,* Nils is ready for it. He takes the lead with his brutal-looking hunting knife held ready. A few wooden seats are on the deck, but he knows most of the passengers would probably have been down below. He edges cautiously toward the top of the staircase, then looks down. "Fuck me."

Paul peers over Nils's shoulder to try to see what he's seen and immediately wishes he hadn't. Dead faces stare back up at him from down below. An unruly heap of piled-up corpses is on the lower deck at the foot of the steps. "They must have died in the crush trying to get out," Paul says, thinking out loud.

Nils descends, jumping the last few rungs to avoid the dead. He crouches and examines the nearest body. It's a young boy, thirteen or fourteen, perhaps. His T-shirt is soaked with blood. He looks back up at Paul and the others looking down. "This kid didn't die in any crush."

"How can you be sure?" Paul asks.

"Because he's on top," Rajesh tells him.

"He died because of this." Nils gently tilts the boy's head to the left and reveals a vicious-looking wound on the side of his neck, like his throat's been ripped open.

Natalie climbs down to get a better look. "This makes no sense. It's like an animal attack. What did this?"

Nils corrects her. "Not what, *who*. Look, there are bruises around the edges of the cut. Finger marks."

Paul and Rajesh are now belowdecks too. The four of them jostle for position in a small, square area, tripping over one another. Space is at a premium with the mound of bodies taking up most of the room.

A single door leads deeper into the boat. Rajesh lifts his hand to open it, then stops. He looks nervous. "Maybe we should stick together? Whoever did this might still be here."

Nils is ready. On his mark Rajesh pushes the heavy metal door open and lets him through. He looks up and down, his eyes quickly becoming accustomed to the different light levels in here. He almost wishes it were darker because then he wouldn't have to look at the hell they've just uncovered. More bodies. Many, many more. Lying at his feet is a kid with a badly broken arm, grossly swollen and misshapen, bone snapped at the elbow and jutting through the skin. Behind him, another child is wedged between two rows of seats like he died trying to either escape or hide. Nils is distracted by something at the window. The rough waves lap against the glass, and a buoyancy aid floats past. Behind it are some tangled netting and other flotsam and jetsam. In the middle of it all is yet another dead kid, long hair splayed out like seaweed.

Thankfully it's quiet and there's minimal movement inside the boat. Blood and seawater drips, dribbles, and flows, and the wreck groans with the effort of staying in one piece. Yet, inside the wreck it remains deceptively calm. It reminds Rajesh of a fairground fun house: all crazy angles and potential jump scares. He's half expecting someone in a fright mask to lunge at him from around a corner.

He thinks, Maybe it'll be the killer who comes at me? The crazy bastard who did all this?

Still waiting in the doorway, Paul feels his guts constrict. His mouth begins to water. He wants to vomit, but nothing is there and instead he can only spit. Natalie moves around him and heads deeper into the butchery. She takes slow, cautious steps, looking for spaces among the outstretched limbs and death masks that litter the ground. This is both heartbreaking and terrifying, yet the impossibility of what they've discovered seems somehow to cushion the blow. From end to end and wall to wall, the entire place is carpeted with death.

"What is this, Nat?" Rajesh's voice fills the cabin. He looks up when she doesn't immediately answer. She just shakes her head and bites her lip, tears flooding down her face.

Nils is squatting down next to another body. The middle-aged woman has a bloody chunk torn from her wrist. "I think the same person did all of this."

"How can you be sure?" Paul asks.

"I'm not sure, but I think it's likely. I've looked at quite a few of the bodies now. Their wounds are varied, but the manner of each attack is similar."

"That doesn't make sense."

"None of this makes sense. Mostly this seems to have been a single sustained attack, but some basic improvised weapons have been used." Nils holds up a length of chain. It's wet with blood, and lumps of flesh and gristle are stuck in and around the links.

"You're saying that one person is responsible for all these deaths? You're telling me a boatful of people couldn't stop one maniac between them?"

"I'm not telling you anything, but that's what I'm seeing. There's a pattern to the killing. You can trace a path through it. Also, all the attacks came from the same kind of height. There are more kids than adults with facial damage. Several of the adults have chest and groin injuries. Look, there's a small girl over there with her flesh ripped down, and a taller guy just here with his skin torn upwards from the belly."

"Fuck's sake, Nils," Natalie says. "That's enough."

"It's important," Rajesh tells her.

"Yeah, I get that, but not here . . . not now. These are *people*. We were supposed to be spending the week with them. Don't talk about them like they're animals . . . like slaughtered meat."

"Sorry," Nils mumbles.

"So where are they now?" Paul asks. "Whoever did this . . . where the hell are they, because I for one don't want to be stuck down here if some fucking lunatic is going to—"

Nils glares at him, and the intensity of his stare immediately silences Paul. "Whoever did this is gone."

"You know that for certain, do you?"

"No, but I reckon we'd probably be having to fend them off if they were still here, don't you? I don't believe they'd stop killing after doing all of this. I don't imagine we're any more or less a threat to them than these people were."

"But why?" Rajesh says. "That's what I can't work out."

"They were out of their fucking minds, whoever they were," Paul says. "Could have been an extremist, maybe? Some kind of deluded vigilante? It's got to be terrorism, hasn't it?"

"I doubt it. It was a high school trip, Paul. They were year eight and nine kids. All under fifteen."

"You wait. They'll find out who it was soon enough, and we'll have their bloody ranty videos and Facebook quotes all over the news for weeks."

No one else is listening. Natalie can't stand Paul's noise. A raised viewing platform is beyond a set of doors at the far end of the cabin, and the light that pours through the porthole windows is welcoming. She walks toward it. The soles of her boots squeak in a puddle of blood, and she reaches out to steady herself on the back of a row of seats. The tattered orange upholstery is stained with so much blood that it appears almost black, and when she looks down, she sees another dead kid curled up tight as if he were trying to sleep through the massacre. In the gap between this row and the next are three more corpses—a woman and two young girls—all huddled together. The woman's face is ashen; her throat torn open and her clothes soaked with gore. She looks at Natalie with dry eyes, and even though they're frozen and unblinking, they still seem to follow her every move. It's like the woman's asking, *Why?*

"Hello . . . is anyone here?" Natalie shouts, and she curses herself when she realizes she hopes no one answers.

Several centimeters of water soak the floor back here. She can see it trickling in around the edges of the door she was trying to get to. She stops and turns back. Now that the light's behind her, it's difficult for them to see her expression.

"You all right, Nat?" Rajesh asks.

"No."

"We should get back to base."

"In a minute."

"Come on, mate. No reason to stop down here any longer than we have to. There's nothing we can do."

"There were supposed to be twenty-two kids on this boat. Seven adults too, including George. Nearly thirty people . . . all gone."

"We could do a head count," Paul suggests. "Try and work out how many of them are here?"

"No point," Nils says. "What would it prove? We don't know how many ended up overboard."

"I'm going back," Rajesh announces. "I've seen enough."

"So what are we supposed to do now?" Paul asks.

"For now there's nothing we can do. We're not going anywhere until the police and the coast guard turn up."

With that, Rajesh climbs back up to the top deck. Paul follows, and Nils isn't far behind. Only Natalie remains for a moment longer. She pauses before leaving, struggling to come to terms with the enormity of what they've discovered here. The ferocity and brutality with which these people have been killed is both sobering and terrifying in equal measure. There was no mercy here, no second chances. Just hate.

7

This time yesterday the mess hall was filled with noise. Good-natured banter. Arguments and laughter. Now the building is almost completely silent save for a few fractious, staccato conversations. No one knows what to say anymore. No one knows where to begin. Ronan Heggarty's staff should have been home by now. Instead, as a result of two inexplicable events, they're stuck here on Skek. Trapped. Vanessa's death may have been a tragic accident, but the massacre on the *Heavenly Vision* was anything but. Both incidents have shaken everyone to the core.

The Hazleton Adventure staff keep themselves busy. Rajesh, Nils, Natalie, and Stuart are in the kitchen. Ruth is in the radio room out back and hasn't emerged since the wreck was discovered.

In contrast, the visitors are lost. Directionless. Gavin, Rachel, Joy, and Frank have been in a huddle for some time. The initial shock of what's happened has left them asking one another endless uncomfortable and unanswerable questions. Joy's becoming increasingly agitated, and her agitation is winding up Paul, who's on his own a short distance away. "Chill out, Joy," he snaps at her when her pointless suppositions and grating voice become too loud to stand.

"Don't you tell me to chill out," she snaps back at him. "These questions need answering, and they need answering now. What happened to those kids, and how are we gonna get home?"

Stuart senses a storm brewing and emerges from the kitchen to try to stave off an argument before it begins. "We'll get you home," he says, but his words sound hollow and perfunctory.

"How?" Joy demands again. "You're all talk. We got no phones, no boat . . . you tell me how we're supposed to get off this damn rock?"

"Give it a rest, Joy," Paul says. "I'm sick of your bloody moaning."

"Don't talk to Joy like that," Frank says. "She's got a point."

"Ruth's trying the mainland again as we speak," Stuart tells them.

"But they should have sent someone here by now," Joy says, spoiling for a fight. "This ain't good enough, us sitting here with all them dead kids and a killer for company." She points directly at Stephen, still sitting in isolation in the far corner of the hall.

"How many times do I have to tell you? I didn't kill her. I didn't do anything. She went for me."

"You two had history."

"We didn't get on, and I made no secret of that, but I didn't kill her. What kind of a person do you think I am . . . ?"

"He could say anything happened out there and we wouldn't know the truth," Joy says. "Poor girl is dead now. Can't defend herself no more."

Stephen gets up and lumbers toward Joy. Ronan's been sitting at his laptop, but he's up equally quickly to stop Stephen from getting any closer. "I told you," Stephen yells, sounding desperate, his voice full of emotion. "I didn't kill her."

"Liar."

"All those kids have been slaughtered, and you want to vilify *me*? Or do you think I somehow did that as well?"

Stuart helps manhandle Stephen back toward his chair, then drags Ronan in the other direction. "Do me a favor and keep your people under control, for Christ's sake."

"I'm doing what I can. We're all under a lot of pressure here and—"

"And you're right, we're *all* under pressure, so let's try and keep everyone calm. You get back to your paperwork or whatever it is you're doing," Stuart says to Ronan, "and you stay over there," Stuart tells Stephen. "And you"—Stuart turns to Joy—"just put a bloody lid on it, will you? You're not helping." He storms back to the kitchen, muttering under his breath.

Rachel's in tears.

"What's your problem?" Joy grunts at her.

"Nothing."

"Then stop your grizzling."

Rachel gets up and sits on the other side of the room, away from everyone else.

"Give her a break, Joy," Gavin whispers.

"And why should I do that? Bloody princess."

"Have you not stopped to think that she might be struggling?"

"We're all struggling. You're struggling, I'm struggling. What's so special about her majesty?"

"Her daughter. You can understand it, after what happened to all those kids. She's going to be worried. Stacey's only three."

"We've all got people we're missing." Joy's voice is devoid of compassion and no lower.

Rajesh and Natalie emerge from the kitchen. The mess hall's quiet now with the only noise coming from Ronan, tapping on his laptop keyboard. "What exactly are you doing?" Rajesh asks.

"Admin," Ronan answers, nonplussed.

"Don't you ever stop? You've been on that thing all weekend."

"I've got a lot to do. I cleared my schedule for the end of last week, but I've got things coming up over the next couple of days. I've got to get in touch with a few people. Important meetings I can't afford to miss. Some emails that need to go."

"There's no internet here. You know that, right?"

"Of course I know that."

"So why are you trying to send emails?"

"I'm getting them ready so I can send them as soon as we get back to the mainland."

"And that's more important than looking after your team, is it?" Rajesh is appalled.

Ronan looks around and whispers, "The rest of the world doesn't stop turning just because we're delayed getting home."

"It's stopped turning for Vanessa," Natalie reminds him, "and for those kids on the ferry." Ronan doesn't know how to respond to that and focuses on his draft emails again instead.

Matt's been sitting on the fringes of these conversations. He clears his throat. "Seriously though, Rajesh, there's got to be another way of getting home, hasn't there? I mean, health and safety and all that . . . there has to be another way of getting back?"

"You've got canoes here, haven't you?" Paul asks. "Is that an option?"

"It's our emergency option, sure, but it's a last resort. Things aren't that bad just yet."

"Exactly how bad do things need to get?" Frank asks.

Matt's thinking about Jen on her own at home. She'll be going out of her mind, he knows she will. "Why isn't there another boat?"

"We have a principle here, something that Rod's always been keen to stick to," Rajesh explains. "When you're on Skek, the whole point is that we want you to immerse yourself in island life as much as possible, without the distraction of everything else."

"What exactly are you saying?" Gavin asks, not liking where this is going.

"The isolation and the lack of external contact is what this place is all about. Rod's philosophy is that while you're here, we try to keep the outside out. Folks like you pay a shitload of money to come to Skek, but what's the point of doing it if all you're going to do is check your emails and spend your time with your faces glued to your phones?"

"I appreciate that," Ronan says, knowing full well that last comment was directed at him. "Rod implied as much when I made the booking, but he didn't say anything about us being completely cut off."

"To an extent we're deliberately disconnected. Normally that's not a problem because we've got a network of contacts back home."

"So where are they?" Matt asks.

"Look, it's no use pointing fingers. It won't do anyone any good. There's no way we could have predicted what happened to Vanessa or what happened on the ferry."

"It's a bit bloody shortsighted if you ask me," Frank says, winding himself up from a stupor. "You're running an extreme-sports center in the middle of the bloody ocean, and you don't have a viable escape route?"

"We have everything we need here," Rajesh counters quickly. "Several of us are medically trained, we've got enough supplies to last—"

"Well, you clearly don't have everything you need," Frank argues. "Because if you did, we wouldn't be stuck here like this, and maybe Vanessa would still be alive."

"Just a minute, Frank, that's bang out of order. I'm truly sorry about what happened to your friend, but short of locking you all in here all weekend, nothing we did or didn't do would have prevented it."

Rajesh turns around and sees Ruth standing in the kitchen doorway. She looks exhausted. Everyone's staring, and she feels pressured into answering their unspoken questions. "I haven't got through just yet. I need a couple of minutes' break, then I'll get back to it."

Frank's still agitated. "What do you mean you haven't got through? What's the problem? Don't tell me your radio's as useless as your contingency planning?"

"I've already told you, it's not our kit. I can get through to the coast guard no problem. It's just that . . ."

"Just what?"

"It's just that no one's answering. No one anywhere is answering."

"Then keep trying," Ronan tells her.

"What about the canoes?" Matt asks. "You said that was a last resort and I understand that, but how viable is it?"

"The last long-range weather forecast I saw showed storms coming overnight and into tomorrow. I'm not risking Rajesh going out there yet."

"How long's it going to take you?" Ronan asks, looking directly at Rajesh for an answer because Ruth's clearly not playing ball.

"Several hours, depending on the tide. And if you think I'm going out there now and risking losing the light, you're very much mistaken."

"I've already got a load of bodies to account for," Ruth says. "Let's not add any more to that number."

An awkward silence lasts seconds but feels like hours.

"But they'll come looking for us eventually, won't they?" asks Matt, rocking back on his uncomfortable plastic chair. "I mean, I know Jen's going to be worried when she doesn't hear from me tonight. All our families will be concerned. And the ferry will have been expected back in the port by now, wouldn't it?"

"He's got a point," says Paul.

"He has," Ruth agrees. "And if they can't get in touch with anyone here, they'll work their way through the emergency contact list until they do get to speak to someone. They'll sound the alarm, a boat will be sent out, and you'll be wrapped up safe back in your precious little homes and offices before you know it."

"This emergency contact list," Ronan says. "Who's on it?"

"Rod's is the first name, then there's a couple of folks in Scarborough, and some others up the coast toward Whitby. Believe it or not, I know about risk management and such stuff. I was a corporate operations manager for almost ten years before Stuart and I came here. Just because we turned our backs on the rat race doesn't mean we've always lived like this. Contrary to what you might be thinking, we don't take unnecessary chances out here. There will be more than enough people looking out for us, and enough people looking out for you too, I shouldn't wonder. And as for those poor kiddies out there and their families . . . the staff from the college . . . it doesn't bear thinking about, but you can be damn sure their disappearance won't have gone unnoticed." Ruth suddenly gets emotional and stops to compose herself. "For now, all we can do is wait. We'll get you home just as soon as we can."

8

"Anybody seen Joy?" asks Frank.

"She was in the dorm, why?" Rachel replies.

"Well, she's not there now."

"Think she might have gone out for a smoke," Gavin says.

"That's what I wanted her for. Need to borrow a cigarette."

Frank zips up his waterproof and heads out to find her.

"Don't rush back with her," Paul says. "No offense, but she does my head in. Can't stand her bloody noise."

"Yeah, she's just as complimentary about you."

Joy is dead.

Frank finds her body facedown in the long grass, halfway between the generator shed and the stores. He yells for help and waves his arms furiously. Rajesh spots him through the window, and he, Nils, Natalie, and Paul sprint out to him. Natalie gets there first and rolls Joy over onto her back. Natalie trips over her own feet with shock, landing on her backside in the wet.

Paul gags when he looks down at what's left of his work colleague's head. Joy's face has been caved in with a rock. Her left eye socket has shattered and collapsed, and her jaw has been dislocated. Fighting to control his own nausea, Rajesh checks for a pulse, but there's nothing.

"What the fuck is going on here?" Paul demands.

Nils scans the scene for tracks and finds footprints in the mud. He traces them back in the direction of the beach and finds yet another body. It's a teenage girl. None of them recognize her. Natalie starts checking her for wounds and vital signs.

"Where the hell did she come from?" Paul asks.

Nils has spotted more tracks. "She must have got off the wreck before we found it and worked her way around the rocks. There's a way to get around the headland, depending on the tide."

"But why she didn't try and get to the base and get help?"

"She probably didn't even know it was here until it was too late. Or maybe she was hiding."

"Hiding from what?"

"From whoever killed your friend."

Nils walks farther away. He's found yet more prints.

"What is it?" Rajesh asks.

"There was definitely someone else here. Look. These tracks are different. Bigger and heavier. You realize what this means?"

Paul looks blank.

Rajesh gets it straightaway. "Whoever killed the people on the boat and Joy and this girl is here on the island."

Natalie's still working on the girl. Her face looks beaten like Joy's, though nowhere near as badly damaged. She's wearing a short, buttoned-up pink crop jacket that's covered with bloodstains. Innocent and helpless.

"We should move them," Rajesh says.

"Agreed," says Nils.

"Shouldn't we leave them where they are?" Paul argues. "This is a crime scene. We need to—"

"All of you shut up and help me," Natalie shouts, silencing their conversation. "This kid's still alive."

9

The light's already fading by the time they've moved Joy's body. Through necessity, during the day the stores building has become a makeshift morgue: Vanessa, the washed-up ferry corpses, and now Joy have been draped with sheets and laid out in line along the center of the drafty, hangarlike building.

Lockdown and roll call.

The loss of the light has emphasized the gravity of the situation. People have died here—been *killed* here—and nothing makes sense. The day's almost over, and they're no closer to finding any answers or getting off the island. In the steadily increasing darkness, home feels further away than ever. It feels surreal, like a bad dream. Collective hysteria.

Stuart sits at a table at the end of the mess hall. He's holding a bunch of papers, and the way they're shaking makes it clear just how nervous he is tonight. He's not alone. They're all feeling it. Matt sits opposite, chewing his fingers. He takes another puff of Ventolin to try to stop his chest's rattling. He's so scared he can barely think straight.

Ronan's pacing.

"Will you just quit and sit down," Gavin shouts.

All that does is make Ronan pace faster. "I'm thinking," he snaps. "I can't sit still when I'm thinking."

"Then go think somewhere else. Jeez."

Rajesh and Nils have been outside, and their sudden return to the building makes everyone stop what they're doing and turn and look, terrified that they're under attack from whoever killed Joy and those poor kids. Nils dumps armfuls of supplies just inside the mess hall, then swings two bows and several quivers full of fiberglass arrows from the archery range off his shoulder.

"All done, Stu," Rajesh says. Stuart nods approval. "We grabbed a few things and did a quick circuit of the buildings. There's no one around. No indication anyone's been around here either."

"Good."

"And your bungalow's clear too. No sign of any trouble."

"Great. Thanks."

"Is that it?" Ronan asks, turning and glaring at Stuart. "That's the full extent of your security checks?"

"It might have escaped your notice, Ronan, but security has never been a major concern here. We had a light-fingered kid on-site a few weeks back who helped himself to another kid's phone and a few quid out of his teacher's wallet, but on the whole, crime rates have tended to be pretty low on Skek."

"There's no need to be sarcastic."

"And there's no need to ask bloody stupid questions."

Ruth appears from the female-staff dorm. In the low light she looks tired, old beyond her years.

"How's the girl?" Matt asks.

"No change. Rachel's sitting with her."

"What's the prognosis?"

"She's catatonic, and that's probably for the best. I've given her something to keep her under and give her body chance to recover.

Poor little thing must have been through hell today. I can't even begin to imagine it . . . escaping what happened on the boat, then getting caught like that on the beach. She had a purse in her pocket with a library card and some cash. Her name's Louise. Only just turned fourteen."

Natalie and Paul have been preparing food. It's not much of a meal, but it's warm and a welcome distraction. "Sorry about the grub," Natalie says as she hands out plates of beans and spaghetti hoops on toast.

"I'm not hungry, thanks," Gavin says. "Not after today."

"You need to eat," Frank tells him. "Keep your strength up."

Rajesh has taken off his jacket and is sitting down. Nils, however, is still on his feet. If anything, he looks like he's getting ready to go out again. "Nils, man, come over here and rest," Stuart says to him.

"Can't rest. I need to go down to the beach in case the coast guard turn up."

"They know where we are."

"I'd rather go and make sure."

Stuart shakes his head. "I know you too well, man. That's not the real reason you want out, is it?"

Nils thinks for a second, almost like he doesn't want to admit it, like the kid caught stealing whom Stuart just mentioned. "I need to find whoever did this before they come looking for us."

"Not tonight, mate," Rajesh says, his mouth full of beans. "We talked about this. We stay here until first light, then we go hunting. It'll be better if we both go."

"I can't just sit here with that maniac running wild out there."

"Yes, you can. Neither of you are going anywhere," Ruth tells them. "Nils, you know this island as well as I do. There's no possibility of anyone getting away, and I'm not having you going out there again tonight. I know you can look after yourself, but you've got to bear in mind that we're dealing with a sick little monster here. Someone who's capable of doing that to all those kids won't think twice about having a pop at you. Like Raj says, wait till morning when it's light. There are plenty of us ready to help."

"I don't need help."

"And I don't need you dead."

Nils smirks. He's taller than Ruth. She's relatively large and far from athletic, he's toned and lithe. He's lived off the land for most of his life, she's mostly worked in offices. "You think I'm at risk from this kid?"

"How d'you know it's a kid?"

"From the wounds. From the bodies."

"That's not conclusive."

"There were supposed to be seven adults on the ferry. I counted six dead on the boat and one in the water. The killer is definitely a kid."

"Okay, but we're still dealing with a seriously deranged, badly screwed-up kid. Look, I'm pulling rank on you here, love. Not tonight."

"We don't have rank."

"I'm Rod's deputy, then Stu. So as your boss and as a friend I'm asking you—*telling* you—that you're not going back out there until morning. Got it?"

It takes Nils a few seconds to consider all the options. He and Ruth have known each other for several years and they have a deep, mutual respect. His instinct says *fight*, but his brain says *stay*. "Got it," he reluctantly answers.

Both Ruth and Nils visibly relax. The respite in the tension is short-lived.

"We should let him go and do it," Gavin says. "There's a killer on the loose out there. I can't believe you're just going to sit here and do nothing about it."

"No one's saying we're not going to take action," Ruth tells him, "just not yet. Not tonight. There's no sense us taking any more risks than we have to. As I said, we'll wait till morning."

"And how many of us will be left alive by then?" A definite hint of panic is in Gavin's voice.

Matt picks up on it. It makes him feel uneasy. "We're safe as long as we stay together and stay indoors."

"You think? You can be so naïve at times, Matt."

"It's logical. Since Joy died we've all been in this building and—"

"Think about what you're saying . . . since Joy died. We don't know for sure who did that to her."

"No, but—"

"We don't know exactly where everybody's been. We don't know anything about these people."

"What's that supposed to mean?" Rajesh asks. "What are you implying?"

"We're just a bunch of strangers, stuck here together. None of us know what the others are capable of or what they've already done."

Gavin looks across at Stephen. For a split second it looks like Stephen's going to react, but all his fight is gone. Instead he remains slumped over the table, head in his hands, trying to block everything out.

"Hang on, you think one of us killed Joy, is that what you're saying?" Paul asks, double-checking because he's having trouble believing what he's hearing.

"No one's saying that—" Ronan starts to say.

Gavin interrupts, "All I'm saying is we can't be sure someone here *didn't* do it, that's all."

"I think we need to calm down and regroup here," Ronan says. "Everything's getting blown out of all proportion."

"You think? Joy and those kids on the boat were murdered,

Ronan, don't you get it? Or is it that your head's so far up your ass you can't see it?"

"You can't talk to me like that."

"I can talk to you how I damn well like."

Paul positions himself between the two of them. "Leave it, Ronan," he says to his boss.

"He needs to learn some respect."

"And you need to learn when to let go. This isn't the time or the place. It's been a hell of a day. We're all on edge."

Frustrated, Ronan leaves the room and looks for somewhere quiet where he can shut everything and everyone out for a while. But there's nowhere.

He's trapped.

They're all trapped.

10

The waiting is endless. Matt sits alone in the mess hall and stares at his outdated mobile phone. Paul calls it Matt's brick, and it might as well be for all the good it's doing him right now. In fact, he reckons he'd probably get better reception from a house brick out here. He keeps willing the NO SERVICE indicator in the top left of the screen to disappear. Just one bar is all he wants, just enough signal to let him get a message home to Jen to tell her he's okay and that he'll be home as soon as he can. It was hard enough coming away for the weekend and leaving her behind, but this is unbearable. He knows she'll be worrying. He'll have to find a way of making it up to her when he gets back.

"That's a fancy case," Natalie says, startling him. Matt's unremarkable, years-old phone is encased within a rugged suit of rubberized armor.

"My girlfriend bought it for me. Waterproof, shockproof, bombproof . . . all that shit. I think she thought I was climbing Everest this weekend or something. It's probably worth more than the phone."

"Bit over the top, isn't it?"

"That's Jen for you. She's very cautious."

Natalie points at Jen's picture on his lock screen. "That her? She's pretty. I'm assuming that's your girlfriend and not just some random woman off the internet?"

"Yeah, that's Jen. And, yeah, she is."

"She's a lucky girl."

"Not sure she'd agree with you there. Anyway, I'm the lucky one."

"That's sweet. And they say romance is dead."

"Don't know about that, but I reckon I might be if I don't get home soon."

Natalie looks at him, not sure how to take that.

"She worries," he explains.

"That's not a bad thing. It shows she cares."

"No, she *really* worries. She suffers with her nerves. She doesn't cope well with unexpected stuff like this."

"But it's not your fault, is it? Life doesn't always go to plan. She'll just be relieved to have you back home safe. It'll be fine."

"Will it?"

There's an awkward pause. Natalie doesn't immediately answer.

Small talk isn't Matt's forte, but he quickly decides he much prefers noise to silence and tries to restart the conversation. "So what about you?"

"What about me?"

"Do you have anyone or . . . ?"

"Nope. I'm very happy on my own at the moment, thanks very much. I've learned my lessons and had my fingers burned by . . ."

She stops midsentence. Matt looks up and sees Ruth standing in the kitchen doorway. She's been gone for some time. All eyes are on her again now she's back, everyone waiting expectantly.

"Everything all right, love?" Stuart asks.

She clears her throat. "I finally got through to the coast guard."

Though they're all waiting for her to expand on that, she doesn't immediately.

"Well?" Frank demands, his nerves wearing thin.

Ruth clears her throat again. "I don't know who it was that I spoke to. I think . . . I *know* . . . something's wrong. There's some kind of problem on the mainland."

Ronan closes the lid of his laptop and asks the obvious question on behalf of everyone else. "You're going to have to give us a little more to go on than that. What kind of problem?"

"That's the thing." She sounds increasingly uncertain. "I don't know. It's hard to explain."

"Well, try," Ronan shouts, unexpectedly aggressive.

"Take it easy, mate," Stuart says, and gets up from his seat to stand alongside his wife.

"The woman on the radio just now . . . she wasn't from the coast guard. She didn't know what she was doing. It was just luck that I caught her. She heard me calling in and managed to answer."

"So who was she?" Stuart asks.

"I don't know. Said her name was Yvonne. Said she worked in one of the offices near the docks."

"What was she doing in the coast-guard building?"

Ruth pauses, almost as if she's doubting herself. "She said she was hiding."

"Hiding?" Natalie repeats, as if there's been a collective mis-hear. "Hiding from what?"

"She wouldn't say. Couldn't say. She was barely making any sense, to be honest. Started talking about someone she knew coming after her, whispering like she didn't want to be heard."

"Was she drunk?" Paul asks unhelpfully.

"Probably stoned," Gavin suggests.

"I've had enough of this," Ronan says, looking like he's about to lose it. "Show me how to use that radio. I'm going to sort this out."

"Be my guest," Ruth says, unfazed. "It won't make any difference. She's gone now."

"Gone? You let her go? Did you tell her where we are and what's happened here?"

"I didn't have a chance. She was the one who ended the conversation, not me."

"You said you thought there was a problem on the mainland," Frank says in an almost-accusatory tone.

Ruth looks exhausted. She leans against the wall and drinks from a half-empty bottle of water. "It's just a feeling. A combination of things. There's the kids on the boat, Joy, that business you were talking about on Friday, Raj, and now this woman. She sounded frantic. Bit more than just coincidence, I reckon."

"And Vanessa." It's the first time Stephen has spoken in hours. They all just look at him.

Matt has a question. "Wait, what did you see, Rajesh?"

Rajesh looks as confused as everyone else.

Ruth prompts him. "You know . . . that trouble you said you saw."

He remembers, but that just seems to make him more confused, not less. "What's that got to do with anything?"

"What happened?" Matt asks, feeling increasingly uneasy, sick to his stomach.

"I went home for a couple of nights last week. There was a bit of trouble on the road when I was driving back here, that was all."

"A bit of trouble," says Stuart. "That's not how you described it. You said it was more than just a bit of trouble. You said it was a deliberate attack."

Rajesh is conscious that he's now the center of attention. "It all happened so fast I couldn't be sure." He looks around and sees that everyone's staring at him, and he feels obliged to keep talking. "It was rush hour, right, so it's not like problems are unusual.

The roads were all snarled up. There'd been a crash and the highways people were clearing it up."

"And?" Paul senses there's more to this. "Road rage?"

"No, this was different. . . . It was on the trunk road into town. I was driving over the top of it on the bypass, the part where it loops down from the motorway. I got stuck at the lights on the bridge, looking down, and . . . and it was just the weirdest thing." Rajesh pauses, checking himself more than anything else. He turns to Ruth. "I don't see how you think this can be connected to anything else though."

"Just keep talking," Ronan says.

"So they'd got two out of the three lanes all coned off, and there were a couple of traffic officers and a few police in the middle lane clearing up the debris. Looked like a truck had clipped a car and shunted it into the central reservation, nothing major. Anyway, they'd got the traffic coming through dead slow along the one open lane, and this one driver just lost it."

"Lost it? What do you mean, 'lost it'?"

Rajesh swallows, his mouth dry. "This guy in an Astra just swerved out of the traffic into the middle lane, then accelerated and hit one of the police full on from behind. Poor fucker didn't stand a chance. The impact threw him right across the road. He ended up in the middle of the traffic coming the other way. But the bloke just kept on driving. Crazy fucker started chasing down the other folks out on the road like it was some kind of game. *Death Race 2000*, remember that film? It was just mad. Surreal. Couldn't believe what I was seeing. The truck that had crashed was blocking the carriageway, and the one open lane had slowed to a stop, so there was no way he was ever gonna get away. Police started swarming out from everywhere and boxed him in, and there were other people getting out of their cars and . . ."

"Just some random crazy?" Paul asks.

"I guess. But you should have seen him. They stopped him and dragged him out of his car and he was kicking and screaming like it was everyone's fault but his. Like the whole world was ganged up on him. Fucking crank. Guy was clearly a psycho."

"Sounds that way."

Ronan's up and pacing again. "Fascinating story," he sneers sarcastically, "but I'd be very grateful if someone wouldn't mind telling me *what the hell that's got to do with what's happened here?*"

"Take it easy, Ronan," Ruth warns.

"Take it easy? Don't you dare tell me to take it easy. Two of my staff are dead and we're stuck on this bloody island because of your firm's ineptitude. Who the bloody hell do you think you are, telling me to take it easy?"

"Like I said earlier," she answers, completely calm, "I'm in charge. So you need to get your ego in check and keep your mouth shut. It's not just your staff who are affected. Don't forget the kids on the boat, and don't forget my people either. We're all in this together, right?"

No response.

"Right?" Ruth says again.

Ronan just nods.

The room falls quiet. It's an uneasy, fragile calm.

Matt coughs and clears his throat, a nervous habit. He's not sure if he should, but he's been going over and over this in his head and he needs to ask Ruth another question. "Sorry, but how exactly do you think any of this is connected?"

"She's talking rubbish," Frank says quickly. "There's nothing to it. It's bullshit. The world's full of crazies, and there's stuff like this happening all the time out there. You can't go trying to find connections where there aren't any. That's the job of the media."

"Don't judge people by your own standards," Stuart says. "There's never any bullshit where my Ruth's concerned. She's the one who keeps the rest of us sane."

Ruth doesn't react to Stuart's flattery. The room is quiet save for the electric hum of the strip lights and the wind blowing across the island, buffeting the building. The place feels distressingly exposed and insubstantial just now.

"That woman I was speaking to," Ruth eventually says, taking her time and choosing her words carefully. "She said there was something going on. She said it was something big."

"Like what?" Gavin demands.

"I don't know. *She* didn't know. She said it was a feeling more than anything else, a thousand tiny things adding up to make one big problem."

"Now you're just talking crap. I don't have time for this."

"Then you explain to me why we've got a ferry full of dead kids out there and why two of your friends are dead too? Come on, Gavin, if you're so bloody smart, quit criticizing and come up with some answers."

Gavin has nothing. He shuts up and looks down at his feet.

Matt's not going to let this go. "Ruth, are you saying that you think the deaths here are connected to whatever's happening on the mainland and what Rajesh saw last week? That's impossible."

"I know it is, but at the same time it's too much of a coincidence for them not to be. The woman on the radio . . . she sounded terrified."

"But do you think she was genuine? Did you believe her? Was she making any sense?"

"I don't know."

"You said she was talking about hiding from someone."

"That's right. Someone she knew. A friend, I think."

"And did she say why?"

"She said she thought they were going to kill her."

TUESDAY

11

The morning comes too soon. Matt's lay awake all night on the bed he thought he'd finished with yesterday, thinking about the bed he should have been lying in instead, and the woman he should have been lying alongside. No matter how bad he's feeling, he thinks Jen will be feeling a hundred times worse. This is exactly the kind of thing she didn't need. She'd been telling him all along he should have refused to go on Ronan's stupid off-site weekend, and he wishes he'd listened. She says he never listens. She said he should have told Ronan where to stick it. He thinks he'll take her advice next time. If there is a next time, that is.

He's been lying still for way too long. He should have got up and gone to the bathroom, but it's too cold and too quiet and he didn't want to be the first to move and wake everyone else. He thought he heard a door creak open a while back, but the more time that passes, the more he convinces himself it was just his imagination.

There's definitely movement elsewhere in the building now though. Light seeps under the dormitory door as the fluorescent lights in the mess hall reluctantly flicker into life. Then he hears the bang and clatter of movement in the kitchen. Probably Stuart and

Ruth, he thinks, beginning their usual morning routine. They're the only ones here who have any semblance of routine left to follow. Half of the people here on Skek should be hundreds of miles away at home, and the rest should be looking after the bunch of innocent kids who are lying dead on the boat on the rocks.

It's like a bad dream. None of it makes sense. How can there be any link between all the deaths here and what he's told is happening back home? Then again, how can there not be?

Matt can't hold on any longer. He's out of bed and on his way to the bathroom before he can talk himself out of it.

He pauses at the door, paralyzed by a sudden, terrifying thought. What if it's not Stuart and Ruth? What if it's whoever killed Joy and beat up that girl Louise? What if it is Louise . . . ?

He checks the hall, feeling completely unprepared as he stands there shivering in his T-shirt, socks, and boxer shorts. There's no one there. The lights are on but no one's home. "Hello . . . ?"

A hand on his shoulder.

He spins around and jumps a mile.

It's only Paul. "Sorry, mate, did I scare you?"

"What do you think?" Matt hisses at him, heart pounding. "You idiot."

Another crash comes from the kitchen, over to their right. A cacophony of noise as pots and pans are moved. The two men look at each other, equally anxious. "Come on, there's two of us," Paul says as he pushes Matt toward the kitchen door.

"Yeah, and there were about thirty people on that boat yesterday, and look what happened to them."

Natalie has bigger bollocks than the pair of them combined. She emerges from the female dorm and goes straight into the kitchen without hesitation. A couple of seconds later the serving hatch opens. It was Stuart after all, getting ready for breakfast.

Paul visibly relaxes. He leans against the wall next to the hatch and watches Natalie and Stuart work. Matt disappears for his long-overdue trip to the toilet. "Morning, both," Paul says. Stuart mumbles some kind of reply, Natalie doesn't even bother. "Anything I can do to help?"

"Don't think so," Stuart tells him. "We've got it covered, thanks."

"How's the girl?"

"Louise? She's still sleeping, far as I'm aware. No change. Ruth spent the night with her."

Stuart's answers are cursory. Neither he or Natalie is interested in small talk this morning, but Paul doesn't get the message. "What's on the menu this morning, boss?"

Stuart barely looks up. "Not a lot. We need to be careful with our supplies."

"But there's enough, isn't there? You told me the other day that you kept plenty of stuff in stock just in case there's a problem."

"Yeah, but there are problems and there are problems, aren't there?" Natalie says. "It's one thing making sure we've got enough food, water, and fuel if we're delayed getting people home for a couple of days, but we don't know how long this is going to go on for. If Ruth's right and things really have gone shit-shaped back home, we all might be stuck here for a while."

The realization is sobering. Paul wonders if they're painting a deliberately dark picture, making it sound worse than it is. "You were expecting a boatful of kids here yesterday. What about all the stuff they were going to eat?"

"Most of it was on the boat with them. And I don't know if you noticed when we were on board yesterday, but there wasn't a whole lot of it left. What hasn't already drifted out to sea will probably be water damaged. I doubt there's anything left worth salvaging by now."

"Then shouldn't we have done something about that yesterday?" Paul asks.

Stuart finally stops what he's doing. "And when were we supposed to have done that, Paul? Before Vanessa fell off the cliff and died, or should we have waited until after Joy was attacked? Should we have gone out after dark last night and risked being killed too? Fuck's sake, man, think before you speak."

"I was just saying—"

"Yeah, well, don't."

Rajesh appears at the serving hatch. "Stu, you got a second?"

"Trouble?"

"Could be."

Stuart's legs weaken with nerves. He tries not to let the others see him holding on to the kitchen counter for support, but he doesn't know how much more of this he can take. Whatever it is that Rajesh has come to tell him, he's not sure he wants to hear it. Mouth dry, he forces himself to ask, "What's up?"

"It's Nils. He's not here. Bloody idiot's gone vigilante. I'm going out to find him."

Ronan emerges, drawn out of the relative safety of his bed by their voices. "Shouldn't we stay in here?" He's doing all he can to keep the door to the outside world firmly shut. "If Nils is stupid enough to go out on his own, he'll have to face the consequences."

"He's out there trying to make things safer for the rest of us. Are you suggesting we leave him to fend for himself? There's a psychopath loose on Skek, in case you'd forgotten."

"Of course I haven't forgotten."

"Or is Nils not as important because he's a member of *our* team and not *your* team?"

"No, of course not. It's just that . . ."

"Just that what?"

Ronan pauses, uncharacteristically tongue-tied. Like the rest of them, he's spent sleepless hours going over and over in his head the events of the past day, trying to make sense of what's happened and looking for explanations. He clears his throat and looks directly at Stuart. "How well do you know him?"

"What?"

"Nils. How well do you know him? Did you carry out full background checks before he started work here?"

Rajesh is appalled. "What are you insinuating?"

Ronan swallows hard and massages his temples. "It's just that we don't know for certain when Joy and that girl on the beach were attacked, do we? Do we know where Nils was all that time?"

"You've got to be fucking kidding me. . . ."

"He keeps going off on his own."

"So does he." Stuart points at Matt.

"This has got to be a frigging joke," Rajesh says.

"Nils didn't want to be here with us last night, did he? We were all pulling one way, he was heading in the complete opposite direction." Ronan turns his back on Rajesh and faces Stuart instead. "I'm just saying that until we know for certain where he—"

Rajesh spins Ronan around and grabs him by the scruff of his neck. The rest of the building falls deathly silent. No one moves. Barely anyone breathes.

"Nils is as much a killer as you or me," Rajesh tells him, his face just millimeters from Ronan's. "I've known him for years. I'd trust him with my life. Put it this way: I trust him a hell of a lot more than I trust you."

Rajesh lets Ronan go, but Ronan just can't help himself. He doesn't know when to give up. "I'm just trying to—"

He shuts up when Rajesh threatens to come at him again. This time Natalie gets in the way, separating them. She holds Rajesh back.

"If Nils was a killer, we'd all be dead by now," Rajesh tells him.

"Come on, ladies," Frank says, pulling on his boots. "Put down your handbags and let's go find your friend."

From some approaches it's hard to believe this tumbledown, ragtag collection of lichen-covered stone was ever anything other than a naturally occurring rock formation. From other angles, though, the illusion is revealed. There are man-made corners and edges. Roughly hewn blocks. Weathered walls with gaps where doors and windows used to be. The crumbled remains of a basic cottage.

Nils has been hunkered down here for hours, since before first light. This is a place he comes to often, usually to find some escape from the kids, creeps, or clowns that Hazleton Adventure Experiences frequently attracts. The ruins offer him a little respite: they're far enough away to drown out other people's noise, but close enough to still be able to see them.

When he was growing up in Denmark, Nils liked to hunt. He'd go out with his grandfather and stalk red deer. His fascination with outdoor life began there, and there Granddad helped a boy become a man. That was what Mother always told him, anyway. Hunting is in his blood now. He'd rather be outside like this, living on his instinct and his nerves, than cooped up indoors with other people. Other people irritate Nils.

Though there's nothing but outdoors here on Skek, there's next to no wildlife to kill. Incessant, blizzardlike flocks of birds nest on the eastern cliffs, but other than that, nothing. Stuart offers a class in clay-pigeon shooting every once in a while, and Nils and Rajesh have taken shots at gulls from the archery range on quiet, drunken nights, but that's all.

Not today.

Today, the hunt is most definitely on.

This morning Nils is watching the killer from a distance. He's seen the kid, but the kid hasn't yet seen him. He noticed his tracks near the beach yesterday, then saw the same footprints outside the base this morning. The killer is biding his time, Nils thinks, waiting for people to emerge from the building so he can pick them off one by one. Nils thinks the kid must surely realize that some people here can handle themselves. You need decent survival skills just to stay sane on Skek if you're here long enough.

Nils is in no rush this morning. He's seen the carnage this little bastard has already caused and is not taking any chances. The killer kid looks like he'd be easy to take down, but appearances can be deceptive. He must be out of his mind to be able to do the things he's done, and Nils knows such craziness could give the kid the edge. The kid's got nothing left to lose.

He's currently sheltering in the small generator shed, hiding like a child playing a game. Nils's plan is simple. He knows the others will come looking for him sooner or later, and as soon as they're up and out of the main building, he'll force the kid out into the open and drive him straight into their arms.

And then he'll strike.

Fucker won't know which way to turn.

*

"That kid could be anywhere, so we stick together, right?" Rajesh says as they peer out from the front of the building. Frank, Paul, and Natalie are close behind him, bunched up tight.

"Stores first, then the beach," Natalie suggests. "Okay?"

"Okay," Rajesh agrees, leading the way.

They set out en masse, heads down into the wind. Behind them, Matt closes up the building as instructed, keeping the heat in and the danger out. He crosses the mess hall and watches the group through the narrow safety-glass windows. Natalie is up front with Rajesh now, both of them all legs and Lycra. They move quickly, well used to the conditions. Frank and Paul have already dropped back. Matt moves to get a better view, but it's much the same through all the windows on this side of the building—bleak scrubland in every direction. Nothingness.

Wait.

What's that?

He sees movement in the near distance, though the featureless landscape makes it hard to gauge exactly how far away it is. Someone moving. Running toward the base.

It's Nils.

Matt's instinct is to go out and call the others back, but he's not sure what to do. He looks around for someone to ask, but no one's around.

Sod it.

Matt opens the door to shout to them and runs straight into a kid he doesn't recognize, coming from the other way at breakneck speed. The two of them collide with brutal force, butting heads and both ending up on their backsides in the mud, staring at each other in absolute terror. Matt scrambles away on all fours. "It's him!" he yells. "It's the killer!"

The kid's face is ashen white, cheeks sunken and eyes wide. He's an awkward, gangly creature; spiderlike limbs everywhere as he rolls over onto his front and picks himself up, using the building for support. Panicking, Matt looks up and sees that although the others have heard and are pelting back toward base, they're too far away to help. Nils is coming from the opposite direction, and the killer kid knows he's cornered.

Matt's up on his feet now. The kid grabs him with unexpected force and the two of them literally roll around the outside of the building together, clattering against the wooden cladding, feet slipping in the claggy mud. Matt locks his elbows and holds his attacker at arm's length, but the kid's squirming and fighting violently. He bucks and flinches constantly, and Matt loses his grip. He instinctively goes for the kid's face and, more through luck than judgment, manages to shove his hand under the kid's chin and keep him at a distance.

"Hold him still," Nils orders, and Matt looks across to see Nils's standing about five meters away now with a bow and arrow. The kid turns his head, then looks back at Matt with wide, fear-filled eyes. Desperate. Terrified. More victim than attacker. He tries to talk but his voice is strangled and Matt won't let go. He can't let go. If he does, the kid will kill him in a heartbeat, same as he did all the others.

An arrow thuds into the side of the building, and the kid's grip immediately loosens. Matt staggers away, and when he looks back, he sees the lanky teenager is still thrashing, but he's now pinned into position. He knows Nils has hit him, but for a second Matt can't work out where.

He realizes the noise the kid's making has changed. No longer being choked, his cries are now muted in a different way. Matt stumbles farther away from the side of the building and backs into Paul, who's coming from the other way. "Fuck me, Nils," Paul shouts. "Great shot."

The killer is tugging at the side of his face. Matt's mouth starts to water and he thinks he's going to vomit when he realizes Nils's arrow has pierced the kid's left cheek, gone straight through his mouth and skewered him to the wall. He's still struggling to get away, and every move he makes rips the viciously torn holes in his mouth open wider. The fiberglass shaft of the arrow acts like a gag. He bites down on it, tries to shout over it and slide himself off it, but he can't get the angle and it's not budging. The boy's making a terrible noise now: a frantic gargle-scream that's both pitiful and menacing.

Matt can't tear his eyes away. He feels an avalanche of emotions:

anger and relief, but tinged with a definite sense of distress and regret as the kid squeals like a pig. Surely there were better ways of doing this?

"Fucker got what he deserved," Paul says.

"Doesn't this make us as bad as him?" Matt says without thinking.

Gavin, who's finally ventured outside now the danger's passed, glares at him. "You saw what he did. He got what was coming to him." Gavin walks right up to him, stopping just short of his flailing right hand, full of bravado now the kid's not going anywhere. He tries to reach for Gavin, temporarily forgetting he's stuck, then yells again as his flesh tears. Gavin barely moves when the kid's clawed fingers rake the air just millimeters from his face.

The kid screams again, and his mutilated cheek rips open like a sagging mouth.

Stuart's nearby, spectating. "How can anyone do that to another human being?"

Matt's confused. Is Stuart talking about what the kid did, or what they've done to the kid? The gang's all here now, Matt realizes. Everyone's outside. They're standing in a rough semicircle as if this were the climax to some savage ritual hunt, as if it were a wild animal they've captured and sacrificed. Right now Matt wouldn't be surprised if someone suggested they skewer the kid and roast him on a spit.

Nils pushes his way through to the front of the group. He grabs a handful of the kid's hair and roughly yanks his head farther back, leaving him looking up at the sky. His legs threaten to give way but the pressure on his punctured cheeks whenever his body starts to sag just about keeps him upright. The pain must be unbearable, Matt thinks, the fear even worse.

Nils takes his vicious serrated hunting knife from its leather holster and slits the boy's throat.

There's a moment of stunned disbelief. Silence. Even the wind seems to drop.

"Nils," Natalie says. "What the fuck?"

"Good man," Frank says, and Rachel, standing just behind him, agrees.

"It's all he deserved," says Gavin.

Even Stephen has ventured out from the base and is nodding approvingly from his position a short distance back from everyone else.

The kid's holding his throat, trying to stem the flow of blood he can feel but can't see. It's everywhere now, all over him. His hands, chest, and torso are dyed bright red, glistening wet. Nils pushes the side of the boy's head against the building, then grips the arrow with his free hand and yanks it out. The kid doesn't have the strength to scream anymore. He doesn't even have the strength to stand. His legs buckle and he sinks to his knees, looking up with flickering eyes one last time. A crowd of emotionless faces stare back, all of them watching him bleed out, no one helping.

He lurches forward and falls face-first into the mud with a sickening slap. Then nothing.

Show's over. Muted conversation as the others start to head back indoors.

Matt doesn't move.

"Problem?" Paul asks.

"No problem. I'll move him into the stores with the others."

Paul goes in and Matt crouches down beside the dying boy. He knows he's not quite dead yet because the blood's still flowing and his body is twitching. His eyes are moving. Fingers clawing.

Matt thinks, I did this, and feels nothing but guilt because he was the one who stopped the kid from getting away. And then he thinks, But I had to do it. He feels like maybe he'd have been lynched if he'd let the killer get away.

Matt thinks again about Jen alone at home and about getting back to her, and he tries to convince himself that if he hadn't done what he just did, he might have been the kid's next victim. He might have killed more people, maybe all of them, given half a chance. Matt imagines never getting back and pictures Jen on her own in the house, and for a few seconds that appeases the guilt. Then he remembers the boy's parents will be sitting and waiting instead. Stomachs tied in knots. Waiting by the phone for news that's never going to come.

The kid looks at him. Barely breathing now, life trickling away. He groans—one last rasp. Then freezes.

The rain's driving down, but Matt doesn't even notice. He takes the boy's hands in his, flips him over onto his back, then drags him down toward his final resting place alongside all the other corpses in the stores.

12

When Matt returns to the base just minutes later, the atmosphere inside the building has rapidly deteriorated. It was bad enough before, but it's impossibly oppressive now. Nauseating. Bilious. There's none of the relief they might have expected to feel now that they know the killer's dead, just a whole load more questions and uncertainties. And worst of all, Matt feels like it's all eyes on him; everyone watching.

Soaking wet, he takes himself off to the dormitory and changes, stripping off wet clothes and putting on crumpled, dirty clothes instead. Everything he brought with him to Skek has already been used. Shivering with cold, he puts on the least dirty trousers, shirt, and underpants he can find, then hangs up the other stuff to dry.

He pauses before he goes back out. The pressure feels unbearable. He leans his head against the wall and breathes in deeply. He tries to think thoughts like *We're okay now that Nils stopped the killer,* but all he keeps thinking is *I watched Nils slit a teenage boy's neck and I did nothing to stop him. I helped him.*

Matt forces himself out. He walks past Ruth, who's standing guard to the dorm where injured Louise remains under sedation, then enters the mess hall and sits on his own in the corner with only a trashy paperback novel for company. He flicks through the pages and finds his place, but doesn't read any more than a few lines. His mind is too full of other stuff to focus, and he looks around the room, wondering if the others are feeling the same way he does, asking themselves the same questions?

Will we still be on this island this time tomorrow, or will someone come and take us home?

When they find the bodies, will we all be suspects?

Are we all killers now?

Before Matt came back into the building, he wiped his boots clean. They were covered with the dead boy's blood. He dragged the corpse a fair distance, and he's sure his clothes and skin will be covered with traces of the boy's DNA. Or his DNA on the dead kid's corpse? Matt thinks there's probably enough evidence to connect him to most of the deaths. He left the body next to Joy's. Will a rogue splash of her blood on his clothing or a misplaced hair be enough to convince the authorities that he was the one who smashed her face in?

"You all right, Matt?" Stephen asks, distracting him from his thoughts. Stephen's more animated than he has been since Vanessa died. Relaxed, almost. He sits down next to Matt uninvited, invading his personal space, and leans in too close, wheezing.

Matt's hesitant. *Should I even be talking to you?* "I'm fine," he says, giving Stephen only the most cursory of replies.

"Yeah, right, sure you are. I don't reckon any of us are fine. I reckon we're anything but fine, actually. But at least we're all in the same boat now."

"What's that supposed to mean?"

"We're all in this together. We're all suspects. They can't put all the blame on me now."

"What are you on about?"

"Everyone was quick enough to blame me for what happened to Vanessa, but at least there's a plausible explanation for how she died. How are you lot going to talk your way out of what happened to that kid? Now you know and I know why you all did it, but it doesn't matter what you tell the police, fact is you've left him with arrow holes in his face and his throat slit."

"I didn't do it."

"You *all* did."

Matt doesn't need to be reminded. When he closes his eyes, the kid's face is all he can see. He tries to focus on his book again, but Stephen won't let him.

"One dead body's the same as the next, isn't it? Way he is now, that lad doesn't look any more guilty or innocent than any of the other corpses. The fingers will point at those of us who are still alive when it comes to finally getting off this rock."

Across the room, Ronan's getting animated again. "You need to calm down, Ronan," Stuart tells him. "You'll give yourself a heart attack."

"I am calm," Ronan says, but he's clearly not.

"You're winding yourself up, and that's winding everyone else up."

"I'm just finding it difficult to understand why you still can't give me any information or any idea when we're going to get home. I'm not prepared to spend another night on this damn rock."

"Feel free to leave at any time," Nils grunts at him.

"Don't treat me like an idiot."

"Then don't act like one."

Stuart positions himself between the two of them and shoos Nils away. Ronan leans back against the wall, struggling to compose himself. "Look, Stuart, I need to get back."

"It's out of our hands, you know that. We have to wait."

"But if what Ruth said last night is true, there's a chance no one will come."

Frank's nearby, eavesdropping. "You were talking yesterday about Rajesh getting help by canoe. When can he leave?"

"Not until the weather lifts. Judging by the wind speed and low cloud, I think it's going to get worse before it gets any better."

"You *think*? You don't know?" Ronan says.

Stuart is exasperated. "Which part of this are you having trouble understanding, Ronan? There's no internet on Skek, all we've got is the radio. And if no one can get through on the radio, then no information's going to get through at all."

"So how long's it take to canoe back to the mainland?"

"You volunteering?" Rajesh asks as he returns to the room.

"No," Ronan says quickly and definitely. "Anyway, where've you been? Why d'you keep disappearing?"

"I was in the quiet room if you must know. I pray, okay? Sorry, I didn't realize I had to keep you updated."

"Can't you do it out here?"

Rajesh just looks at him aghast. "No."

"So what about the canoe? How long's it take?"

"It's a kayak," Rajesh corrects him, "and like Stuart says, I'm not going anywhere until I've got calm seas, blue skies, and plenty of daylight ahead of me. You want to get home quicker, feel free to take the boat out and try it yourself."

"He's right, Ronan," says Matt, looking up from the book he still isn't reading. "It's too much of a risk."

"When I want your opinion, I'll ask for it," Ronan snaps.

"I wouldn't listen to anything he has to say," Gavin says, giving Matt daggers.

"What's the problem?" Matt asks.

"You tell me."

Frank looks as confused as Matt clearly is. "Did I miss something? What's wrong, Gavin?"

"Ask him. He's the one who spent an age fussing over that murderer out there."

"Have you completely lost the plot? Matt just got rid of the body, nothing more than that. There's nothing to worry about with him," Frank continues, talking as if Matt were not even there. "I reckon there's other people you need to worry about more. He's not the one who slit the boy's throat."

"I just put the body with the others," Matt says, not sure why he's being singled out.

"Have you been drinking, Gav?" Paul asks. "Let's get this straight. Joy and Vanessa are dead, you watched Nils slit that kid's throat, and it's Matt you've got a problem with?"

Frank's had enough. He's older than the others, and the constant bickering is wearing him out. "Give it up, for bloody hell's sake," he tells them. "Seriously, all of you give it a rest. Haven't we got enough to worry about already without turning on each other?"

🖋

The day drags.

Minutes feel like hours. Hours feel like days.

Paul thinks sitting waiting like this is harder than anything else. It emphasizes the total lack of control he has right now. It reminds him of being on the start line of a race, or of the minutes leading up to an important meeting or job interview. It feels like everything's going to kick off at any second, and all he can do is wait for it to happen. The longer the wait, the more pressure he feels building up inside.

It's dark in here, and only now does he sit up and look outside and realize how late it's getting. Another day drawing to a close. He gets up off his bunk, eager for a change of scene, and is distracted by voices coming from the small room behind the kitchen. He finds Natalie and Nils there, hunkered over the radio, desperately searching for hidden voices amid the endless waves of static. Natalie acknowledges Paul when he enters, then returns her full focus to the task at hand.

The radio set they use on Skek is cumbersome and ancient looking. Paul knows little about tech like this (if this can even be called tech), and he struggles to place its age. He wonders if it was a relic left behind by the scientists in the eighties or the military before them? "This is the twenty-first century," he grumbles. "No wonder you can't get through. There can't be anyone else in the world using kit as old as that thing."

"Radio waves are radio waves," Natalie tells him dismissively. "Doesn't matter how you receive them, as long as you shut up long enough to listen."

He's been standing there for a good few minutes, wondering how long they've been at this, when it happens.

"Back up," Nils says. "Did you hear it?"

"I heard nothing," Natalie tells him.

"It was a voice. I'm sure of it."

"I heard it," Paul says.

Natalie reverses through the wavelengths. The room is silent save for the hissing of static. They strain to pick out anything that sounds even remotely man-made amid the white noise and distortion.

But there it is again. A brief burst, less than a second. Just a faint flicker of noise.

Natalie's face is a picture of concentration as she operates the radio with hands shaking with nerves. It seems the harder she tries, the more her fingers tremble, but she eventually, locks onto the source. The wash and fade of the radio waves makes the man sound as distant as he inevitably is. The language is hard to decipher. It sounds Nordic.

"... *är attackerad av flera personer. Mina barn är med dem. De har dödat mannen som ...*"

Both Natalie and Paul instinctively look at Nils, but he just shrugs his shoulders. "Sounds like Swedish. I'm Danish."

"Danish, Swedish ... what's the difference?" Paul says.

Nils ignores him, returning his full attention to the radio. "He's saying something about being under attack. Something about his children ... ?"

"Can you hear me, over?" Natalie hands the mic to Nils. "Here, you try."

"*Kan du høre mig?*"

A pause, then a reply: "*Hallå ... Hallå ... är det någon där?*"

"*Kan du høre mig?*" Nils repeats. "*Kan du fortælle mig hvor du er?*"

"What's that?" Natalie asks.

"I'm asking him where he is."

"*Jag talar inte danska. Kan du tyska? Franska?*"

"Great," Nils says off-mic. "He doesn't speak Danish. Either of you two speak German or French? I think that's what he's asking."

"Barely," Natalie says. "I did GCSE French, but that was years ago. I've forgotten most of it now."

"*Hvor er du?*" Nils asks again. This time there's no answer. Just one more crackle of static, then nothing.

Silence. Collective breath being held in anticipation. Seconds evaporate. The pause becomes a wait, then a delay. He's gone.

"And that's it?" Paul says, less than impressed. "You lost him?"

Nils throws down the handset and leaves. Natalie rubs her eyes and massages the bridge of her nose. "Sounds that way."

"Aren't you going to try to get him back?"

"Did you see me doing anything to the controls?"

"So is your equipment crap, or do we have a bigger problem than we thought here? Was your boss right?"

"The radio's not the best," she admits, "but we don't usually have this kind of trouble making contact. I don't think this is a technical problem."

She gets up and leaves, and Paul follows her out through the kitchen, into the mess hall. "So you're saying you think there *is* a problem elsewhere?"

"I'm saying there might be." She doesn't slow down.

"What's up?" Rajesh asks when she sits down next to him.

"We heard something on the radio. A guy in Sweden. He wasn't making a whole lot of sense."

"What did he say, Nils?"

"I couldn't understand it all. Don't you people get it? I'm Danish, not Swedish."

"Same difference," Rajesh says. He swigs from a bottle of water, then wipes his mouth on the back of his sleeve. "This is getting stupid. I'll have to try to kayak back if the weather's not too bad first thing. I'll take my chances."

He finishes a packet of crisps, then helps himself to an apple. "You can take whatever chances you want with the weather," Ruth tells him, "but do me a favor and take it easy with the supplies."

"We've got enough," he says dismissively.

"We've been through this already. Enough for now, maybe, but we don't know how long we're going to have to make it last."

"It'll only be a couple of days at most."

"How do you know?"

"I've told you. I'll kayak back."

The lights are on in the mess hall. The bright electric glare is starting to concern Matt. "What about fuel?"

"What about it?" Ruth answers.

"How long can you keep the generator running?"

"A few days, maybe as long as a week if we're careful."

"And then?"

"Then the same principle applies as with everything else. We run out."

"And that's it?"

"Unless you're thinking about drilling for oil and setting up a refinery, then, yes, pretty much. And I don't reckon you'd have much luck. That's why the scientists left this place untouched. Skek is as barren as it looks."

"Great," Matt says.

"I thought you lot were supposed to be survivalists," Paul goads. He seems anxious tonight. On edge. Antagonistic.

"We'll survive," Rajesh tells him. "You might not though, if you carry on like this."

"Is that a threat?"

"Oh, come on, boys." Natalie sighs. "Grow up, will you? We can ration power if we need to, only use the lights when we don't have any choice, turn the heating off at night . . ."

"As if this place isn't cold enough already," Ronan complains.

"Like I said, I'll try to get back tomorrow," Rajesh says, doing his best to quell their collective nerves.

Ruth disappears to check on Rachel, who's still sitting with the kid in the dorm. Paul watches her leave. He does a silent head count, working out who's where. He notices Frank is lashing the handle of the front door with a length of climbing rope. "What's he up to?"

"He's the security guy," Matt answers. "I guess he's making the place secure. Just doing what comes naturally."

"And look at him." Paul gestures at Ronan, who's standing alone at a window, staring out like a nosy neighbor. It's almost pitch-black out there, barely anything visible at all, but he keeps looking all the same. "What's he looking for? We're all inside."

"I can hear you, Paul," Ronan says. "Sometimes it pays to be visible. I'm being proactive in case anyone lands here and starts looking for us. Front-foot positioning."

"Give me a break. The only people left out there are dead."

"But others will come looking for us eventually. We need them to know that we stand together, that we dealt with the killer and we did it in collective self-defense. Portraying a united front is important."

Stuart's exasperated. "We're on an island a couple of miles wide in the middle of the ocean and the storeroom is full of bodies. It'll take more than a united front to explain away what's happened here."

"You're not listening to me, are you? All I'm saying is it doesn't matter that Nils was the one who actually killed that boy, we're all complicit by virtue of the fact we all have the misfortune of being stuck here together at this precise moment in time. We need to make sure we give the right impression."

"This isn't a popularity contest, you jerk," Natalie snaps. Matt watches her with admiration, wishing he had bollocks as big as hers.

"No, you're right, it isn't. Whoever lands here is going to tar us all with the same brush."

"Those who are still alive," Frank adds unhelpfully.

"Even in battle you have to be aware of how you portray yourself," Ronan continues. "I read that somewhere."

"In battle?" Matt is barely able to believe the continual tirade of bullshit he's hearing from his boss.

"You know what I'm talking about, don't you, Paul?" Ronan continues, aiming his comments at his company's second-in-command for support.

Paul doesn't respond.

"This is getting ridiculous," Matt continues. "We can Skype, we can text and email, we have computers in our pockets, yet we can't get in contact with someone back home to get us away from this godforsaken place?"

"That's exactly what we're saying," Stuart tells him, his deceptively calm tone belying his frustration. "You can spend all the money in the world on high-tech communications equipment, but it all counts for nothing if there's no one at the other end to receive your message."

Gavin is leaning against the wall, nervously chewing his fingers. "Do you think we're looking at this the right way?"

"What other way is there?" Paul asks.

"All I'm saying is, if things are as bad back home as I'm starting to think they might be, then might being isolated out here actually be a good thing?"

"I get what you're saying, but what about when we run out of food and water?" Stuart reminds him.

Gavin doesn't have an answer to that.

"He's got a point, though," Frank says. "Right now there's a part of me that thinks we might be better off waiting a while before we try and get back."

"Just because we can't get through on the radio doesn't mean the rest of the world really has fallen apart," Stuart says.

Gavin's mouth is dry with nerves. He clears his throat. "No, but it might have." He's staring at the entrance door handle that Frank just secured. "The more I think about our situation, the more confused I get. I mean, are we sure it's such a good idea locking the door like that?"

"Of course it is," Frank says without hesitation.

Gavin looks increasingly uncomfortable. He has more to say, but he's not sure how to say it. Deep breath. Here goes nothing. "But we still don't know exactly what happened to Vanessa."

"I told you," Stephen says from the opposite corner of the room. "We were near the edge of the cliff and she just—"

"She just came at you. Yeah, I heard that much. Look, I know what you said. . . . Thing is, though, the kid that Nils killed, he was nowhere near here at the time, was he? Nessa died before we found the boat and the bodies."

"I didn't do anything. How many times do I have to say it?" Stephen gets up to try to argue his case yet again, but the effort's too much and he has no more words. He slumps back down and lays his head on the table, too tired to keep fighting. "I can only tell you the same thing again and again. I didn't push her. She came at me and she fell."

"What are you implying, Gavin?" Frank asks, concerned.

"I just think we need to be careful, that's all. What if he's telling the truth and she really did try and attack him? None of this adds up, and we'll never be able to prove what happened to Vanessa now." Gavin looks directly at Stephen, but Stephen keeps his head down. "Thing is, locks work two ways, don't they? They keep things out, but they also trap things in."

"You do have a point," Matt says, and now all eyes are focused on him. "That lad Nils killed . . . he didn't look like he could fight his way out of a wet paper bag. How could he have caused all the carnage you found on the boat? He was massively outnumbered. There were adults on there too."

"The kid was fucking crazy," Paul says. "He was off his head. Anything's possible when you're in a state like that."

"Crazy or scared?" Matt asks.

"Is there a difference?"

"You tell me. It's getting hard to tell."

"From what I've seen and what Stu's told me, those kids were probably dead long before they reached Skek," says Ronan.

"And how d'you work that out?" Gavin demands.

"Because we had bodies washed up, remember? I think those poor buggers would have had to be facing something pretty bloody terrible for them to want to take their chances in the water."

"He's right," Natalie interjects. "I looked into the faces of those kids yesterday, and even though they were dead, I saw sheer bloody terror on every single one of them. The one thing I know for sure is that I don't want to come face-to-face with whoever did that to them, so if Nils really has killed the killer, so much the better. Now I'm happy to sit here and wait until help arrives, but if any of you would rather go out there and take your chances, be my guest."

WEDNESDAY

13

Hardly anyone sleeps properly. Tuesday evening takes forever to end, and the first hours of Wednesday pass equally slowly. Stuart switches the generator off before midnight to conserve fuel, and the silence and darkness that follow are disconcerting. It's not like the night back home where streetlamps and cars and harsh electric lights take the edge off the gloom. Here, the pitch-blackness has a suffocating choke hold on everything. When the moon and stars disappear behind the heavy cloud cover, all illumination is gone. Your eyes don't get accustomed to this level of black. It's relentless. Isolating. While they're in their beds, the people left alive here are as good as alone, and only when the first telltale signs of morning become visible do they start to look around for one another again. It begins with the faintest glow on the horizon, and as the light gradually begins to strengthen, shadows and shapes slowly start to form. Rather than go back to their very basic prefabricated bungalow, Stuart and Ruth have bunked up in the male-staff dormitory. With Rachel still looking after Louise from the beach in the female-staff dorm, Natalie has chosen to sleep near the kitchen serving hatch, her backside wedged onto one uncomfortable plastic chair and her feet stretched out and propped up on another. Rajesh is sprawled facedown on an adjacent table, his face sleep-scarred by the map he was studying before lights-out. Nils is beside him, flat out on a wooden bench. Frank, Ronan, and Gavin have commandeered the female dorm, leaving Paul and Matt with the whole of the male dorm to themselves.

What the hell was that?

Rajesh sits up with a start, immediately awake, certain he just heard something. He rubs his blurry, sleep-heavy eyes and stretches his neck, aching because of how he's been sleeping. He straightens his spine and massages the small of his back, wincing with pain.

There it is again.

There's a definite noise outside. Something rustling in the long grass around the side of the building, behind where he's sitting. He might have thought it was some kind of animal if he didn't know better, but there are no animals on Skek.

Maybe I imagined it, he thinks. *Probably just one of the others moving about . . .*

He was in the middle of a dream he wishes he could return to. His dad was in it, and his dad's been dead for a couple of years now. It's always good to see him again, if a little disorientating. Rajesh thinks the human brain is an incredible thing. All that time since he last saw his old man, yet in the dream he moved as he always did, spoke how he always did, and looked exactly as Rajesh remembers. Dad was giving Rajesh hell as usual, criticizing his westernized lifestyle. . . .

The dream and its lingering aftereffects are a momentary distraction: a subconscious coping mechanism. Another noise outside brings him back to reality in a heartbeat.

Someone's definitely trying to get in here. . . .

They're at the door now. Rajesh feels sick with nerves. He gets up to look for something to use as a weapon, and he misjudges the available space and clips the corner of a table with his hip, shunting it forward. Its feet drag noisily, immediately waking Natalie.

She sits up fast, immediately alert. Heart pounding. "What the fuck?"

"Someone's outside," Rajesh replies in an exaggerated stage whisper. He keeps edging forward.

"That's impossible."

Eyes adjusting to the darkness.

Natalie on his shoulder.

They bunch up near the door, crouching down like characters from a *Scooby-Doo* cartoon. Nils is with them now, and Matt appears at the other end of the mess hall, making more noise than the rest of them combined. "What's going on?" he asks, struggling to make out who's who in the gloom.

"You sure you didn't imagine it?" Natalie asks perfectly reasonably.

"Fuck's sake," Rajesh replies, annoyed. "Do you think I'm stupid?"

"I heard it too," Nils says. "I think it was—"

His words are abruptly truncated when someone tries to open the front door. It has to be some*one* and not some*thing* because the handle goes up and down repeatedly and the whole door shakes. Then there's an ominous thump: a body hurling itself against the woodwork, desperate to get inside.

"We all here?" Paul asks, his eyes slowly adapting to the environment.

"Yep," Gavin answers, having done a quick head count. Even Rachel's left the sedated teenager's side momentarily.

The person outside smashes with full weight against the door again, and though no one can make out what they're saying, they can hear voices. Shit. There's more than one of them.

"Open the door," Stuart says.

"Are you out of your bloody mind?" Ronan protests, panicking. "Could be the coast guard or the police. Better late than never." Nils picks up a fire extinguisher and holds it ready to use as a weapon, just in case. Brutal, but effective. He'll either club them with it, he thinks, or set it off in their faces to confuse them.

The door's rattling and shaking furiously now. Whoever's out there, they're not going away. Rajesh unties the ropes Frank secured around the handle last night, then steps back when he's done. He takes a sheath knife from the inside pocket of his jacket. Natalie stands to one side of the door with her hand on the handle. Nils and Rajesh steel themselves for a possible attack, then give her the nod and she opens it.

Gray light floods inside—more than expected—and in a sudden flurry of shadows and movement, a figure rushes into the building. Nils raises the extinguisher, ready to bring the base of it down on the now-cowering intruder, but then he stops.

"Don't!" A man's breathless voice pleads. "Please, Nils, don't . . ."

Stuart recognizes the voice instantly. He runs forward to stop Nils from attacking. "Don't, Nils, it's Rod."

Rod Hazleton picks himself up and brushes himself down. "Thanks, Stuart."

"What are you doing back here, Rod? You're the last person I expected to see."

Rod turns around and beckons to someone who's still waiting outside, obviously unsure. A teenage girl reluctantly enters the building. She looks absolutely terrified; white as a ghost.

Once they're inside, Rajesh sticks his head out, looks up and around to check all's clear, then slips out and fires up the generator. He's back in less than thirty seconds, and he closes the door behind him equally quickly, shutting out the rest of the world. Harsh artificial light fills the building now, stealing away the shadows and making it impossible for anyone to hide.

The girl is Rod Hazleton's daughter, Jayde. She sits at a table with her dad, and they're quickly surrounded. Matt thinks she looks as lost as he feels.

"What's going on, Rod?" Stuart asks.

Rod can't bring himself to speak at first. He's in his late forties and is badly out of shape. It's clearly taken an inordinate amount of effort for him to get here, because he's sweat soaked and panting hard. Although his daughter is sitting right next to him, she's a million miles away. She stares dead ahead, not looking at anything, completely traumatized.

Natalie sits down opposite and reaches out and takes her hands. "You okay, Jayde?" Natalie has worked for Rod for a number of years and has known Jayde virtually all that time, and though she doesn't say anything when Natalie speaks, Jayde reacts when they make physical contact. She jumps at first, then visibly relaxes.

The silence lasts too long. "Come on, Rod, talk to me," Stuart pushes again.

Ruth puts a couple of cold drinks on the table and Rod knocks his back. He looks around the room. Some faces he recognizes, others he doesn't know. He again tries to speak but he has to stop and compose himself, still overcome.

"It's all gone to hell out there."

"What has?" Ruth asks.

"Everything."

"Pull yourself together, Rod, you're not making sense. How come you're here, and why have you brought Jayde with you? You told me her mum was trying to stop you having contact."

"Jayde's mother is dead." Rod's voice is finally clear enough to be audible, strangely emotionless and detached now. Beside him, Jayde starts to cry. Her face remains impassive. There are no sobs, just tears. "Her partner killed her."

Jayde starts to say, "Caleb was just—"

Her father interrupts, unnaturally calm, "He killed your mother in cold blood. He'd have killed you too if you hadn't managed to get to the neighbor. Thank Christ Mr. Oakes still had my number."

"What happened?" Rachel asks, pushing her way to the front of the group. She doesn't have a clue who this guy is, but the things he's saying are beginning to sound uncomfortably familiar.

"He hacked her to pieces, that's what happened," Rod answers with scant regard for the effect his words might have on his daughter. "No word of warning and no mercy, by all accounts. Just took a kitchen knife and sliced her up on the street outside his house. Bloody psychopath."

"When was this?" Stuart asks.

"Couple of days ago." Rod looks distracted and tries to find Ruth's face again in the crowd. "Who are these people?"

Ronan squeezes through a gap and offers his hand. "Ronan Heggarty. We've spoken on the phone on a number of occasions."

Rod just looks at him. "But you should have left by now. Why are you still here?"

No one answers. A few exchange glances.

"There was a group of kids booked in for this week, wasn't there? Where are they?"

His eyes move from face to face, looking for answers. Some people look away, avoiding his gaze.

Natalie doesn't. "They're dead, Rod. All but one of them, anyway."

"Jesus Christ . . ."

"The boat ran aground on the east of the island. By the time we got anywhere near them, it was too late."

"How?"

"Killed. Murdered. Those that didn't drown."

"We got the little bastard that did it, though," Paul adds.

Matt watches Rod's face as he absorbs the news. There's none of the shock Matt expected to see, no disbelief, just a strange look of acceptance and a nonchalant nod of the head. "You've seen this before, haven't you?"

Rod takes his time to answer. "It's spreading like an epidemic back home."

"What is?" Ronan asks.

"The violence . . . the killings."

"So is it terrorists or something like that?" asks Paul.

"I wish it was that simple. No . . . this is different."

"Did that kid look like a terrorist yesterday?" Frank asks. "Come on, Paul, get a grip."

"How am I supposed to know? He might have been radicalized. He looked the type."

"The type?" Rajesh says, appalled. "What's that supposed to mean? Do I look the type as well? I'm Muslim, mate, I reckon I probably tick more of your boxes than that kid did."

"Nah, I'm thinking he was like one of those loners who go apeshit. Remember that guy in Norway?" Paul looks at Nils as he speaks, digging himself an ever-bigger hole.

"I'd shut up if I was you, Paul," Gavin warns. "Quit while you're ahead."

Rod raises his voice and silences the chatter. "It's not terrorists."

"What then?"

Another pause. Rod's struggling to explain the inexplicable. "This is different. There hasn't been anything like this before. It's not terrorism, it's not radicalization or extremism or whatever you want to call it, it's . . . it's random."

"Random?" Rachel repeats. "What's that supposed to mean?"

"I don't know. No one knows. It's hard to describe."

"Well, try," Ronan says angrily. "Two of my staff have died while in your company's care."

In a measure of how used to death Rod seems to have become,

he doesn't even ask how. He accepts news of these further fatalities with another resigned nod of the head. "Where are their bodies?"

"In the stores," Stuart tells him. "Some of them, anyway. Didn't seem a lot of point trying to get the rest of the kids off the boat. We'll leave that to the specialists when they get here."

"No one's going to come," Rod says quietly.

"What?"

"I said, no one's going to come. Stuff like this is happening everywhere."

"What do you mean 'stuff like this'?" Matt asks.

Rod's distracted, struggling to process everything. "You said you dealt with the killer." He looks at Paul. "What did you mean? Have you got him locked up? Christ, if there's one of them here, then we have to—"

"He's dead," Nils interrupts, keen to reassure his boss. "I killed him. It was all he deserved."

"Good. And I know that sounds wrong, but I reckon it was most likely the only option you had."

"Damn right it was," Nils agrees.

"What's the supplies situation like?" Rod looks around until he picks out Ruth's face in the crowd.

"Pretty grim," she tells him. "Pretty much nonexistent, if I'm honest."

He nods and thinks. "I thought as much. How long can we last?"

"Depends how many of us are still standing," Paul says.

Rod ignores him.

"A week at the most," Ruth answers.

"But we'll be home well before then, won't we?" Ronan asks, sounding nervous. Rod just looks at him, and when he doesn't give any reassurance, Ronan pushes further. "You're responsible for what happens here, don't forget that. It's your name on the paperwork,

Hazleton. You have to do something. You can't just sit back and do nothing. You need to get me and my people back to the mainland before—"

"We're going nowhere."

"But you can't just—"

"I abdicate all responsibility," Rod says, cutting across Ronan. Rod's voice is louder yet bereft of emotion. "Sue me, bankrupt me, sell your story to the papers . . . do whatever you want. None of it matters now."

"For Christ's sake, all this is irrelevant," Matt snaps, his voice full of uncharacteristic anger. The rest of the group turn and look at him, shocked by his sudden outburst. "Look, I'm sorry, but we need to know what's happening on the mainland. You're sitting there telling us we're going to starve or stay stranded out here and that it's okay that Nils killed a child. . . . If that kind of thing is acceptable now, then what exactly is going on back home?"

Rod takes his time to answer. "I wish I could tell you, but I can't. This isn't a disease, it's not an infection or anything like that. It's not political or religiously motivated. It's like some kind of mass psychosis . . . a contagious delusion if you like."

Ronan balks. "You're not making any sense."

"That's because the whole fucking world has stopped making sense," Rod immediately replies. He tries to speak again but then stops. Another pause. A moment for composure. Juddering inward breath and long exhale. "When I heard about Jayde's mother, I didn't make the connection at first. I was so focused on what had happened, on getting my daughter to safety, that I just didn't think. It was only once I'd seen the senseless brutality of what her mother's partner had done that I started to realize how fucked-up everything was getting.

"You don't even realize it's happening at first. You get so used to seeing stuff like this on the news . . . murders, fanatics, beheadings, shootings . . . it seems almost normal, like you're immune. It's only when it starts affecting you that you realize something's seriously wrong. Jayde's mother lives—*lived*—near Carlisle. I decided to drive Jayde down to the flat in Bristol because I had some business there first thing Monday. It was late and we were looking for somewhere to stop. We were heading for a hotel I've used a couple of times before, but there were police swarming all over the place and we couldn't get anywhere near.

"We eventually found somewhere to stop—this little B and B at the back end of nowhere—and I didn't think anything more of it. I was too busy thinking about Jayde to give any thought to anything else. Next morning we'd only gone about twenty miles before we hit another snarl-up. The roads were gridlocked. Same kind of thing again . . . police everywhere. Army too. There was a massive pileup north of Manchester 'cause some idiot had driven the wrong way down the motorway. By that stage I wasn't joining up the dots. I was still thinking, 'It's just bad luck.' But then we saw it for ourselves firsthand, didn't we, love?"

Jayde continues to stare straight ahead, her expression unflinching. Natalie still holds her hand in hers, gently stroking it. Natalie squeezes until Jayde makes eye contact, then mouths, *You okay?* Jayde nods, but it's clear she's far from all right.

Stuart voices the question everyone wants to ask. "What exactly did you see, Rod?"

"I'm freezing. Can I get another drink?" Rajesh fetches Rod a coffee. He sips it gingerly, wincing at the heat and the bitter taste. "We realized it was going to take us a while to get to Bristol, so we stopped for something to eat. So we were just sitting there, eating breakfast and keeping ourselves to ourselves, when . . ." Rod pauses, barely able to keep a lid on his emotions, the wounds still raw. He looks around at the circle of faces. "We were sitting in a booth right over in the corner farthest from the door, and thank Christ we were. They had these big, tall plastic-backed seats so no one could see us. I just wanted some quiet, you know? Just a bit of head space. Anyway, I was looking at the paper and Jayde was checking her phone and . . . and it was just surreal. It happened so fast we didn't realize until it was done. There was a girl working behind the counter, cooking on a grill, and she just snapped. And it's not like she suddenly lost all self-control and went crazy. . . . This was different. She was controlled. She knew exactly what she was doing. You could see it in her face. . . ."

"See what in her face?" Natalie asks.

"Fear. Absolute bloody terror like there was some great conspiracy against her. I was watching her out of the corner of my eye. She had a knife, but I never thought she . . ."

He stops speaking. Drinks more coffee. Hands shaking with nerves.

"Go on, Rod."

"I had my back to the rest of the restaurant, but I knew something was wrong. So I stuck my head out around the side of my seat, and the girl was standing right in the middle of the restaurant with the knife. I was trying to work out what it was that had freaked her out."

Jayde pulls her hand away from Natalie, gets up, and walks to the other end of the room and stands at the window, staring out at nothing. Natalie goes to follow her, but decides against it. Jayde looks back. Natalie smiles at her fleetingly, but she doesn't react.

"She didn't look that much older than Jayde," Rod continues. "Fresh out of college, probably. She just started attacking the people in the restaurant around her, hacking at anyone who got in her way. There was a couple sitting in a bay not far from us, and she went for both of them without a word of warning. The guy had his back to her, and I watched her just thump the knife down in the middle of his back and yank it out again. Right between the shoulder blades.

He reacted like she'd punched him. Didn't even realize he'd been stabbed. She pushed him out of the way, then dived across the table to have a go at his missus, and she was just slashing at the woman's chest again and again. Must have sliced her six or seven times before she stopped and moved on to the next one."

"And did no one stop her?" Frank asks. "Surely someone must have done something?"

"One bloke did. Dumb hipster tree hugger he was, all sandals and tweed and this big bushy beard. He tried to talk her down and get the knife off her, but he didn't stand a bloody chance. She was savage, I tell you. An absolute fucking maniac, but still with enough control to know exactly what she was doing. The bloke tried to wrap his arms around her from behind, but she got one arm free and stabbed him in the leg. He started screaming and went down, and by the time anyone could react, he was on the floor and she was kneeling on his chest stabbing him again and again, shredding him to ribbons.

"By then the noise was pretty bloody terrible . . . people screaming and running and trying to get away. I dragged Jayde down onto the floor and we hid under the table. I knew that if that girl saw us, if she knew we were there, she'd have killed us too. You could see it in her face, clear as anything, but she was acting like she was the one who was in danger. I could hear people screaming at her to stop and she was screaming back at them, and I knew I couldn't risk doing anything to help because if I tried, then she'd have . . ."

Rod stops. His words dry up.

"So, basically, what you're saying is we're fucked," Gavin says.

"Not as long as we stay here."

"Other than the fact we'll starve to death," Paul reminds them.

"It explains why we haven't been able to get through to anyone on the radio," Ruth says.

"No one?"

"No one of any worth."

"They're probably too busy trying to stay alive themselves to give a shit about what's happening out here," Rod mumbles.

Paul's not convinced. "Wait a second, let's see if I've got this right. You're saying that ordinary people have started just flipping out and killing each other when they feel like it."

"I know how it sounds," Rod says, "but, yes. That's exactly what's happening."

No one argues, and the lack of any response seems to hammer home his point. "It fits," Natalie says. "It's the best explanation we've got for what happened to the kids on the boat. It's the only explanation, come to that."

Frank's not buying it. "Bullshit. That's no explanation at all."

"It's not bullshit," Stephen says from the back of the group, his voice low and nervous. "I told you. Natalie's right. The exact same thing happened here and on the boat. I told you all but you wouldn't listen. Vanessa attacked *me*. I didn't do anything to her."

"Who's Vanessa?" Rod asks.

"One of my staff," Ronan explains. "She fell from the cliffs."

"She was pushed," Rachel sneers, unable to help herself.

"You lot were quick enough to lynch that kid yesterday," Stephen argues, marginally louder and increasingly confident now. "So if you believe he killed Joy and all those others on the ferry, why won't you believe Vanessa was trying to kill me?"

"Because you two had history," Rachel quickly retorts. "We all knew it. You had it in for her."

"I wanted her job, sure, but not enough to kill for it."

"All right, all right, cut it out," Stuart says. "Carry on, Rod. So what happened after the restaurant?"

"We waited under the table for forever, until I thought it was safe to move, then got ready to try to make a run for it. Except we didn't need to run, 'cause by then we were the only ones left. Everyone else was either dead or gone. There was blood everywhere. We got outside and the place was in chaos. The car park was half-empty and some prick had totaled my car trying to get away, so we just walked."

Matt's not satisfied. "You're not telling us much we haven't worked out for ourselves already."

Rod glares at Matt, then looks at the others, still searching for familiar faces. "It's as much as anybody knows. It's all connected . . . but at the same time there are no connections. These people act like someone's flicked a switch. One minute they're normal, the next they're batshit fucking crazy. It makes no sense, I know. I wish I could explain it better, but I can't."

"It's got to be people just copying each other, hasn't it?" Ronan suggests. "Like those riots a few years back, remember? It all kicked off in London, then a few nights later it was Manchester, then Birmingham, and before you knew it, you'd got trouble in every major city up and down the country. I remember being stuck in the office with a crowd of bloody maniacs outside. Thought I was going to lose everything that night."

Rod's shaking his head. "I know what you're saying, but this is different. The things these people are doing . . . it's not like looting a TV from a smashed shop window because your mates are watching and posting a picture on Twitter, these people aren't stealing or smashing things up, they're *killing*. It's brutal. They're unstoppable. It's like they have to kill."

"But there has to be some kind of connection, doesn't there?" Ruth says, siding with Ronan. "It can't really be as random as you're making it sound, can it?"

"That's exactly how it is. No rhyme or reason, Ruth. If there is a connection, no one's saying anything. It's hell out there, though.

It's like there's two kinds of people now. There's normal people like us, and there's *them*."

"Haters." Jayde's still standing by the window, keeping her distance, but she turns around to face the group. "They're calling them Haters. I seen it on the TV."

Paul can't help himself. He laughs out loud. "Haters! Jesus, you've got to be kidding me. Isn't that some shitty American street slang or something? Might as well call them Thugz spelled with a zed . . . or a *zee* if you want to be really fucking pedantic about it."

"You laugh all you like," Rod says. "You wouldn't be so glib if you'd seen what we've seen."

"You're forgetting, mate, I *have* seen it. I was standing on that boat with Natalie, Nils, and Rajesh yesterday, surrounded by corpses."

"Then you should have more respect and be less of a gobshite," Rod tells him.

"I don't have to stand here and listen to this. Who the hell do you think you are?"

"I'm the bloke who owns this place, and actually you *do* have to stand here and listen to this. What else are you going to do? Where you gonna go?"

Rachel moves closer to Rod. "You need to get us off this bloody island. I need to get home to my daughter. Ronan's right, it's your responsibility. *We're* your responsibility."

Rod leans back in his chair. "Not anymore."

"What's that supposed to mean?" she demands, incensed.

"I don't care what any of you do, but I'm not going anywhere. I'm not going back to the mainland, not for a long time. Not until whatever's going on over there has sorted itself out."

"Things aren't going to get back to normal," Jayde says, suddenly much more animated. "Don't you get it?"

"Maybe she's got a point." Matt immediately regrets speaking as he's become the center of attention. He wishes he'd kept his mouth shut.

"I'm not staying here," Rachel says. "I can't."

"Bad news, love," Gavin says quickly. "Have you not been keeping up? There's no way we're getting off Skek. The boat's fucked, remember?"

"How did he get here then?" She points at Rod. She gives Gavin half a second of silence to think, then answers for him. "Was he dropped here from a height? Did he tunnel under the ocean and dig his way here?"

"Yes, I've got a boat," Rod says, "but it's not big enough for all of us."

"I'm not bothered about all of us," Rachel says.

"Did you not hear what I said? I'm not going back."

"And did you not hear *me*?" Rachel yells at him. "I'm going home. I'll take your damn boat myself if you're not going to use it."

"The boat stays here. We'll need it eventually."

"But you just said you're staying here."

"My boat, my rules." Rod takes a key from his jacket pocket and dangles it in front of her. "Anyway, you need this to start the motor, and do you know anything about navigation? Point yourself the wrong way and you could end up anywhere. You'll die drifting out to sea."

"I'll take someone with me who knows."

"Listen to me, you silly bloody girl, it's too dangerous to go back."

"And it's too bloody dangerous to stay here!" Rachel yells. Frank puts a hand on her shoulder to calm her down, but she angrily shrugs him off.

"You're forgetting, we killed the killer, Rach," Gavin tells her. "Get a grip and chill out."

"You really think that's the end of it?" She looks around the group. "You think we're safe now we're all tucked up nice together? Have you not been listening?"

Only Natalie picks up on the implications of her comment and her sideways glances. "Wait, wait, wait . . . back up a little, Rod. These so-called Haters . . . who are they exactly?"

"That's the whole damn point. No one knows. They're everybody. *Anybody.* Like I said, there's no connections between any of them that I know of. There was no indication that girl was going to go crazy in the restaurant or that Jayde's mother's partner was going to kill her. One minute they're normal, the next they're fucking psychos."

"And you're certain this isn't a media thing like Ronan said? Copycats?" Frank asks.

"And it's not some kind of disease?" Paul says. "People aren't catching it from dirty toilet seats or whatever?"

"Come on . . . ," Matt says.

"Or bites?" Paul continues, on a roll. The rest of them just look at him, unimpressed. "I'm kidding, okay? It's just that this sounds like the start of a shitty zombie movie, that's all. It sounds fucking stupid, if I'm honest. We're miles from anywhere here and there's less than twenty of us. We should be all right."

"Did you really just say that?" Matt asks. "It's already happening here, don't you get it?"

"No, it's *already happened* here. That kid must have brought it here with him from the mainland."

"Have you not heard anything I said?" Rod says. "Like I told you, it's random. Everybody's struggling to join the dots. As far as I can tell, this can happen to anyone at any time, and even if you don't become one of them, there's every chance you'll end up getting caught up in the carnage of someone else's meltdown. There's no trigger that I know of, and once it starts, there's no stopping it.

I saw that girl in the restaurant go from cooking breakfasts to slitting throats in a matter of seconds."

"That's my point exactly," Rachel says, "but you lot aren't seeing it."

"Spell it out to us then," Frank says, getting annoyed.

"My point is that this is just the beginning. It could be any one of us next. If what he's saying is true, any one of you could be the next to change and start killing."

14

Food.

Supplies are limited and appetites are poor but, as Ruth takes great pains to point out, they have to eat. She's cobbled together another hot meal from the food she already had in the kitchen: basic provisions she kept in reserve. Stomachs are churning, tensions are high, but everyone's here.

Rachel's the final one to arrive. She emerges exhausted from the dorm where the girl they found on the beach is still resting and sits down on a bench between Gavin and Frank. "No change since you gave her that last shot earlier," she tells Ruth when she asks how Louise is doing. "She opened her eyes a couple of times, but that was all. Poor little bugger's still in shock. She's shut down, I reckon."

It's a basic stew for midafternoon lunch, overseasoned and undernourishing, but tasty and warm. Watery gravy. Tinned meat. More potato than anything else. Copious amounts of bread that's on the verge of going stale. Eat it now, Ruth's already told them, otherwise it gets binned. Black teas and coffees all round. There's no more milk.

The mess hall is subdued and has been since Rod and his daughter arrived. Matt's sitting with his back against the wall, struggling to concentrate on his paperback. Paul's opposite him. Rod and Jayde are several empty tables away. Natalie, Stuart, Rajesh, and Nils are eating with their boss. "Weird how it's changed the dynamic, isn't it?" Matt says, looking over the top of his book.

"What?" Paul replies, slurping his stew.

"That bloke Rod turning up here. Before he arrived, it felt like we were all in this together. Now it's like they don't want to mix with us."

Paul shrugs. "Who cares? You going to eat all that bread?"

Matt has four slices of white piled up at the side of his bowl. He halves his stash and passes two of them over, then prods and pokes at what's left of his lunch. "Don't feel like I can say anything. My mouth's as dry as that bread."

"What are you on about?"

"All this stuff that's going on . . . it makes it hard to start conversations, doesn't it?"

"Then don't."

Matt ignores him and keeps talking anyway. "I mean, I don't want to talk about home because I don't know when we'll get back there. Can't talk about our friends and families because if what we've heard is true, they could be in all kinds of grief. Can't stand thinking about Jen on her own."

"She's in a better place than you are, mate. You're under the bloody thumb, that's your problem."

"Says the bloke who thinks commitment is buying a girl a second drink."

"Get lost. Anyway, I'm still not convinced. I don't reckon this is half as bad as they're making out."

"You can't be serious? After everything we've seen and heard?"

"Coincidence."

"You're still holding on to that? What's it gonna take? One of this lot coming at you with a meat cleaver?"

"Something like that. Hope it's you. I wouldn't have a problem then. I'd snap you like a twig."

"Nice. Thanks for that."

"Pleasure."

"You can't just dismiss everything, though. Can't you feel it?"

"Feel what?"

"The tension? The nervousness?"

"Yeah, but I still reckon it's manufactured. It's one of those self-fulfilling prophecies. Go on about something for long enough, and it'll start to happen. I learned about shit like that on that business-psychology course Ronan sent me on last month."

Matt ignores Paul. "I feel like we're just waiting for it all to kick off."

"Don't reckon it'll be long." Paul gestures back toward the others. Voices are raised again. Matt looks past Paul and sees that Ronan and Stuart are squaring off against each other near the kitchen serving hatch.

"There's no need to question my priorities. Of course I'm concerned about the safety of my staff, how could I not be?" Ronan says.

"Then put your damn laptop away. Focus on your people, not your paperwork," Stuart tells him.

"It's a distraction."

"They're scared."

"I'm scared."

"People are starting to think they might not get back."

"We'll get them back," Rod says.

Stuart responds without hesitation, turning on his boss. "How? You won't get Joy back. Vanessa won't get back. Those kids aren't going home."

"Then we'll get the rest of them back!" Rod says louder. "I want them gone. This is my island. I'm staying here with Jayde and I really don't care about anyone else."

"All for one, eh?"

"You know what I mean."

"Yeah, I know exactly what you mean."

"So my people are just going to be discarded, is that what you're implying?" Ronan says. "Are you going to start splitting us up? If we can't get home, are you going to start giving us less food than your team?"

"Don't give me ideas," Rod grumbles. Ronan's really starting to annoy him.

"We're *all* screwed if we don't do something," Stuart says. "It doesn't matter how many of us are left here if we all run out of food. Doesn't matter if you divide nothing by ten or by a hundred, you get the same results. No one gets anything."

"There are as many of my people here as your staff," Ronan continues, his anger unabated.

"What, are you considering a coup?" Rod laughs, leaving Ronan temporarily bewildered.

"I don't reckon you could handle the responsibility," Stuart sneers.

Matt laughs involuntarily, enjoying seeing his boss on the ropes. Ronan turns on him. "Well, thank you for your support, Matthew."

"I didn't do anything."

"You never bloody do, and that's the problem."

"What's that supposed to mean?"

"You know exactly what I'm talking about. You're hardly a team player, are you?"

Matt is flummoxed, genuinely surprised. "Where's this coming from?"

And now Gavin has him in his sights. "It could be him next."

"What are you on about now, Gav?" Frank asks, confused.

"You keep your cards too close to your chest for my liking. I never know where I stand with you, Matt. We did that personality-test thing at the last managers' meeting, remember? You came out in a completely different section of the results to the rest of us."

"So?"

"So you've never really fitted in, have you?"

"That's a bit harsh," Paul protests, but Matt doesn't need his support.

"Yeah, and do you remember after we'd got our results when the facilitator was talking about how having different personality types benefits an organization? I'm an introvert, not a pervert."

"Are you saying I'm a pervert?" Gavin gasps, his emotions getting the better of him.

"I'm not saying anything of the sort." Matt looks around for support, but feels like he suddenly doesn't have any. "What, so now you think I'm one of *them*? You think because I'm less vocal than the rest of you that I'm somehow one of those Haters?"

"I don't know what I think anymore," Ronan says, eyeing him up and down. "Gavin's right, though, you've always been something of an outsider. Even this weekend when there's only been a few of us here, you've still done all you can to keep yourself to yourself."

"Are you serious? I think you've mixed up being an introvert with being a psychopath. Just because I'm not always shouting my mouth off like most of the rest of you doesn't mean I'm about to flip out and kill someone."

"So what have you been doing when you've been hiding away on your own here?"

"Reading my book, mostly," Matt answers, waving his paperback at his boss, well aware of how dull he sounds. "I like my own company. Is that such a bad thing?"

"You do spend a lot of time away from the group," Frank says.

"Yeah, and like I said, I like my own company. That's not a crime. Just listen to what you're implying. And you think I'm the one who's lost their mind?"

Suddenly a noise is coming at Matt from all directions. Ronan, Gavin, Rachel, Stephen . . . they're all ready to put the boot in. Paul stands up and gestures for them all to shut up. "Matt might be a bit of a dick, but he's no killer."

"How d'you know?" asks Gavin, sounding almost disappointed. "He's the one who was fussing over that kid's dead body yesterday."

"I couldn't have left him out there like that," Matt explains, trying to dig himself out of a hole he's still not sure how he ended up in. "Regardless of what he did, it wasn't right. If you must know, I wanted to make sure he was dead, and I also wanted to move him because we don't know how long we're going to be stuck here. I didn't like the thought of there being a corpse on the doorstep."

Matt has a point. There's another brief pause in the arguments and counterarguments as the others consider his words.

The next voice is quiet and unexpected: Jayde Hazleton's. "You wouldn't all be talking like this if you'd seen them. They look at you and you know that all they want to do is kill you. I've seen them hunting down innocent people like dogs. All they want is to kill. They can't help themselves."

But still Gavin won't give up. "And all I know is he showed more care and consideration for that killer than anyone else. He's got the potential to be one of them, I know it."

Matt remains in his seat, listening to this baseless character assassination, too numb to fight back.

Paul turns to face him. "Come on, mate, show a little backbone. I've said my bit. Are you just going to sit there and put up with this shit?"

Matt feels himself starting to panic. His skin is prickling with nerves. He wants out, but there's nowhere to go. He's not good at dealing with confrontation, never has been. Matt glares at Gavin as he rips Matt apart, thinking maybe he's right about me, because all I want to do right now is kill him.

"Matt's sound, leave him alone," Stuart says, taking everyone, especially Matt, by surprise.

"So who are you going to pick on next?" Matt asks the group, taking his life in his hands. "Maybe Rajesh 'cause he's Muslim? Or you, Gavin, because you're gay?"

Matt visibly relaxes when the attention starts to shift elsewhere.

Rod's been watching the cross fire. "Who you sleep with doesn't matter, nor who or what you pray to, come to that. The killers have *nothing* to do with each other. There's no common denominator. Like I told you, that girl cooking breakfasts didn't look like a murderer, and neither did the old fella we saw beating on his missus just before we got off the mainland."

"What old fella?" Gavin instinctively asks, even though he knows the details are largely irrelevant now.

"He must have been in his eighties. He was so frail he looked like a decent gust of wind would break him in half. I presume it was his missus, anyway. Whoever it was, she was in the middle of the road, and he was laying into her like someone half his age."

"And you just stood back and watched?"

Ronan gets to his feet to try to take charge of the situation but fails miserably. "Gavin, please quiet down. We've all been through a lot these last couple of days. You need to take a time-out and—"

"And you're as bad as the rest of them, if not worse," Gavin screams at him. Gavin's right in his face now, showing no mercy, yelling till his voice is hoarse. "All you're interested in is your bank balance."

"That's not true. . . ."

"It damn well *is* true. You think you're something special, but you're not. You say all the things you think people want to hear. You flip and flop with the wind, changing your mind depending on who you're gonna benefit the most from. There's nothing behind your words. You're at the office all hours 'cause you don't have anyone at home to go back to. Work's all you've got and it's pathetic."

"This isn't helping anyone," Paul says. "You've said your piece, Gav, now just—"

Gavin stands up and tries to get to the dormitory, but his way through is blocked. "All of you just stay away from me."

He pushes through a tangle of chairs and collides with Stephen, who cowers in anticipation, figuring he's the next to be subjected to Gavin's wrath. Now Frank does his best to intervene. "Come on, Gav, it's like Paul says, we're all under a lot of pressure. Maybe you should just—"

In pushing Frank away, Gavin loses his footing and, because of his size, trips over his own feet and falls against an empty table. The collision sounds far worse than it is, but it's enough to make Frank wonder if it's Gavin who's about to turn.

In frustration Rod slams his fists down on the metal counter outside the kitchen serving hatch. Cups and crockery jump up with surprise and clatter back down, filling the mess hall with even more noise. "For fuck's sake shut up, all of you."

Now Gavin's incensed. Everywhere he looks stupid men are blocking his way.

And now he's alone in the middle of the room.

Everyone's watching him.

No one's moving. No one's reacting.

"Just stay away from me, all of you."

With that he storms out to the dormitory, shuts the door, and locks himself in.

15

The calm is somehow worse than the chaos. Rachel and Ruth take turns to sit with Louise, who's barely moved. It's almost two days since they found her, and she remains virtually catatonic.

In the mess hall, people are continuing to struggle. The lack of answers combined with the lack of action is hard to take. It's like they're balanced on a knife edge; nothing to do but sit and wait. Matt's hidden himself away in the male dorm, wishing he could lock the door because the only escape from everyone else is sleep.

With the curtains closed he's managed to doze, and according to the time on his phone, a couple of hours have passed. He opens his eyes and rolls onto his back, feeling disoriented, wondering what he's missed.

"You're awake then?"

Matt sits up fast and hits his head on the underside of the top bunk. "Christ, Paul, do you have to?"

"They told me to come in here and keep an eye on you, just in case you started acting weird."

"You're kidding, right?"

For a moment he's unsure, the shadows and the silence hiding Paul's true intent. The deception doesn't last long. "Course I'm kidding. Just wondered what you were up to, that's all."

Matt swings his feet out over the side of the bed and sits up properly, still nauseous with sleep. "What's going on out there?"

"Not a lot. Gavin's calmed down. Bloody queen."

"Leave him alone. He's just worried like the rest of us. What are the rest of them up to?"

"Most folks are taking your lead and keeping themselves to themselves. Frank tried to get a card school going a while ago but ended up playing solitaire. Probably for the best."

The sleep is starting to clear from Matt's head. "I was dreaming about being back home."

"We'll be off this rock soon enough," Paul says without thinking.

"And how d'you figure that out?"

No immediate answer. After a while, Paul says, "You could get us home though, couldn't you? Didn't you say you used to go sailing?"

"For a few months in the Sea Cadets when I was a kid, but that was a long time ago. I can read a compass, if that's what you mean."

"So you could get us back to the mainland if we had Rod's boat?"

"Maybe. We haven't got Rod's boat, though. Rod's got Rod's boat, remember."

Matt's had enough of talking. He picks up his book and heads for the kitchen. His heart sinks when Paul follows him out like a tireless puppy.

"Want a coffee?"

"If you're making one. Look, Matt, I don't know why you—"

A sudden noise comes from near the entrance to the building. It's loud like a gunshot, and it's followed by a few seconds' calm as all stop what they're doing to listen. Paul goes out to the mess hall and Matt follows, but they're both held up by a sudden stampede of people trying to get the other way. Ronan, Frank, Rachel . . . they all fight to get past Paul as he tries to get through. He knows in his gut that whatever's happened is bad. Really fucking bad.

But when the two men finally push through the crowd and see it, it's far worse than they could have imagined.

Nils has Gavin pinned up against the door. At first Matt thinks Nils is repeatedly punching Gavin in the stomach like they've just fallen out and are having a dustup, but when Matt sees blood, he knows it's far more serious than that. And the longer it goes on, the more blood he sees.

Nils isn't punching Gavin, he's stabbing him. He's driving a shiv up into his gut again and again. Shredding his flesh, calm as anything. Both men are soaked with gore from the waist down. Innards splatter on the linoleum like someone's emptying a slop bucket.

No one tries to stop Nils.

No one does anything to intervene.

Instead the entire group moves farther and farther back—Paul and Matt too now—putting maximum distance between themselves and the unnervingly calm and controlled attack. Ronan finds himself pressed up against the wall with Frank tight on one side and Rod on the other and can't move. Ronan starts to panic, grabbing hold of other people to try to get away, but they're all doing the same and there's nowhere left to go. "Do something," he hisses, but no one does and no one will, because each of them is thinking, I could be next. . . . Please don't let it be me next.

Back at the entrance door, Nils has finished with Gavin.

Panting hard with effort, he lets go of the dead man. Gavin slides down and lands in an uncoordinated, blood-soaked heap at Nils's feet. For several more interminably long seconds Nils just stares at the corpse.

Rajesh watches his friend Nils—*ex-friend . . . enemy?*—and tries to make sense of the incomprehensible scene he's just witnessed.

Still no one moves. They're all frozen in position. Too scared to react. Watching. Waiting.

Nils lets out a deep and sorrowful sob and wipes his eyes.

Then he looks up.

He sees them all watching him. The expression on his face is hard to read: equal parts terror and rage. The distance between Nils and the others is just a few meters. They each know he could go for any of them in a heartbeat, and they also know there's nowhere for any of them to go. He's between them and the building's only exit.

Nils charges at the rest of the group.

Frank yells and Ronan squeals as the newly turned killer comes at them, but Stuart remains impossibly calm. He's got hold of one of the bows and arrows from the back of the room, and he pushes his way through the group. He pulls back the string and lets the arrow fly before he can talk himself out of it.

Point-blank range.

The arrow hits Nils's chest with a loud *thump*, sinking deep and piercing his right lung. He stops, looks down, then tries to pull the shaft free. His hands are greasy, still drenched with Gavin's blood, and he can't get a grip.

Progress slowed but not stopped, he lumbers forward again, legs a little heavier now.

Another arrow. This time Stuart aims higher. Straight through Nils's neck, front to back.

Still he keeps coming, but after a couple more half steps his legs finally buckle. He falls forward onto a table, then slides off it and crashes facedown to the floor. His head hits the deck with a nauseating crack. The arrow in his throat snaps. The other one is shoved right through his chest and is left sticking out of his back like an antenna.

Stuart's shaking. Ruth weaves through the crowd of dazed onlookers and puts her arms around her husband. "You had to do it, love. He wasn't Nils anymore. He'd have killed us all if you hadn't done it. All of us."

"That doesn't make me feel any better." Stuart shakes with nerves and is unable to look anywhere but at the corpse lying just in front of him.

He was my friend.

People are milling around the top of the mess hall in a daze.

Two more dead.

"You believe me now?" Rod says to Ronan. He gestures to Paul and Frank, and the three of them carry the fresh bodies outside.

16

Matt has a scrap of paper and does all he can not to let any of the others see what's on it. He's trying to work out who's what and who's where. He's divided his scribbling into three columns: *Rod's people, Ronan's people,* and *Dead.* He adds a fourth column as an afterthought: *Others.* He writes *Louise* under that heading.

Dead: Gavin, Nils, Joy, Vanessa, the killer kid, all the passengers and crew of the *Heavenly Vision* (apart from Louise).

Rod's people: Rod, Jayde, Stuart, Ruth, Rajesh, and Natalie.

Ronan's people: Ronan, Paul, Frank, Stephen, Rachel, and himself.

We're all even, he thinks, six a side. He wonders if a slight numerical advantage might have come in useful.

But the real purpose of his idle scribbling is to look for connections, because he thinks they have to be there. This can't be as random as they're being led to believe, can it? He looks around at the people he's trapped in here with and draws a few exploratory lines on the page . . . people who are a similar age, people with similar beliefs, people with the same hair color, ethnicity, overweight or underweight. He tries any and every link, no matter how obvious or how tenuous, but gives up quickly. He realizes there's no point, because for every similarity he finds between two people, he can just as easily find half a dozen differences. Living, dead, male, female, Christian or Muslim, short or tall, a Rod Hazleton employee or one of Ronan's staff, none of it seems to matter. The only thing of which Matt is certain now is that this does make as little sense as he originally thought.

He starts idly ticking off the names of the people he can see. There aren't too many of them, as it happens. Ronan's sitting at a table by himself, still distracting himself with his laptop. Jayde's sitting at another table, playing games on her phone. Rod, Stuart, and Rajesh are in the kitchen, thick as thieves. Stephen's sitting on his own and hasn't moved for hours. Paul emerged from the bathroom a few minutes ago, and Frank's just disappeared into the one of the dorms. Elsewhere he can hear Ruth on the radio again, still trying to make contact with the outside world, and Rachel's with Louise.

Wait. Someone's missing.

Matt gets up to double-check. He acts nonchalant, trying to make it look like he's lost his book or something equally trivial, not that he's checking up on his captive colleagues.

Everyone's on edge. He notices Jayde flinch when he nears her, even though she does everything she can not to let him see. He realizes he flinched when she flinched. It's getting so they're all afraid of one another.

He looks through the small square windows in the doors of each of the dorms, then goes back to the mess hall. "Anyone seen Natalie?"

"I thought she was in one of the bedrooms," Rajesh answers.

"I just checked. She's not there."

Matt looks in the bathrooms and checks all the individual cubicles and showers, then returns to the mess hall again.

"Any sign?" asks Rod.

"Nope. She's gone."

People start hunting around, calling out for her like they're looking for a missing pet. They check all the places Matt's already looked, even under tables and behind doors, but she's nowhere to be found. "She must have gone outside," Frank says, stating the obvious.

"That's a pretty safe bet if she's not in here," Paul quickly responds. "Shit, Frank, no wonder you're head of security."

"When did anyone last see her?" Ronan asks.

"Can't remember," Matt replies. "An hour ago? Maybe longer?"

"Just after Nils," Frank adds. "She must have left when we were getting rid of the bodies."

"Don't you think we should try and find her?" Matt looks around, but the reaction to his question is muted at best.

"Suppose," Franks says, sounding less than enthusiastic.

"What if it's her next?" Jayde says. "What if she's one of them?"

Matt shakes his head. "No way. She's no more a killer than I am."

"This time yesterday I bet Nils would have said the same thing," Rajesh says in an almost accusatory tone. "And Stuart's a killer too now, if you want to be pedantic about it."

"Why are you so keen to find her?" Ronan asks.

Matt regrets having spoken out loud. The others are looking at him weirdly now. He imagines that their minds are working overtime. He can almost hear the cogs turning.

"She can look after herself," Rajesh says quickly.

"I know that. It's just . . ."

"Just what?"

Matt shakes his head. "Nothing."

Everyone's back in the mess hall now. Rod's looking directly at him. "What have you done to her?"

"What?"

"You heard me."

"Are you serious? You think I've hurt Natalie?"

"I don't know what to think. I don't even know you."

"So let's rewind a second. You think I've attacked her, maybe even killed her, dumped the body somewhere, then started asking questions to throw you off the scent?"

"Like I said, I hardly know you. I don't know what you're capable of."

"Matt's not capable of anything," Paul says a little too quickly.

Matt laughs involuntarily. "You think I'm one of them? You've got to be kidding."

"Maybe Gavin was right about him," Frank says, now talking about Matt as if he weren't even in the room.

"Wait, I need to get my head round this. We've got people on this bloody island dying all over the place, Nils turns out to be a killer, Stuart's a killer too because he dealt with Nils, Natalie's gone AWOL, and yet I'm the one who's getting another character assassination? For Christ's sake, this is an absolute bloody joke."

Matt laughs again in disbelief, but no one else thinks it's funny. Stony, emotionless faces all round.

"What have you done to her?" Ronan demands, deadly serious.

"Come on, Ronan, get a grip. This is ridiculous even by your standards."

Matt starts to question himself now. Normally that's the kind of comment he'd wish he could say but would keep to himself or would mumble deliberately quietly so no one else could hear. Talking back to Ronan like that was out of character. Are they right? Am I changing? Did I do something to her?

"This is crazy," he says, his head clouding with confusion. "I haven't killed anyone and I'm not about to. Just listen to yourselves. Bloody ridiculous."

"So where is she?" Rod asks, deadly serious.

"I told you, I don't know. I was the one looking for her first, remember?"

"We should lock him up," Frank suggests. "Just to be sure."

"Makes sense," Stuart agrees, and because he's nearest, he goes to take hold of Matt.

Matt snatches his arm away. "Get off. Leave me alone."

He's acutely aware that the balance in the building has shifted. Whether they realize it or not, the others have closed ranks on him.

"Keep calm and you won't get hurt," Stuart says. "This is for your own good, just until we're sure what's what."

Stuart comes at him again, but Matt slips out of the way. He weaves between tables and chairs, backing away from the other man. The rest of the people gathered in the mess hall are reluctant to get involved. Whenever he gets close, they scatter as if he's infected.

Matt's backed up against a wall with Rod, Stuart, and Rajesh closing in. His head's all over the place now: panicking that he's about to get a beating, and trying to work out an exit strategy. He can't focus. Can't think straight.

"Get hold of him," Stuart says.

Matt scrambles to the entrance door. He unlocks it and yanks it open.

One foot in and one foot out.

"You go out there and you're not coming back in," Rod warns.

"I'll go and find her," Matt says, his confidence gradually returning now he thinks he's found a way out. "If that's what it's going to take to sort this out and prove I'm not a Hater or whatever you call them, I'll go find her and bring her back."

"Dead or alive?" Rajesh says with no hint of irony.

"Alive," Matt immediately answers. "Either that or I won't come back at all. I've got nothing to hide. I'm just like the rest of you, just trying to get through this so I can go home to my missus. That's all I'm interested in right now. I just want to get back to the other half and put this whole bloody mess behind me."

Surely they'll see sense now, Matt thinks, still quietly surprised by his sudden confidence. But they don't.

Stuart forces Matt's hand. "We can't afford to take any more chances than we already have. Get out, Matt."

Matt knows that if his options were limited a few seconds ago, they're virtually nonexistent now. He tries to convince himself he's doing the right thing by going out and looking for Natalie, but what if she has turned? What if he finds her and she tries to kill him? Every available option feels like the wrong choice.

"I need my jacket." He takes a couple of hesitant steps forward. Jayde visibly recoils and Rod blocks his way.

"Leave. Now."

"Come on, this is a bit extreme, isn't it?" Matt hears Paul say, just about coming to his defense. "Matt wouldn't hurt a fly."

"The kid Nils killed was the same, and look what he did to Joy and the people on the boat," Rajesh reminds Paul.

Matt knows the decision has been made, and that to fight or protest would only make matters worse. He braces himself against the wind and rain, then starts walking and doesn't look back.

It's not the end of the world, Matt thinks, but he's starting to wonder if it might actually be. He's only been outside a few minutes, and already he's soaked and shivering with cold. He surveys the barren landscape he's a prisoner of and considers his depressing lack of options. Looking for Natalie is his obvious priority, but he can't risk being stuck out here alone for too long. He could try to break into Stuart and Ruth's bungalow and shelter there if needs be. Or, if it comes to it, he can hang out with the growing crowd of corpses in the stores.

He stops when he literally stumbles upon Nils's and Gavin's bodies, which have been dumped in the long grass not far from base, wrapped in blood-soaked sheets. He's suddenly found himself in a situation so bizarre it feels unreal—the baseless accusations and his unplanned eviction being the cherry on the cake—but seeing the corpses again helps him focus on the seriousness of what's happening. He crouches down and peels back a corner of the sheet covering Gavin, feeling compelled to check it's really him. His dead colleague's face is gray-white and splattered with blood from his eviscerated torso.

Should I take his jacket? He doesn't need it now.

If parts of it weren't as slashed and torn as Gavin himself, Matt thinks he probably would.

Back to Natalie.

Where the hell did she go?

Matt walks a circuit around all the other buildings. It's slow going because whichever way he walks seems to be head-on into the breeze. In the absence of trees and other natural windbreaks here, the weather is relentless, constantly blustery. The wind races across the island virtually unopposed, and now that Matt knows there's no way back into the main building, he's feeling the cold more than ever.

He reaches the stores and lets himself inside. The doors are permanently unlocked. No matter what the value of the equipment the Hazleton Adventure staff keeps in here, until now it's always been safe. Until Monday morning there'd never been any real trouble on Skek, save for the petty pilfering Stuart mentioned a while back. Matt looks around the building for as long as he can stand, helping himself to a spare waterproof and gloves. There's probably more here he could take, but the stench and his nerves get the better of him quickly and he has to get out.

Back outside again, Matt slowly trudges north, retracing his steps back toward the bungalow. When he looks up this time, he sees that the people in the main building are watching him. Their faces are pressed against the windows. What do they think he's going to do? Crack up? Go crazy? Try to break back inside so he can finish the job Nils started and kill the rest of them? He skirts around the building at a distance, then stops at the bungalow. The out-of-place, strange-looking building is locked tight. No lights, no life, no one home. He moves on, figuring he might come back after dark when he's not being watched.

The day is being steadily eaten away. He decides to head for the ruined fishing cottages up near the northeast of the island. Maybe Natalie will have reached the same conclusion and she'll be sheltering there too? Better the protection of crumbled walls and weathered stonework than no protection at all. Or maybe she knows about somewhere he doesn't? The overgrown army lookout near the beach perhaps? He resigns himself to doing a complete circuit of Skek before nightfall. But what if Jayde was right about Natalie? What if she's turned and now *she's* following *him,* poised to attack? He's tying himself up in knots again. He doesn't relish the prospect of being stuck out here on his own overnight. If the cold doesn't get him, then something or someone else might. For Christ's sake, he orders himself, man up.

What about the wreck?

The more he thinks about it, the more it makes sense. It's a relatively safe place—as safe as anywhere on Skek, anyway. As far as he's aware, nothing is on the ferry but death and destruction. It's reasonably solid (providing it's still afloat), and there will likely be some supplies he can scavenge. Most important, there's no fresh blood left to spill there. Everyone on the *Heavenly Vision* is already dead. No more killing. No one else left to turn. He sets off with pace, keen to get there fast. If Natalie's not there already, he'll claim it for himself.

When he finally reaches the cliffs on the east of the island, he stops. He crouches in the long grass, both to catch his breath and settle his stomach. He suffers with vertigo, but now's not the time. He looks down at the *Heavenly Vision* far below and tries to decide whether the ferry's in any worse condition than when he last saw it. It looks pretty much exactly the same, and that's something of a relief. It will be cold and uncomfortable, and it'll be fucking horrible belowdecks, but spending the night on the boat feels like his only option just now. Is Natalie down there? He can't see any indication, but he thinks she probably must be.

Nothing's ever straightforward, he thinks. Getting down to the boat is going to be a problem. He looks for the footpath Nils and Natalie took when Vanessa fell near here on Monday. He finds the beginning of the precarious route, but the way down is narrow and far from straightforward. He's struggling to see where the path actually goes and has just decided that taking his chances and abseiling is a marginally safer option when he stops and spins around, sensing someone behind him. He's immediately tense, braced for attack, weaponless but ready to defend himself if he has to.

He relaxes. It's only Paul.

"What do you want?"

"I've come to kill you," Paul says, deadpan. He holds Matt's terrified gaze for a couple of uncomfortable seconds longer before breaking into a broad grin.

"That's not funny." Matt reverses back up the path and then steps away from the edge of the cliff on the off chance Paul actually has lost his mind and really is about to shoulder-charge him over the edge. "Why are you here?"

"I figured you and Natalie had the right idea. I'd rather take my chances with you than Stuart and Frank and the rest of them. It was getting a bit oppressive in there. Ronan's winding himself up again. Never mind the Haters, I reckon it's only a matter of time before the whole lot of them gang up and attack him."

"Great."

"Seriously, though, it's getting out of hand back at base. They started having a go at Stephen again after you'd gone. I figured it would probably be my turn before long." Paul walks toward the drop and peers over the edge. "Natalie's down there then?"

"Not sure. Think so."

"Shall we?"

Paul starts to put on one of the climbing harnesses that have been left on the cliff top. He hooks himself up to an anchored rope, takes the strain, and starts to slowly walk back toward the edge.

"You sure about this?" Matt is on the verge of talking himself out of it and trying the path down again.

"Rajesh showed me how to properly rope up on Saturday. Come on, mate."

Several permanently hooked-up climbing points are here, complete with all the necessary metalwork. In the hurry to get back after Vanessa's death, Rajesh and Nils left the harnesses and ropes. Paul shows Matt how to secure everything, then shows him how to feed the rope through as he abseils down. Matt tugs on the rope and checks it's secure. The harness is tight around his waist and crotch. Almost too tight. He readies himself for the drop.

Paul casually disappears over the edge. Matt's vertigo is threatening to kick in, but he makes himself do it. He takes a deep breath, then steps out, and suddenly nothing but air is below him. He plants the soles of his boots against the rock face and steadies himself as the swirling wind buffets him from every direction. He looks around for Paul and immediately wishes he hadn't because he's already descended halfway with almost semipro speed. Matt's looking past him now, all the way down to the rocks. Bodies from the wreck are there, several of them tangled together in a rock pool like human-shaped flotsam and jetsam. He makes himself focus on his feet as he walks painfully slowly down the sheer rock wall. "I should be wearing a safety helmet," he chunters pointlessly to himself, complaining to take his mind off the nerves.

When he's had enough of looking down, he looks up. Dark clouds swirl ominously overhead, heavy with rain. His head feels heavy with the pressure of an impending storm.

Another few minutes and he's almost made it. A sudden gust of wind threatens to blow him into the cliff face before he takes the last downward steps, but Matt just manages to keep his balance. It's a massive relief when he finally plants both boots on solid ground again, and he wastes no time disentangling himself from the rope and harness.

When the two of them finally turn around, a bow and arrow points at them. The tip of the arrow moves from face to face. "Fuck off," Natalie tells them. "Both of you turn around and fuck off right now and leave me alone."

Matt knows she means business. She has that no-nonsense look in her eyes he's seen a few times before, and he thinks she'd let that arrow fly in a heartbeat. "Come on, Nat. Please . . ."

"I said fuck off. I came here to be alone. If I'd wanted to be surrounded by dickheads, I'd have stayed in the warm."

Despite that she's aiming a lethal weapon at his face, her comment is enough to make Matt laugh out loud. His reaction disarms her momentarily, but she immediately regains her composure and increases the tension in the bowstring.

"We were worried about you," Paul says.

"Bullshit. Worried about yourselves, more like."

"It's true." Matt does what he can to present a united front. "I didn't like the thought of you being out here on your own."

"I'm fine, thanks for your concern." It's clear that she is. "Anyway, how do I know you're not here to try and kill me?"

"Says the girl pointing the arrow at us," Paul answers quickly. She's not impressed.

Matt looks from face to face and clears his throat. "Because if one of us was going to try and kill you, I reckon we'd have probably done it already. And from what I've seen and heard this last couple of days, I reckon we'd have tried to kill each other too. We wouldn't have turned up here together like a bloody double act."

"A really shit double act at that," Paul says, noticing that the tension she has the bow string under is making the muscles in Natalie's arm tremble. "Come on, Nat, please."

She relaxes slightly—just slightly—and lowers the bow. The arrow's still ready to fire, her fingers still tightly gripping the cord.

"He got kicked out," Paul tells her, gesturing at Matt.

"What?"

"They threw me out. Reckoned I was probably a Hater."

"And are you?"

"No, of course not. That's stupid."

"How do you know?"

"He doesn't," Paul says quickly. "To be fair, though, neither do I. Or you. None of us do, come to mention it. All three of us could be Haters, if Haters even exist."

"Of course they exist." Natalie lowers the bow still farther. "What do you think happened to Nils, for fuck's sake? Cabin fever? Have another look inside this boat. Normal people don't do that."

"Or maybe they do," Matt says.

Natalie just glares at him. "Are you trying to be deliberately awkward?"

"No, it's just that we don't know what's normal anymore. We all turned on Stephen, and they all just turned on me. We don't know who to trust now, so no one trusts anyone. But you know that already. That's why you came back down here, isn't it?"

"Maybe. But look at Nils . . . he killed that kid, then he turned himself and killed Gavin. Explain that?"

"I can't," Matt says. "I can't explain any of this. I'm just doing what I can to cope with it."

Natalie lowers the bow completely now, arrowhead pointing straight down. "I don't know who to believe. I figured any one of us might be the next to turn. I thought I'd be safer out here on my own, which is why I'd be very grateful if you two would just turn around and fuck off back to base."

"I'm not going anywhere." Matt sounds more defiant and confrontational than he actually feels. "Don't reckon I could, as it happens. They probably wouldn't let me back in."

"Three is the magic number," Paul announces.

"What's that supposed to mean?"

"I'm serious. I think three is the optimum number to keep us alive. I was thinking about it just now. It's one of the reasons I followed you out here, Matt."

"You never said anything."

It's clear Paul's making this up as he goes along, but he seems to think he's onto something. "Think about it . . . if there's just the two of us and one person changes, the other one is likely completely screwed. You agree? But if there's three, there's a better chance of two of us making it if the other one loses their mind."

"He's got a point," Natalie says.

"So can we stay?"

"No."

"Come on . . ."

"No. One is my magic number. If I'm on my own, there's no

problem either way. Doesn't matter what side I'm on if there's no one else here with me."

"Please, Nat." Matt wonders if he sounds as desperate as he's starting to feel. "I'm not going to give you any trouble."

She looks him up and down. He's not like the other blokes left on the island. Not cocky. Not arrogant. Not full of himself like the rest of them, talking in business-speak or trying to impress her with exaggerated machismo. She weighs the pros and cons. "Okay, you can stay. Your mate can piss off, though."

Paul protests. He can't help himself. "What the hell? That's completely out of order." He points at Matt. "He's fucking useless."

"And you're fucking irritating," she tells Paul.

Matt maneuvers himself between them, well aware that he'll be first to get it if she changes her mind and decides to make use of the bow and arrow. "I'll keep him under control, I promise. We won't cause you any problems."

She thinks for a few seconds longer. "Okay, you can both stay. Short term. And you keep well out of my way, right?"

"Right."

"And I reserve the right to kick both of you off the boat if I change my mind, got it?"

"We get it," Matt tells Natalie. "Understood."

"Good."

She turns her back on them and returns to the wreck of the ferry. Matt takes that as a sign of implied trust, because right now he thinks there's a good chance that if he turns his back on anyone on this damn island, he or she will stab him as soon as look at him.

The two men follow her onto the *Heavenly Vision*. It feels like it's listing at a more acute angle than before, and everything looks different. As soon as Paul gets belowdecks, he can tell that Natalie's been working hard since she got here. "She's shifted a load of the bodies," he whispers.

"Has she? Fair play to her. Must have taken some guts to do that."

Paul has a bad joke on the tip of his tongue, but for once he keeps his mouth shut. Some of the corpses are in pretty bad shape, and all of them have started to rot. A sickly sweet stink is in the air, slightly tempered by the salty sea spray. Matt gags and spits. "Bloody horrible, isn't it?" Paul says. "I remember hearing people on TV talking about the smell of death, but I never experienced it until now."

Matt's focused on trying to keep control of his stomach. He can taste the decay above everything else. "I reckon if we were stuck here for a year that smell wouldn't even have started to fade."

Natalie's busy, doing everything she can to keep to herself, but she notices Paul looking at the unruly mound of bodies she's hastily assembled near the stern of the *Heavenly Vision*. It's a waist-high heap. "I had to move them. I couldn't leave them like we found them."

"Don't suppose they're too bothered," Paul says dismissively.

"It matters to me, though." For a split second he thinks her demeanor is about to change. He detects a chink of vulnerability, but it's almost immediately covered up with armor plating and aggression. "Couldn't stand having all those dead faces watching me."

Matt hasn't been in here before. He does what he can to hide how badly he's affected by what he's seeing. He can only begin to imagine how terrible it must have been to have walked into this slaughter unprepared. He's still feeling bilious and grabs a nearby wooden handrail for support. As if the blood and the bodies weren't enough, the constant unsteady rocking of the beached ferry and the unnatural angle at which it's come to rest have combined to increase the violent churning in his guts. Nothing's level in here. The deck is sloped downward and is tilted to one side. It's like something out of a gothic horror movie, but this is real, not a camera trick.

"You okay, mate?" Paul asks. "You're looking a little green around the gills."

Matt takes a deep breath of ice-cold, salt-tinged air to compose himself. He's in a short and narrow space, almost a square, with a door on either side. He feels increasingly claustrophobic. To his right are the toilets, to his left some kind of office. He reaches for the office handle, but Natalie stops him. "Not in there. That's my space. Keep out."

He holds up his hands in submission. "Whatever you say."

Paul's more confident than his seasick work colleague and stands on tiptoes to try to look in through the porthole-shaped window. "What are you hiding in there?"

"*My* food, *my* clothes, *my* stuff. Butt out." She makes it clear she's still ready to use the bow and arrow if Paul doesn't back off.

Fortunately, he does. "Where are we supposed to go then?"

Natalie gestures back toward the main cabin and the rows of empty, blood-soaked seats where the majority of the bodies were found. "Plenty of space down there."

"You're fucking kidding me."

"Well, it's either that or you go back to the others. Your choice."

"Jesus, Natalie, why be such a bitch about it?"

"Leave it, Paul," Matt warns, his nausea beginning to subside. He walks deeper into the sarcophagus-like shipwreck. "We'll be fine here. Honestly, Nat, it's okay. We don't want any trouble."

She mutters something unintelligible under her breath at Paul as she pushes past to get into her room. Paul tries to snatch a proper look inside, but the door is slammed shut in his face before he has a chance. He hears her blocking it from the inside. "Stay away, right?" she yells, her muffled voice still loud enough to be audible.

Paul shrugs. "She's a bit highly fucking strung, don't you think?"

Matt sits down on a relatively stain-free seat and holds his head in his hands. "She's scared, Paul, don't you get it? The aggression is how she deals with it. It's an act, I think, but you're not going to do any of us any good if you keep winding her up."

"Silly cow. Like she's the only one who's got problems."

Matt slumps forward, shoulders hunched. He stares at the wooden floor between his feet and traces a watery gore stain that trickles along the planks then disappears between them. "Leave her alone. She's done things here that I don't know if I could have done."

"What, shifted a few bodies? Give me a break."

Matt doesn't bother arguing, because he knows there's no point. He makes himself as comfortable as he can on the seat and tries to rest. Paul's still chuntering about Natalie, but Matt makes a conscious attempt to change the conversation. "It's already getting dark out there."

"It tends to do that at this time of day. Thanks for stating the bleeding obvious."

Another day already drawing to a close.

Another day they didn't make it back.

"What do you reckon things are really like back home?" Matt asks.

"Honest answer?" Paul replies after a few seconds' thought. "I don't think it's as bad as they're all making out. There's something going on there, sure, but they're all starting to talk like it's the end of the world. It's paranoia. Things just feel worse here because we're stuck and because this bloody island's so small, know what I mean? Everyone's feeling a thousand times worse because everything's confined and we can't get away."

"Suppose."

"And when you're in a situation like this—"

"You make it sound like you've been in situations like this before."

"—when you're in a situation like this"—Paul ignores Matt—"it's easy to let your mind run away with itself. Every little thing gets multiplied by a factor of ten thousand."

"What, every little thing like Joy or Nils? One minute he's normal, the next he's carving out Gavin's innards in front of us. . . ."

"You know what I mean."

"Yeah, I know what you mean." Matt sighs, unconvinced.

The conversation falters. Just the noise of the waves now.

"So what do we do now?" Paul asks after a minute or so.

"You tell me. You're the one who reckons he's usually got all the answers."

Paul is uncharacteristically reserved. "Yeah, but what do *you* think we should do?"

"Right now I think we should get some rest. As for the morning . . . who knows? I think Natalie's got the right idea. Keep away from everyone else as much as we can until we find a way of getting home."

"Sounds logical."

"And for what it's worth, I also think she picked the right place to stay. Why would anybody bother coming back here to kill when everyone's dead already?"

THURSDAY

17

Natalie doesn't emerge from her office hideout all night. Matt knows because he spends hours watching the door, waiting for her to move. It's freezing in here, so cold that it hurts his bones. He's lying across a couple of seats a short distance from where Paul is sleeping, and Matt only gets up when he absolutely has to because he needs the bathroom. He slowly shuffles toward the hull of the boat. Every step he takes in the gloom feels fraught with danger. He convinces himself the bodies are closer than he remembers, or that maybe he'll stumble on a couple Natalie missed. Perhaps they were hiding in the toilets while their friends were being massacred out here? He pictures himself finding a kid still trapped in a cubicle, cowering. What if some are still alive? Right now he can't decide if it would be better or worse to find them dead.

He scares himself so badly he occasionally freezes. What if he takes a step in the wrong direction and treads on outstretched fingers? He imagines the sickening crack of young bones beneath his boots, and it makes him feel sick to the stomach. Or what if he trips in the darkness and finds himself flat on the ground, face-to-face with one of the dead . . . ?

A couple of times during the long hours now ending, the ferry itself seemed to sob with grief. It reminds him of the way the rented house he shares with Jen seems to moan and sigh under its own weight at night, floorboards and pipes expanding and contracting with changes in temperature, cracking and popping. But, here on the boat, the noises are different and far more ominous. The ruptured metal hull groans as if it's in pain. The exaggerated grinding sounds are like prolonged, distorted screams, and Matt's left in no doubt that, sooner rather than later, something's going to give. It all feels uncomfortably close to collapsing under the strain. Three times now since nightfall the beached belly of the boat has dropped. It's probably only millimeters each time, but to Matt each movement feels like the beginning of a stomach-churning free fall. He reckons the wreck of the *Heavenly Vision* probably weighs several tons, but it feels painfully lightweight. Fragile, even. He imagines a chasm opening up along the center of the dead ship as it buckles and bends, then pictures himself falling through the gap into the ice-cold waters below. His mind continues to wander, and in his head he's deep below the waves and still sinking, unable to breathe or get back to the surface. The water-wrinkled, ghost-white fingers of dead kids reach out for him from the murk, pulling him deeper down as quickly as he tries to swim up. Desperate for breath. Lungs burning . . .

Focus. Snap out of it.

The light levels and the temperature have slowly changed, but the stench remains the same. It's as bad now as it was when he and Paul first got here. He thinks he'll never get used to it, no matter how long he's here. In fact, the longer that is, the worse it seems to get. He pees at speed in the pitch-blackness, and when he leaves the bathroom, he realizes just how much brighter it is outside now. The first tendrils of dawn's early gray light have started to creep in through the windows and add detail to the shadows.

Rather than sit back down and wait for the nightmare to come into full focus, he instead climbs the slippery metal steps up onto the deck.

He's drenched in seconds. Sea spray and driving rain combining to leave him completely waterlogged. He doesn't want to go back down again and so looks for alternative places to shelter. He spies the bridge of the ship and half-walks, half-slips along the wooden decking toward it. If only he'd thought of this last night. It would have been an infinitely better place to have spent the time; though ice-cold it would have been fresher and less enclosed and oppressive than the morguelike lower level. He finds the body of a crew member on the floor near the back of the small cabin, but once he's covered the dead man's face with a fire blanket, it's easy to convince himself the body isn't there. He tries not to dwell on having recognized the face. Matt remembers him skippering the boat when it carried them over to Skek last Friday morning. Christ, that feels as if it were a lifetime ago.

The control panel Matt's now leaning against is as dead as everything else. He idly flicks a few switches and presses a couple of buttons, but nothing happens. Wait. There's a key. He never imagined you'd start something as big as this ferry with the turn of a single key like his heap of car that's sitting on his front drive back home, he hopes. He goes to turn it, but then stops. What's the point? They're not going anywhere. It'll just make a load of unnecessary noise and attract unwanted attention, if it does anything at all.

"Do it." The voice takes him by surprise.

He turns around and sees Natalie standing behind him. "Oh, so you're talking to me this morning then?"

"As long as you don't do anything stupid."

"What are you doing out here?"

"I could ask you the same question."

"Couldn't stand it down there any longer. It's all right for you in your little cabin. All I'd got was a load of corpses and Paul for company. Don't know which was worse. What about you?"

"Just wondered where you'd disappeared off to," she nonchalantly answers.

Matt notices that she's still carrying the bow and arrow. "Will you put that damn thing down? You're making me nervous."

"There's other things on this island for you to feel more nervous about, believe me. Now turn the bloody key."

He does as he's told, and it is just like starting his car because as he moves the key a quarter turn clockwise, a couple of the lights on the panel in front of him illuminate. The single lightbulb above his head starts to glow too. He's about to turn it farther but stops himself. "No point, I guess. Don't need the engine. We're not going anywhere."

He looks around for Natalie, but she's already on her way back belowdecks. She moves at double his speed, and by the time he's reached the bottom of the staircase, she's back in her room again. Paul's still where Matt left him—sprawled out and fast asleep—so Matt knocks on Natalie's door like a kid waiting to see the head teacher. He gingerly opens it and sticks his head round. "Mind if I come in?"

She doesn't answer, but she doesn't object either, and he takes that as a positive. She's sitting on an office chair at a stunted, rubbish-strewn desk, messing with a computer and waiting for it to boot up.

"Did you not think to try the power before now?"

"I was too busy keeping my head down, trying not to be found." She doesn't look up. "I'd have got round to it eventually."

Matt lets himself into the room fully. It's so small that they're at opposite ends but are almost touching. He watches her as she stares at the computer screen, arms folded and impatient.

"What are you doing?"

"What do you think I'm doing? I'm trying to get online. Thought I might be able to get a message out to someone."

"You might struggle. I haven't had a phone signal since I got here."

She looks over her shoulder at him despairingly. "You think I don't know that? I have to try, though, don't I?"

He leans back against the wall and looks out the grubby window to his right. The water feels perilously close here, washing up against the glass, far higher up the hull than it should be. Yet this little room feels safe. It's still warm from last night. He can feel the residual heat from the cocoon of fire blankets and life jackets Natalie used as bedding. "Nice pad."

"Fuck off before you get any ideas. It's mine." Her answer comes quickly, and he thinks he detects the faintest glimmer of a smile in her reflection in the monitor. He's relieved. The Natalie he got to know over the weekend is still there. "It stinks, it's small, and it's uncomfortable, but it's a little oasis in here. Just enough room for one. Perfect."

The outer wall is white-painted metal; the others are covered to shoulder height with dated faux-oak cladding. A notice board dead ahead has all kinds of rubbish pinned to it. Sun-curled notices and faded safety posters.

"You reckon any of that was important?" Matt anxiously fills the silence with noise. "That rota's six weeks out-of-date."

"Does it matter?"

"I don't know. It might. What if there's something up there about the kids that were on board? Some contact details or something?"

"Maybe."

"That could be useful though, don't you think? There's probably all kinds of stuff that might be useful on here if we can get to it before it gets too waterlogged. We should have a look through it at least. In fact, I reckon we should strip the boat. We could do it between us." Now his mind is racing. "Hey, what about flares? You think if we set off a flare someone would see us?"

"We've already got flares. Be quiet, Matt. I've never heard you talk so much. Are you nervous or something?"

"Yes," he answers without hesitation. He thinks there's no point beating around the bush anymore.

The computer's finally ready. A familiar boot-up chime in an unfamiliar environment. It sounds out of place and unexpectedly reminds them both of home. Thankfully no passwords are required to gain access. Natalie digs the mouse out from under a pile of papers and shakes it to find the pointer. The clunky old machine is slow to respond, and it takes more effort than it should to drag the arrow down to the browser icon. It's made worse by the uneven angle of the desk, but she gets there in the end. She pauses before clicking.

"Come on, Nat, we don't know how long the power's going to last."

She waits a second longer because she knows how much this matters.

Deep breath.

Click.

It takes an inordinate length of time for the program to open.

For a while there's hope as the window fills with graphics and text, but it's just a cached page, and when Natalie clicks on a new link, all she gets is a message that no network connection is available. "Fuck." She clicks again and again and again and again in frustration, like she thinks the computer will have a change of heart and connect. Now the machine asks if she wants it to try looking for other available networks nearby. "There's nothing nearby, never mind a fucking network."

She throws the mouse across the desk. Matt slumps against the wall. His heart sinks, and the bitter disappointment makes him realize he'd staked a hell of a lot on being able to get a message home. "Shit. Shit." He hides his frustration, clenching his fists.

Natalie has turned around and is watching him. "Stop holding it in."

"What?"

"It's okay to be angry. Let it out or you'll give yourself a coronary."

"I can't."

"You *can*. I know you're an introvert, but you'll choke on it if you're not careful."

She's right and he knows it. Matt punches the wooden cladding, leaving a fist-shaped indent in the cheap woodwork.

"That's more like it," she says.

It hurts but it feels good, so Matt does it again. And again. And again and again . . .

"What the hell's going on in here?"

They both look around and see Paul standing in the doorway, staring at Matt and the hole he's punched in the wall.

"How long have you been there?" Matt asks.

"Couple of seconds. I heard you knocking seven shades of shit out of something and I panicked. Thought you might have been killing each other."

"We were trying to get online," Natalie explains.

"Well, that's not gonna happen, is it?" Paul says unhelpfully. "Want me to take a look?"

"All yours." She gives up her seat willingly. "I hate computers."

"All due respect, Paul," Matt says, rubbing his throbbing knuckles, "what difference is you looking at it going to make? Doesn't matter who's sitting at the keyboard, there's no network connection."

Paul takes the chair and stretches his fingers like a concert pianist about to start a recital. He opens a few windows on the screen, checks some settings, then closes them again. "You're right."

"Yeah, I know we're right."

He stares at the screen. "Doesn't make sense, though. If there's no network, why was there a computer here?"

"Who cares?" Natalie says.

"I do."

Paul flicks through folders and directories, opening and closing documents and spreadsheets.

"What exactly are you looking for?" Matt asks.

"Don't know. Anything, really. Probably nothing . . . just looking."

Matt's had enough. The small room feels overcrowded now with three of them. Despite everything, he's hungry. His empty stomach growls for attention. He heads back into the main part of the ferry. He has it in mind that there must be something here to eat. There might have been some kind of snack machine or concessions stand selling confectionary and drinks to pacify the kids being ferried to and from the island. Failing that, he thinks, there might be something in the abandoned luggage that's lying around. Is it too soon to be turfing through the children's belongings? It feels wrong, but he knows he probably doesn't have any choice if he wants to stay alive.

They're dead, I'm not.

Yet.

He has to be mercenary, even though it's against his nature. None of this stuff is of any use to the kids now, but a little food might mean the difference between life and death for him and the others. The more he thinks about it, though, the more he realizes it's probably not so much a choice between life and death, it's more about choosing between dying now and dying later. As long as they're stuck on this bloody island, it feels like they're just prolonging the inevitable.

He's standing right on the edge of the mountainous pile of bodies, trying to work out if he's really going to do this, if he *can* do it, and whether it'll be worth it. Frozen, ice-white faces are looking in his direction like cursed porcelain dolls, glazed eyes fixed on him, unblinking. It's like they're warning him, *Don't touch our stuff . . . we'll get you if you touch our stuff.*

Matt leans down and teases a kid's brightly colored rucksack out from under a corpse. He's gentle at first, but when it doesn't move, he's forced to tug a little harder. A dead arm flaps over and slaps down onto another body like cold meat on a butcher's counter, and for a second he thinks he might be about to trigger a gruesome avalanche of dead flesh. He takes a few steps back just in case, but only one more body is disturbed. It rolls over onto its belly and lands on top of another, locking the two of them together in an uncomfortable and unnatural embrace.

The bag he's picked up is wet. The floor's wet here too, he notices. The wreck is slowly flooding. Matt takes the rucksack to drier ground and mooches through its contents, regretting his intrusion into its late owner's brutally truncated life. There's a lifeless mobile phone, its case plastered in faded boy-band stickers. A well-used hairbrush. A rolled-up magazine and a copy of one of those YA books that's become an increasingly unsatisfactory movie franchise. He went to see the first film in the series with Jen. He quite enjoyed it, though Jen wasn't impressed, so he tempered his enthusiasm.

Now he holds a waterlogged diary with a padlock holding the clasp secure, all its secrets locked away forever. Such innocence. Such naïveté. He wipes his eyes and continues his grim scavenging, figuring that he should take whatever he can find here, no matter whom it belonged to or how the person died. He pockets a Mars bar he finds in the pocket of a discarded jacket, and a packet of throat lozenges from inside another dead child's coat. Some crisps. A packed lunch in a plastic box labeled GEORGIA PETERS— YEAR 8. He uncovers a mound of drenched luggage and is about to start working his way through it when he's disturbed. He looks up, feeling guilty like he's been caught stealing. Natalie's calling to him from the other end of the wreck, and he walks back toward her, already making excuses. "I was just looking for some food. I thought there might be something to eat. It's not like they're going to need it anymore and I—"

"Not interested," she says abruptly, and she pushes him back into the little office. "Look at this."

Paul's gotten something up on the computer screen. It's a low-res, black-and-white camera image. The quality is desperately poor.

"What is it?"

"It's here," Paul replies. "The boat. Basic CCTV."

Matt squints at the screen, trying to work out what exactly he's looking at. It's like doing one of those old Magic Eye 3-D pictures he used to like as a kid: a mass of visual static until you squint at it in a certain way, with a certain focus. Once part of the picture starts to become clear, the rest takes form. He now recognizes that the tramlines running up the center of the screen are the edges of the aisle between the rows of seats running the length of the *Heavenly Vision*'s lower deck. He ducks out of the office and looks up. A small, cheap-looking camera is mounted above the door where the wall meets the ceiling. He instinctively waves.

"Yeah, yeah," Paul says. "We see you. Stop dicking about."

"So what are you thinking? Does having CCTV make this place any safer?"

Paul clicks through a series of three camera icons near the bottom of the screen, and each time the image changes. Another camera looks back along the inside of the boat, and a third is up on deck near the bridge. "We might be able to use it if we can keep the power running long enough."

"Do these cameras stream or record?" Natalie asks.

"No idea. What difference does it make?"

"A massive difference. I think you're both missing the point."

"Enlighten us then." Paul is still idly cycling through images.

"Isn't it obvious? If these cameras were running before the boat hit the rocks, we might actually be able to see what happened here."

"We know what happened. A fucking bloodbath is what happened. What's done is done."

"I think we should watch it," Matt says. "Natalie's right. It won't change anything, but if we can find the kid Nils killed on the footage, we'll be able to watch him and figure out when he flipped. There might be some kind of signal, some kind of giveaway. Shit, we'd be in a much stronger position if we can tell when someone's about to change."

"And what if it's one of us?" Paul says, focusing on the computer again.

"What?"

"What if we work out how you can tell if someone's about to turn, and then it happens to one of us three? What do we do then?"

Natalie shuffles nervously from foot to foot. "I've still got the bow and arrow. I'll do what I have to do."

Paul doesn't look up. "Yeah, I don't doubt it. That's all well and good, but what if you're the one who's lost control?"

"We'll cross that bridge when we come to it." Her answer is reassuring and disconcerting in equal measure.

Paul focuses on the computer, sensing this is another impossible conversation they could probably all do without. His eyes are darting around the screen now, checking the cluttered desktop for a shortcut to the camera program or some kind of archive. "Got it." His mouth is dry with nerves. His hands are clammy. He double-clicks and opens up a separate viewer with a long list of date-stamped video clips, then scrolls through the files. Natalie pulls down a blind to reduce the light coming in from outside.

"Try and find early Monday morning," she suggests as Paul wheels through the surprisingly long list of dates and times. "It had to have happened when they were close enough for the currents and tide to drag them onto the island. Chances are they'd have drifted out to sea otherwise."

The file-naming convention is difficult to fathom. Paul goes back way too far initially, and the screen fills with a scene neither he or Matt expected to see. It's their own trip to the island late last week. Matt sees himself sitting reading, with Joy just in front of him leafing through a magazine, face like thunder. Ronan is bending Frank's ear, and Rachel and Gavin are laughing about something inconsequential. . . .

Paul clicks another file without comment.

It doesn't take long for him to find what they were looking for.

The next few clips Paul loads up all look pretty much the same: a scene of devastation, captured shortly after the *Heavenly Vision* hit the rocks. He keeps backing up to a while before impact, and as the boat cuts through the waves, subtle changes occur in the shadows and lighting. Everything else on the screen remains unnaturally still. Frozen. Dead. Paul glances back for reassurance.

"This is after the attack but before the crash. Keep going," Natalie tells him.

Paul jumps further back in time at five-minute intervals until he sees movement on board. It's jerky and indistinct, almost like a time-lapse. He goes back a little further still.

"Sweet Jesus," Matt says as another file opens and pixelated black-and-white chaos fills the computer screen. They're watching from the outside camera now as three young kids scramble up onto the deck from down below, desperately trying to escape their inevitable deaths. One of them loses her footing and crashes down onto her backside, only to end up tumbling to the edge of the deck as the boat bucks the waves, then falling overboard in an uncontrolled flurry of arms and legs and panic. Somehow Matt finds watching the girl falling more disturbing than the massacre he assumes was taking place elsewhere at the exact same time. He can't get the image of that poor child out of his head. She was only a dot: no older than the kid who lives next door to him and Jen. He imagines the shock of the unbearable cold. The terror as her lungs filled with salt water and the current dragged her down. Unable to scream. Fighting to get back to the surface but sinking ever deeper, knowing she was going to die. Petrified. Helpless. Alone.

It's hard watching this stuff, but they know they have to do it.

A handrail chain being used like a whip.

Kids and adults sacrificing each other to get out of the way of the killer. Every man, woman, and child for themselves. Role reversals. Adults hiding behind kids. Kids hiding behind one another. In the chaos it's impossible to discern who's the killer and who are the victims.

After viewing a few scenes the initial shock wears off and they start to become immune to what they're watching. After all, they've seen worse firsthand this week. They start looking for details in the destruction.

"Where's that kid?" Matt asks. "The one Nils got rid of. The killer."

"He shouldn't be that difficult to spot." Paul selects another file to open. The boy was awkward and gangly limbed, uncomfortable in his own skin. Floppy hair. Bum-fluff chin. Spots. Loose-fitting, baggy clothes. Paul cycles through the cameras repeatedly, but never quite manages to catch more than a glimpse of any of the killings. Victims stumble in and out of frame, corpses are pushed away to the side or trampled underfoot. The camera resolution is low (Matt thinks that's not a bad thing), and *the deed* remains largely unseen.

Paul's close to giving up when Natalie spots something. "Wait," she shouts, making both him and Matt jump with surprise. "There. Back up."

Paul does exactly as he's told, and then he sees it too. The kid. He's standing in a doorway, little more than a silhouette with little visible detail apparent, but it's irrefutably him. "Yep," Paul says, even though Natalie doesn't need his confirmation, "you're right. That's our man."

"How can you be sure?" Matt's still squinting.

"Because he's the only one left moving," Natalie says. "He'd killed all the rest of them by this point."

Paul's not sure. "No, wait a minute. . . ." He replays the last few seconds of footage again and taps his finger on the bottom right-hand corner of the screen. A brief flicker of movement is there, little more than a fleeting shadow. Paul notes down the file reference, then navigates to another camera feed—same time, different perspective. Now they're watching from the next nearest camera angle. A girl, half the killer's size, is running for cover. She's wearing a coat that looks too big, and its size emphasizes her childish fragility.

"I can't watch this." Natalie looks away. "Poor little mite. I've seen enough. I don't want to watch her die."

The girl moves with far more speed than the gangly youth who's hunting her down. She's remarkably stealthy and races through the stillness with athletic ease, clearly desperate to get away. Again, Paul's not sure. He feels like he's watching a horror movie, waiting for the inevitable jump-scare. "Jesus, she's not running away. She's running straight toward him."

"Wait, what's that?" Matt asks. "Quick, freeze it."

Paul does as he says. Backs up a few frames. "What's the problem?"

"What's she got in her hand?" Matt leans in closer and adjusts the angle he's watching from. "Can you sharpen the picture? Change the contrast or something?"

"Give me a sec." Paul adjusts a slider at the top of the screen that controls the brightness, then messes with the contrast.

"What is that she's holding? It looks like a metal pipe, something like that? It looks like a weapon."

"Smart kid," Paul says. "Self-defense. Looks like she wasn't ready to go down without a fight."

Natalie shakes her head. "I think you're wrong."

"What are you saying?"

"For fuck's sake, don't you get it? She's not interested in self-defense. Look at her! She's on the prowl. She's on the attack!"

As they watch, the girl on the screen is distracted by something happening beyond the reach of the camera. She sprints out of shot with sudden predatory speed like a hunting animal about to pounce.

Cut to the third feed. Overexposed. Too much light. The brightness balances out when the girl springs into view. They watch her chase down a man who towers over her, holding on to his legs the way a cheetah hangs on to the flank of a gazelle it's caught, jaws locked and teeth sunk deep into flesh, never letting go. The man hits the deck with a body-shaking thump that's not audible but is certainly visible, and though he tries to fight her off, the girl dodges his clumsy attacks with ease. She's lightning fast, anticipating his every desperate move. Before he knows what's happening, she's on his back and he can't reach her or defend himself. With one foot planted down hard between his shoulder blades, she caves in the back of his skull with the metal rod.

Another frantic flurry of movement, then it's over.

There's just the girl left moving on-screen now. A Hater. No one says it out loud, but they all know that's what she is.

Paul flicks between feeds again. It all looks deceptively calm. There's barely any other movement. Shifting shadows. Rolling waves. No one else left alive.

"So there were two of them," Natalie says. "That's how they managed to do so much damage."

"Still, two wild kids against about thirty normal people. They should have been able to stop them, shouldn't they?" Paul says, sounding unimpressed.

"You'd have thought."

Paul continues to stare at the computer screen as he chews over the situation. He flicks through the camera feeds, advancing through chunks of time, then stops suddenly, his attention piqued. "Wait a sec."

"What is it?"

"Not sure . . ."

He flicks backward and forward—same camera shot, different time stamp. It's one of the cameras belowdecks again now, post-wreck, and everything appears motionless. The violent impact of the ferry and its unnatural listing has thrown the corpses around. Front and center is the pile of dead kids they found when they first boarded the boat. He taps his finger on the image of a girl lying sprawled on her back on top of the pile, staring up at nothing. A dark smear of blood is splashed across her white T-shirt. "Look. These bodies have moved."

"So?" Matt says. "That was a hell of an impact. Anything could have happened."

"Yeah, but that doesn't explain this. That girl fell up."

"What?"

"Look at this." Paul takes a couple of screen shots from the same camera at slightly different times and compares them. Same angle, same bodies, one major difference. In the earlier footage the girl they're looking at is facedown on the floor. Later, she's on her back on top of the heap. "So how did a dead body manage to fall up the pile?"

He goes back to the clip where the body's facedown, then lets the footage run.

There's movement among the dead.

"What is that?" Natalie asks.

"Can't see . . ." Paul struggles to make it out.

All becomes clear.

It's the boy they saw earlier, the boy Nils killed. He's burying himself under the bodies, trying to hide. Clearly struggling with her weight, he drags the girl in the white T-shirt on top.

Paul cycles forward now, eating up time in large chunks, advancing way past the moment of impact until the image changes again. He clicks PLAY and they watch the boy crawling back out. Blood-soaked. His movements are the polar opposite of those of the murderous girl they were just watching. Where she prowled, he creeps. Where she was confident, he's afraid. Where she seemed to have the strength of someone double her size, he has half. He can barely move now, the weight of his nightmare situation dragging him down. He edges cautiously forward, then waits, then he runs for his damn life.

Matt's struggling to get his head around all of this. "So what was he hiding from?"

"That girl. Has to be. She was the only one left."

"Wait, so are we saying he's *not* a Hater?"

"Looks that way."

"We don't know for sure," Paul quickly interrupts. "The cameras are really limited, don't forget. There could be loads more going on that we're not seeing."

"I didn't see him attacking anyone," Matt says.

"Like I said, the cameras are limited."

"But he was *hiding* for Christ's sake."

"We don't know that for sure."

"No, you're right, we don't. It's a pretty safe bet, though."

"It would explain why Nils didn't think twice about killing

him, wouldn't it?" Natalie suggests. "Nils was one of them, the boy wasn't."

Paul cycles backward, then stops when the camera begins shaking uncontrollably, the brightness and contrast temporarily off the scale. The moment of impact.

When the picture settles again, it all looks familiar, like it is now. The same unnatural angles. Paul leaves the footage running. "I reckon we've seen enough."

"We've barely seen anything," Natalie says.

For several minutes the same picture remains on-screen. Nothing happens. Nothing moves. Paul double-checks that the video is actually playing, that they're not staring at a freeze-frame. Then there's movement in the bottom right-hand corner, almost out of shot.

"What is it?" Paul asks.

"It's that girl again."

There she is—the killer. She's sprawled on the ground, only coming fully into view when she finally picks herself up. "What's she doing?"

"She looks hurt. Must have happened when the boat hit the rocks."

As they watch, the girl staggers forward, then drops to her knees. She manages to get up again and takes a few more unsteady steps. Her oversize, blood-soaked coat falls from her shoulders leaving her cold and painfully exposed. This is the first clear view of her they've had. The first time she's been relatively still and fully in shot.

Natalie freezes. "Wait, wait, wait . . ." She's panicking. "Oh, no. Fuck, no . . ."

"What is it?" Matt asks.

"Don't you recognize her?"

"No."

"It's the girl we found. It's Louise."

"It can't be."

"It *is*."

"Jesus. Are you sure?"

"As sure as I can be with these shitty images."

"But she'd been attacked, hadn't she?"

"That was what we assumed. Nils said he reckoned she'd been hiding near the top of the beach and then she got attacked, but what if the opposite happened? Look at her, she's hurt. What if she managed to kill Joy, then was overcome with the cold and exhaustion and collapsed?"

They watch as she disappears from view again. She can just be seen climbing down the side of the boat, her arms and head visible briefly before she drops from view.

"But she could never have got up off the rocks in that state," Matt says.

"She could if she used the path around the headland. It branches off. One way heads up, the other takes you right round from here to the jetty."

"Shit, Nat. It must be her."

Natalie doesn't need his validation because she knows she's right. She makes for the door, pausing only to snatch up her belongings and her weapon. Matt's close behind.

"Where are you going?" Paul asks.

Natalie's dumbfounded. "What? Do you really need me to spell it out to you? There's a Hater in the base with them, a bloody psychopath. We have to tell them about Louise before she comes around."

"Fuck 'em."

"You can't be serious," Matt says.

"They didn't seem to give much of a shit about you yesterday, did they?"

"None of us knew what was going on. Heat of the moment and all that. . . ."

"We can't just leave them," Natalie says. "If she wakes up and kicks off, who knows how many people she'll kill."

18

Three people need to get off the beach with only two climbing ropes. Matt takes the long way around. The narrow footpath is no less precarious. The rocks are craggy with plenty of foot- and handholds, but the constant rain and the spray from the crashing waves leave every surface feeling unnaturally slippery, like they're covered with grease.

It's a lot easier to spot the route from the bottom looking up than it was from the top looking down. Matt's passed the fork in the path, but while the route around to the main beach and the jetty appears relatively gentle and clear, the option he's taken feels almost as steep as the rock-face climb he came this way to avoid. He's barely halfway up, and a hell of a drop is already to his left. The narrow footway curls and weaves around the edge of the headland, constantly climbing, but never direct. There's barely enough room to put one foot in front of the other in places, but he can't go back. The way ahead is largely hidden by the mist and the swollen bulge of the rock face, but his only option is to keep climbing.

The other two are waiting impatiently when he finally reaches the top. He drags himself over to them on his hands and knees, thankful, and not a little surprised, that he's made it in one piece. "I hate heights," he says, but there's no chance of any sympathy. One look at Natalie immediately focuses him on the task at hand. She has her bow and arrow ready.

The three of them march across the island in silence, grouped together against the tireless wind and rain. They're in full view of the base because there's nowhere to hide and no way of approaching unseen. "Stay close," Natalie tells them. "United front and all that shite."

Panting with effort. Racked with nerves.

The buildings look just as they left them yesterday, and that's a relief. Lights are on and they can hear the steady chugging of the generator in it's shedlike outbuilding. "Reckon they'll let us back in?" Matt asks, genuinely unsure.

"Who knows," Natalie replies. "Anyway, it's not them we need to worry about."

The door to the main building is shut. They approach it with caution. Matt reaches for the door handle, then stops and looks to the others for reassurance. Paul nods at him, urging him on, but Matt changes tack and decides to knock first. He hammers with his fist. "We don't want them freaking out and going off at us half-cocked."

When there's no immediate reply, he does try the handle. That the door's not locked catches him off guard. Opening it takes a fraction of the effort he expected, and he grunts with surprise, losing his balance and almost falling into the building. He picks himself up and goes inside.

"Hello . . . ?"

Nothing.

His eyes adjust to the harsh lighting. He takes a few steps forward, then stops.

"Oh, Christ."

He finds Frank first.

He looks like he's been in one hell of a fight. The right side of his face is swollen and misshapen, broken teeth mixing with bloody drool, which dribbles down his chin and drips into his lap. He's sitting in a heap on the floor like a Saturday-night drunk who's lost his battle with the booze outside a club. Natalie crouches down to see to him, even though she already knows she can do nothing. She carefully puts one hand on either shoulder and pushes him back, but she can tell from the way his head lolls forward heavily and without any control that he's dead.

"Watch out for the kid, she could be anywhere," Paul whispers. He's hanging back near the doorway, looking around for something to use as a weapon and feeling hopelessly underprepared.

Matt walks farther into the building. It's deathly silent in here. The occasional creak. Dripping. Natalie calls him back. "Wait, Matt. Be careful."

At the end of the dining area he finds a table that's awash with blood. There's barely an inch of its surface that's not been dyed deep red. Everything's coated. There's an abandoned mug and bowl. The bowl's half-full, and the blood looks like soup, unidentifiable lumps floating in the semisolid liquid. He walks around to the far side of the table and finds a chair on its side, two of its legs broken. More blood, too. A snail trail curves out past the chair and along the walkway like someone's been dragged away. He wonders whose blood this is. It could belong to anyone. Could be from more than one of them.

Natalie's on his shoulder, but he's so preoccupied trying to make sense of everything he's seeing that he doesn't notice her until she touches him. He jumps out of his skin and slips in the gore. "Christ's sake," he gasps, heart racing. "Don't do that."

Natalie has more important things on her mind. "Louise might still be here," she whispers ominously, and she points out a trail of bloody footprints that snake away toward the kitchen and the dorms. They're smudged and hard to make out. Some look like they were made by boots, others by the soles of bare feet.

Instinctively, Matt follows the prints. He glances around and sees a bread knife lying on the counter just inside the kitchen. He reaches in through the serving hatch and snatches it up, then carries on.

"What are you doing? Are you out of your fucking mind?" Paul hisses at him, standing his ground from a relatively safe distance back. "Have you never seen a horror movie?"

"Grow up," Matt tells him, but Paul's too busy remembering all the horror clichés he's always joked about before. This is no joke, though.

"Don't split up, don't go into the dark . . . for fuck's sake, just *don't*."

Now Natalie's the one who's holding back. "He's got a point, Matt."

Matt stops. Did he just hear something? It could be a rat or some other vermin, he thinks, but he knows he's kidding himself because there are no rats or any other similar-size animals on Skek. There's just people, and right now those people seem intent on tearing one another apart.

He braces himself for an attack, which doesn't immediately come. "Where are they all?" he asks, thinking out loud. "If they're all dead, where the hell are they? The kid couldn't have moved them, could she?"

"Why would she even have bothered?" Natalie asks, reluctantly edging closer.

Matt continues toward the dormitories. Natalie checks that her arrow is correctly loaded onto the bow and takes up the tension in the string. More blood is on the linoleum here.

"I don't reckon there's anyone here," Paul says.

"There must be," Matt whispers, and he peers around the first door. The dorm he and Paul slept in is empty. The dorm next door is too, as is the third—the room where Louise was being kept under sedation. His heart's in his mouth for a second when he uncovers a body-shaped bulk on the floor, but it's just pillows and bedding, turfed off the mattress in a hurry.

One dorm left. It's the only one with a door that's closed. The key's still in the lock, and the back of a chair has been wedged under the handle to make sure it stays shut.

"Leave it, mate, just fucking leave it," Paul whines.

"She in there?" Natalie asks. Matt looks through the small rectangular window, but he can't immediately be sure. The lights are off in the dorm. He squints into the gloom. The room's a maze of tall bunks and wooden wardrobes.

"This is a really fucking bad idea," Paul says, and Natalie can't help but think he might be right.

"We have to check," Matt tells them both. "Don't see that we have any choice."

His hands clammy with nerves, Matt grips his knife tight, then moves the chair, trying to make as little noise as possible. Natalie stands a short distance back with the bow and arrow, ready to fire.

"You sure about this?"

"We have to be certain."

"Just do it," Natalie says before she can talk herself out of it. "You're right, we've got to deal with her one way or another."

"The kid's a fucking killer," Paul protests. "We're better off leaving her locked up."

"Do it," Natalie says again.

Matt turns the key, then drops the handle and pushes the door open. There's a rush of stale air, but the immediate rush of violence they're fearing doesn't come.

"Anybody in here?"

Knife held ready, Matt takes a few tentative steps forward.

"What's happening?" Paul asks, his view restricted.

"You'd be able to see if you weren't hiding," Natalie sneers.

Matt treads in a pool of something tacky on the linoleum floor, then notices a bloody trail snaking away around a corner, disappearing between two bunks. "Looks like she's hurt," he whispers.

There's that noise again. Someone moving?

"Careful, Matt," Natalie says.

Another noise. More movement.

Matt panics and starts to reverse. "Get back, get back."

But it's too late.

Natalie's already followed him into the room and Paul's close behind, and between the two of them, they're blocking the way out.

"Move!" Matt yells at them both because he can hear her coming for him now. "The kid's in here. Get out!"

There's a sudden burst of movement from the other side of the dorm. A frantic flurry of arms and legs as the killer kid picks herself up and comes at Matt.

But it's not little Louise.

Too big. Too heavy. Too powerful.

It's Ruth.

She's hurt. Lots of blood. Dragging one leg behind her.

Weakened. Wounded.

"Thank Christ, Ruth. We thought you were—"

She hurls herself at Matt with vicious intent but barely controlled direction. She skids in the blood, then smacks her knee on the corner of a bed and crashes into Matt off-balance, forcing him back up against the wall, winding him. She's carrying Nils's serrated hunting knife and holds it up high, ready to bring it thumping down into his unprotected flesh.

Yet she doesn't do it.

She freezes and stares at him, eyes fixed on his and filled with hate, time slowed down to a virtual stop.

Matt pushes her away and she staggers back with the kitchen knife he'd been carrying sunk into her gut at an awkward angle, just below her sternum. Buried to the hilt.

One lung punctured and filling with blood. Deep, rasping breaths.

"I didn't mean to do it," Matt says quickly. He's instinctively apologizing and overcompensating, worried that the other two will think he's something he's not. "I'm not a Hater, I swear. . . . I was just holding the knife . . . she ran onto it . . . she came at me."

Coordination gone, legs numb, Ruth trips farther back into the dormitory. She's trying to pull the knife out of her flesh, but it's in too deep and the angle's all wrong, and with hands slippery wet with blood she can't get a grip. She topples over and hits the deck hard. She tries to scream, but can only make a sickly wheezing sound as the air escapes through the hole in her chest before reaching her throat. Blood pools across the floor, spilling out from underneath her like an oil slick, an unstoppable flow. Her arms and legs flail furiously, slipping in the flood, splashing and splattering.

Gurgling. Gasping. Another half-choked dry scream. Then silence. No movement.

Ruth somehow maintains eye contact with Matt, who's standing over her now, feeling confused—terrified and guilty in equal measure. He wants to tell her he's sorry, but he's not. He knows if his knife hadn't come between them, hers surely would have.

A couple more twitches. The death rattle. A split-second strained face, then nothing.

Matt looks up and sees the other two watching him from the doorway. "What does that make me?" he demands. "I killed Ruth. What does that make me?"

Paul's not sure what Matt means. "What?"

"What does that make me? I'm a killer now. . . . Does that mean I'm one of them? Like Nils? Like the girl?"

Natalie marches up to him, bow now slung over her shoulder. She's face-to-face with Matt, holding his chin up to keep him from looking at the still-spreading wave of gore. "Look at me, Matt. She attacked *you*. You didn't set out to hurt her. You didn't have any choice. You had to do it."

Matt's voice is unsteady, full of emotion. "You think? I don't know if it was an accident or if I did it on purpose . . . if I *wanted* to do it. I don't know if it was self-defense or if I just knew I had to get her before she got me. I don't know if I hate myself for doing it, or if I'm proud. . . ."

"She was a Hater," Natalie says, connecting the dots and vocalizing what all three of them are beginning to think. "That's the only explanation. Why else would they have locked her in the dorm? You just did what you had to do."

"It was luck." Paul tries to sound more confident than he feels. "Whatever the reason, you did it, and it's just luck that she's the one lying dead at your feet and you're still alive."

Matt's panicking. "Yeah, but what if I do it again? What happens if it's one of you two next time?"

"What, you think you're going to get a taste for it?"

"I don't know. How am I supposed to know?"

Natalie wraps her arms around him and whispers, "I reckon I'm safe with you, mate."

What starts as a casual hug lasts longer and feels more important than either of them expects. It makes them both realize how fucking terrified they are. Physical contact—*friendly* physical contact—with another human being says more today than a thousand words ever could.

"Very touching," Paul grumbles, feeling excluded and less than impressed. "So what's the plan now? Clean this place up and hunker down, or try to find the others?"

"We need to hope they haven't all crammed into Rod's boat and fucked off without us," Natalie says.

"Think they have?"

"I think they might have. If I was in their position, I reckon it'd look like a pretty good option. What do you think, Matt?"

Matt doesn't answer. Instead he just walks back to the mess hall in silence, his legs feeling heavier with every step. He makes it as far as the nearest blood-free table and collapses into a chair, no longer able to support his own weight. "I don't know how much more of this I can take." His voice echoes around the alien stillness of the building. "I think I've got my head around what's going on, then it all goes to shit again."

Natalie fetches a drink from the kitchen, then sits down with him. "It's shock. Here, have this."

Overstrong fruit cordial. Matt winces at its unexpected sweetness as he stares at Frank's body slumped at the other end of the building near the front entrance. "Every time I think things can't get any worse, they do."

"It just feels that way because it's been so relentless. It'll slow down soon. It has to."

"Yeah, when there are none of us left," Paul unhelpfully suggests.

Matt sips his cordial, beginning to regain his composure. "I've lost track. Who actually is left?"

Paul's been asking himself the same question and has the answer ready. "Assuming they're in hiding and not dead, from our side there's Ronan, Stephen, Rachel, and us." He looks at Natalie. "From your lot there's you, Rajesh, Rod and his kid, and Stuart."

"Jesus Christ, Paul, sides?" Natalie says.

Matt's keen to head off another pointless argument before it begins. "So there's nine left in total."

"And Louise," Natalie adds.

"Forget that little freak," Paul says. "So, if they are still here, do we try and find them and stick together, or do we keep our distance?"

"We stick together," Matt answers without hesitation. He sips his drink again and swallows hard. "It makes sense."

"You reckon?" Paul says, obviously not impressed. "I think Natalie had the right idea last night."

Matt shakes his head. "I've changed my mind. Think about it. . . . So far the three of us have managed to not kill each other, and the longer we don't, the more chance I think there is that we won't."

"That's just speculation," Natalie says.

"I know, but right now that's all I've got."

"And you just killed Ruth," Paul adds.

"Yeah, but I didn't kill you, did I? I don't know about you pair, but I'd feel better knowing where the rest of them are. Let's find out for certain if they've gone. There's so few of us left now it should be easy to keep an eye on everyone."

"Fair point," Natalie admits. "And with fewer of us we should have a better chance of working out who's who."

"Or who's *what*," Paul corrects her.

"I think we need as much information as we can get," Matt says. "I know that's not going to be a lot, but knowing where the others are is a start. Otherwise we'll just be sitting here waiting for them to find us."

"And kill us?" Paul asks.

"Maybe. Who knows."

"Or maybe we'll kill each other first."

The conversation stalls. No one has anything to say. It all sounds ridiculous. Or it would if it weren't so fucking terrifying.

Matt looks at the other two, almost demanding answers with his stare, but there's nothing coming. It's an impossible, illogical situation they've found themselves trapped in, with no obvious way out. When the lack of response becomes too much to stand, Matt tries again. "Okay, I reckon we need to get what's left of us together, see what's what, then work out how we're going to get us all off this bloody island."

"And how exactly are we going to do that?" Paul asks.

"Like I said, Rod's boat," Natalie says. "It'll be down at the jetty. We'll take it. He said he wasn't ever going back, remember?"

"He also said something about being light on fuel."

"We can use kayak paddles," Matt suggests.

"For now I think we should just get down to the jetty and stake our claim, make sure no one can leave here without us."

"How?"

"I don't know . . . sabotage maybe? We steal something that'll make a difference. Something crucial. Something that'll stop them sailing."

"Like what?"

"It doesn't matter. A part of the motor, the rudder . . . whatever it takes."

"Spark plugs?" Matt suggests.

"Something like that. Anything. Just enough to disable it and stop anyone getting away and leaving us here. Something we can put right when we're ready to leave. As far as I can see, the person who's got control of the boat right now is the person who has all the power. We just have to make sure it's one of us."

They make their way down to the jetty at speed. Natalie outruns the two men. She's naturally quick as it is, but she's even faster when her neck's on the line.

She stops on the brow of the hill and looks down. Matt and Paul catch up a few seconds later, and they both see what she's seen.

Nothing.

There's no point running any farther.

The jetty is empty.

The boat's already gone.

19

If anyone else is left on the island, there are only a few places where they're likely to be. They could hide in the crumbling ruins of the cottages to the north or the abandoned and overgrown military defense turret near the south coast, but neither option seems particularly practical. With both the main building and the stores being filled with corpses, Stuart and Ruth's bungalow seems to be the only sensible choice remaining.

Someone's definitely been here recently, that much is clear. Fresh muddy footprints are in the well-worn path that leads from the base to the front of this neighboring building. Quite a few footprints. Different sizes, different directions.

Neither Matt or Paul have given the bungalow much thought before now. The squat, shoebox-shaped, grim-looking building is quite a distance from everything else, and Matt can't understand why it wasn't built closer when the buildings are already so far from the rest of civilization.

The cottage sticks out. It looks like a bland 1960s-era prefab that was cast out of concrete before being literally picked up and dropped onto the middle of Skek. It's a surreal, almost comical sight. During the time they have lived here, Stuart and Ruth have clearly tried hard to imbue the place with some of the comforts of home. "It reminds me of something out of one of those fake villages the army used to build so they could practice blowing the shit out of stuff," Paul says, and Matt knows exactly what he means. Matt's seen the footage on TV documentaries: fake houses lining fake streets filled with cardboard-cutout pedestrians, the artificial calm frequently being shattered by squads of real gun-carrying soldiers practicing fighting, and by very real tanks firing very real mortars.

A low picket fence defines the (presumably arbitrary) extent of Ruth and Stuart's smallholding and keeps the (almost nonexistent) neighbors at bay. The cottage has a pea-green front door, and a weather-faded, hand-painted wooden sign has been hung next to it: WELCOME TO OUR HOME. But when Matt looks at it, he feels anything but welcome. He tries to remember the self-assured, effusive, and hospitable Ruth he met last Friday evening, not the crazy, psychopathic bitch who attacked him less than an hour ago. The crazy, psychopathic bitch he then killed. How the hell's he going to explain that to Stuart? If the others thought he was trouble before, they're going to want to crucify him now.

I've killed someone. . . .

The guilt is hard to handle. It stops him in his tracks and makes him question everything.

Am I a Hater?

He's still not sure.

"So do we just rock up to the front door and knock?" Paul asks.

"Yep." That's exactly what Natalie does. She raps on the door with her knuckles, then tries the brass knocker above the post flap when there's no immediate answer.

"There's a postbox." Paul sounds nervous and is talking crap again. "Why the hell is there a postbox? Did you get many deliveries round here?"

She ignores him and crouches down. She lifts the flap and shoves her fingers through to prop it open so she can see inside. "Anybody in?" she yells. Though there's no obvious response, she thinks she catches a glimpse of fleeting movement, most likely someone trying his or her best not to be seen. Or was it a shadow? Just a trick of the light? It's hard to be sure from her restricted viewing angle. She holds her breath—because her heavy breathing is making it harder than it should be to hear anything—and concentrates. There it is again. Someone is definitely in there, and whoever it is, is doing all he or she can to stay hidden. Natalie can sense someone watching her, and the building definitely doesn't have the hollow air of an empty place. She shouts again to try to force the person's hand. "Anyone there? Come on you fuckers, let us in." She listens again, this time not necessarily waiting for a response, just for any kind of reaction.

And she hears it.

Shuffling noises. Someone giving almost silent instructions to someone else—trying too hard to stay quiet and making enough noise to be heard outside by default.

Matt's up at the window now, but the curtains and blinds are pulled shut. "Anything?" he shouts across to Natalie.

"They're definitely in there," she shouts back, not worried about the volume of her voice. If anything, she wants them to hear her.

"Break the fucking door down then," Paul suggests. Matt gives him a couple of seconds to see if he's actually going to do anything other than bark out instructions, but he's clearly not. Natalie beats the pair of them to it. She puts down her bow and arrow and starts barging at the door, trying to get it open. It looks old and flimsy but it's surprisingly firm. When she's had a few attempts and got nowhere, and Matt's also had a turn and failed, Paul finally steps up. "Here," he grunts, readying himself. "This is how you do it."

He takes a couple of paces back along the path, then takes a run up with his shoulder dropped. Before he can hit the door, though, it opens inward. He tries to stop himself but it's too late, and he trips over the low step and ends up on his hands and knees halfway down the bungalow's narrow hallway, coming to rest in an unruly heap at Rajesh's booted feet. Ronan's peering out from behind the door, but no one pays him any attention because they're all focused on the ax Rajesh is holding just above Paul's head.

Rajesh is poised to strike. "Don't move a fucking muscle."

Natalie takes a step forward, half in and half out of the building now, and raises her hands in submission. Rajesh lifts the ax higher, leaving her in no doubt he'll use it if he has to.

"Raj, mate, don't . . . it's me."

"I can see that, but thinking you know someone doesn't count for much anymore. You ask Stuart."

"Where is he?"

Rajesh gestures back deeper into the cottage with a flick of his head. His eyes remain fixed on Natalie and the ax is unmoving. "He's in the bedroom, bleeding out over the bed."

"What happened?"

"His wife happened, that's what. She's one of them. She went fucking mental. Killed Frank when he tried to stop her, then turned on Stu and damn near killed him too. We managed to get her into one of the dorms. It was all we could do to shut her in and get the hell out of there. I mean, Frank had hurt her but . . ."

Natalie nods and Rajesh shuts up.

"We saw what she did."

"You've been back to base? Fuck, you didn't let her out, did you?"

"It's okay. She's dead."

"What? How?"

"Matt did it."

"Matt? Jesus. Didn't think he had it in him."

"Well, he has. He killed her."

Rajesh can't work out how to respond. "So is he one of them?"

"Seriously? If he was a threat, would I be standing here with him now? He'd have killed me too."

Natalie takes another step forward and is fully inside the building now.

Matt tries to follow her lead, but Ronan shuts the door in his face. Matt stops it with his foot and pushes back, forcing it open. "Come on, Ronan. Don't be stupid."

Paul tries to get up, but Rajesh is having none of it. He plants his boot between Paul's shoulder blades and exerts enough downward pressure to keep him still and make him yelp with pain. "I told you, don't fucking move."

Matt manages to open the door a little farther. "You can trust us," he says, though even he doesn't sound convinced himself. "Well, as much as we can trust you," he adds, not knowing if that strengthens his argument or makes matters worse.

"Trust you?" Rajesh says. "You're a killer."

Matt answers quickly, thinking on his feet. "No, Raj, I'm a survivor, exactly the same as you. Exactly the same as Stuart, and he killed Nils, remember?"

Rajesh thinks for a couple of seconds longer. It seems to take forever for him to make his decision. "Get in here fast," he finally says, lifting his boot off Paul's back. "Don't try anything stupid. One wrong move and I'll be the one who starts killing next, right?"

"Got it," Matt says. If I don't get you first, he thinks but doesn't dare say. I've got form.

Closing the front door behind them brings a blessed relief. It gives them a temporary illusion of safety and blocks out the constant wind outside. It's also warmer in here and more comfortable than anywhere else left on Skek. But what catches Matt off guard for a few dangerous moments is the sheer normality of the place. It's like a bubble, both a bizarre time capsule and an inextricable link with the distant mainland. The bungalow feels like a proper home from home: wallpaper, paintings, cushions, family photographs, ornaments, a TV and a pile of DVDs, a bookcase full of well-read paperbacks, and a sink full of washing up. The sense of normality, however, is fleeting. Matt only has to remember that he killed one of the owners of this place—after she'd attacked him and almost killed her own husband, apparently—for the surreal reality of their inexplicable situation to return with full force.

The little house is crowded, but not quite as crowded as they'd hoped. Rajesh waits at the living-room door, still standing guard after he's ushered Paul, Natalie, and Matt inside. He's a little calmer, but he steadfastly refuses to put down his ax. Stephen and Rachel are also here.

"Where's everyone else?" Natalie asks.

"Stuart's in the back," Rajesh tells her. "Leave him alone, though, and for Christ's sake don't tell him about Ruth. Poor sod's in a bad enough way already."

"I can imagine." Natalie's fighting back tears herself. "They'd been together since they were teenagers. He was always telling me that, going on about how much he loved her, and you could tell he meant every word. You can't even begin to imagine how much that's gotta hurt. To be attacked like that by the person you love more than anything . . ."

"So who else is missing?" Matt wonders, struggling to keep track of who's still alive. He works his way through the faces. "Just Rod and his daughter?"

"We lost them when we cleared out after Ruth kicked off."

"There's no boat at the jetty," Paul tells Rajesh. "Looks like your boss did a runner on you after all."

"Looks that way," Rajesh is forced to admit.

"The girl from the beach. What happened to her?"

"She's in the back with Stuart," Rachel replies. "She's okay."

Nervous glances are exchanged. "Okay?" says Paul. "Just okay?"

"She hasn't come around yet. We managed to get her out of the way when Ruth kicked off. Rachel's been looking after her. We're still keeping her drugged up."

Natalie's furiously shaking her head. "No, no, no . . . you don't get it, Raj. She's one of them. We have to get her out of here."

Natalie moves for the door to the back rooms, but he blocks her way with the ax. "What are you on about?"

"She's one of them." Natalie's genuinely afraid. "Did you not hear me? She's a Hater."

"Have you lost your mind?" Ronan asks, laughing nervously. "She's just a child. A child who's barely alive at that."

"You don't understand," Matt says. "Back on the boat. There was CCTV. We saw her. We saw her killing. . . ."

"You're confused," Ronan sighs. "Nils killed the boy who did all that, you know he did."

Rachel crosses the room to stand alongside Rajesh and block the way through, a show of solidarity. "That poor kid's been through hell. She's no more a threat to you than I am."

"And how do we know you're not a threat?" Paul says. "Seriously, how do we know about any of us anymore?"

"He's right," Matt says. "Nils wasn't a threat before, nor was Ruth. We just don't know, and we can't risk having her here."

"What do you expect me to do?" Rajesh says. "Dump her outside? Lock her up?"

"Yes!"

"No way. She's just a kid, and she's still out cold. I reckon she's a lot more vulnerable than any of us."

"She's staying here. Deal with it or get out," Rachel warns.

"Let me see her," Natalie demands.

"Lay a finger on her and I'll . . ."

"You'll do what, exactly? Attack me? *Kill me?* Jesus, it's all getting a bit predictable, don't you think?"

"Come on," Matt says. "Let's calm things down a little."

"Don't waste your breath," Stephen says from the far corner of the room where he's been watching the argument brewing. "They won't listen to you. I should know. There's been killing after killing after killing on this island since Vanessa died."

"Jesus, don't bring that up again," Rachel moans.

"No, stop. We need to shut up and listen to them," Stephen shouts at her. He turns to Paul and pulls him closer. "What did you see on the CCTV?"

"There was a basic setup on the ferry," Paul explains. "We found Nat there after we left you lot yesterday."

"I figured it would be the last place a killer would go. It had already been cleared out," Natalie explains. "Fact is, I was trying to get away from everyone else. Fat lot of good it did me."

"There were a few static low-res CCTV cameras on the boat, nothing fancy," Paul continues. "We used them to try to work out what happened. We thought we'd look for clues . . . try and see if there was any kind of trigger we could identify, any obvious behaviors. We just wanted to try to work out who was what."

"And?" Ronan impatiently demands.

"And there's nothing. As far as we could see, one minute everything was okay, the next it all went batshit crazy." They're all staring at Paul. He feels uncomfortable, as if he's being interrogated. "It wasn't the boy who did all the killing on the boat, it was the girl you've got lying in the back room. It was Louise."

"Bullshit," Rachel says.

"I wish it was. We saw her do it. The three of us watched her doing all that fucking terrible stuff on TV. The kid Nils killed, he was just hiding, doing everything he could to keep out of sight until she'd gone."

"He didn't come looking for us to kill us," Matt says. "He came to us for help."

There's a moment of quiet as the others absorb this news.

"See," Stephen says. "Easy to jump to conclusions, isn't it?"

"I need to see her," Natalie says again, and she pushes past Rajesh, who this time moves to the side. Rachel offers a little more resistance, but she too moves out of the way on Rajesh's instruction.

The solitary bedroom at the back of the cottage is as twee as everywhere else. It's overcomplicated and overfussy. Drapes and throws. Scatter cushions. A gore-stained hand-crocheted blanket. Pools of blood. Stuart's lying in the middle of the bed he used to share with Ruth. A deep puncture wound is in his side. It's been strapped up, but the bandages and makeshift dressings are hard to see because they're also soaked with crimson. His face is the same insipid color as the pale curtains hanging listlessly at the windows, off-white. He manages to open his eyes when Natalie enters the room, but clearly every single movement, no matter how small, severely saps his already substantially depleted reserves. He just about manages to lift his arm from the bed to try to acknowledge her. She puts her hand on his shoulder and he relaxes. "Hi . . . ," he croaks.

"Hi yourself. We're all here now, Stu. Get some rest while we work out how to get us home."

"Yeah, right . . ."

His eyelids flutter and close. She doesn't know how much he's heard them talking, or if he's heard anything at all. The dire condition of her good friend is another momentary distraction, but she quickly remembers why she's here.

The room's filling up: Matt, Paul, Rajesh, Rachel, and Ronan are all crammed in here with her. Natalie has to push past the others to get over to the far side of the bed.

Louise is lying on a thin makeshift mattress made up of cushions and blankets. She doesn't move, but Natalie can see her chest rising and falling even from a distance. Deep, unsteady breaths. Natalie tries to get closer, but Rachel stops her. "She's been like this the whole time. We haven't heard a peep from her. She's no threat."

"You haven't seen what we've seen," Natalie tells her.

"She's no threat," Rachel says again, but Paul has other ideas.

"I wish I could show you the video. You wouldn't be so sure if you'd seen her in action."

"If what you're saying is true and she kicks off, I'll sort her out myself."

"If she kicks off, you won't have a chance," Natalie tells her.

"Like I said, I'll sort her out."

Natalie knows there's no point arguing. "Tie her up, then."

"What? Are you serious?"

"Deadly. You got a rope in here? Just tie one end around her ankle and the other around the foot of the bed. Just enough to give us a head start when she comes around."

"Are you mental?" Rachel smirks.

"I'm not so sure anymore." Natalie turns to face Rajesh. "Come on, Raj. Please."

Rajesh thinks hard for a couple of seconds. He's treading a fine line: he thinks this can't be happening, but he trusts Natalie more than just about anyone else left alive on this island. "There's an extension cable in one of the cupboards in the kitchen. We'll use that."

Rachel's less than impressed, but Natalie couldn't give a damn. "Thanks, Raj." She gently touches his arm as he squeezes past. "What's the worst that can happen? So we'll have to explain to her why we've tied her up? So what? I reckon that'll be the least of her concerns when she wakes up."

"She's not an animal," Rachel says.

Natalie's not so sure.

Rajesh fetches the flex, and the others return to the living room, leaving Rachel to watch Louise. Rachel sits on the edge of Stuart's bed, and he groans with pain when the mattress moves. Every little movement causes him waves of untold agony.

A definite air of mistrust and animosity remains inside the bungalow. Natalie puts down her weapons, doing it in such an overly dramatic way that it's clear she's trying to do what she can to get the others onside. "It's time to stop pissing about. We've all seen and done some really fucking awful things, but we're all in the same position here. We need to work together and pool our resources. Rebuild bridges, not burn them."

"I thought he was the one with all the clichés," Stephen grunts, gesturing at Ronan.

Ronan doesn't take the bait.

"I'll try and get back to the mainland in one of the kayaks tomorrow," Rajesh says on his way from the kitchen back to the bedroom. He lays his ax down on the mantelpiece above the cottage's electric fire, matching Natalie's actions. "I'll get help."

"I'll go with you," Paul says.

"Have you kayaked on open water before? Thanks for the offer, Paul, but I'll be better off on my own."

"And how do we know you won't get back to the mainland and just stay there? Fuck the rest of us?"

"You don't, you'll just have to trust me." Rajesh is clearly offended. "Stop judging everyone else by your own low standards, pal."

"At least I have standards. . . ."

"For Christ's sake, Paul, give it a rest, will you?" Natalie sighs. "Way I see it, right now we're all screwed. Raj is our only hope, and we have to trust him to do the right thing. If you go and don't come back, Raj, then fair play to you and thanks for trying. If you go and you do come and get us, well then, that'll just go to prove you're as decent a bloke as I've always believed you are."

Rajesh looks down at his feet, embarrassed and unexpectedly emotional.

Matt looks around the room. The conversation has drifted into somewhat safer waters. The immediate fear feels like it's dissipated somewhat. "It's like Nat says, we're all in the same boat, so to speak. There's no point fighting with each other. No one knows any more or less than anyone else. None of us know the full picture, and I don't reckon we ever will."

"He's right," Rajesh agrees. "This is a truly fucked-up situation. You only have to look at poor old Stuart. His wife did that to him, for crying out loud."

"I'd never met a couple more nauseatingly in love than Stuart and Ruth." A rogue tear rolls down Natalie's cheek.

"It was enough to make you sick," Rajesh agrees with a flicker of a wry grin.

"Honestly, you should have seen them . . . so loved up all the time. Ruth told me that they sold up and moved to the island because they'd realized that all they needed in their lives was each other."

"Vomit inducing," Paul says.

"Pretty sweet, actually," Natalie corrects him, unimpressed. "Anyway, it doesn't matter now. It scares the shit out of me, though, because if what's happening is enough to do that to a couple as in tune and devoted to each other as Stuart and Ruth, then I think we're all in trouble. None of us are safe."

Rajesh and the others brought the radio over with them when they left the main building after barricading Ruth in the dorm. Seven of them are now crowded around the tired old transmitter, which they've placed on a coffee table in the middle of Stuart and Ruth's living room, each of them praying they'll finally be able to make contact with the rest of the world. It feels like they've become co-cooned here, locked away until the last one's left standing. It reminds Matt of that Japanese film he saw once . . . *Battle Royale,* he thinks it was. It feels like they've been here forever, though it's not yet been a full week. Tomorrow, he realizes, it'll be seven days since he last saw home and spoke to Jen. This unwanted and unexpected anniversary makes his personal situation feel all the more out of control. It feels like the two of them might as well be on different planets.

It's getting dark outside. Another day is drawing to a close. Ronan counts up the number of people who died today and wonders how many of them will be left by morning. He can see the main building from where he's sitting. A dull yellow glow is coming through the windows of the empty base. It looks disarmingly cozy, though he knows inside it's anything but. "Shouldn't we turn the generator off?"

"Why?" Matt asks.

"Save fuel. Keep the noise down."

"Does it really matter? We need to keep the power running for the radio."

"Suppose."

"And it's not like we're trying to stay hidden," Rajesh adds. "Everyone left alive on the island is here already."

Ronan nods, then slides down the wall and sits in the corner. Not on a chair in the corner, but literally right in the corner of the room instead. Knees drawn up to his chest and head bowed down like a frightened kid.

The door to the bedroom is fully open, and Natalie keeps an eye on what's going on next door. Stuart's sleeping fitfully, occasionally trying to move and growling with pain like a dying bear. Louise hasn't shifted. Natalie's ready for when she does, one hand resting on the bow and arrow at her side. She keeps telling herself she'll do what she has to do when the time comes, but her guts churn whenever she thinks about it. She can't imagine killing a child. She can't imagine killing anyone.

Stephen and Paul are sitting at either end of a three-seater sofa like a married couple who've fallen out and aren't talking. They're watching Rajesh and Rachel intently. Rajesh has been messing with the radio for the last half hour, but Rachel has just taken over. They've lashed the antenna to the side of the bungalow and have fed the cable through a narrow opening in the window. It's only a slight crack, but it's enough to let the wind whistle through. It howls tirelessly, rattling the glass in its frame.

"You sure you know what you're doing with this?" Rajesh asks Rachel as she messes with the controls and dials on the dashboard of the radio.

"I watched Ruth. And I grew up with these things. My grand-dad used to have an interest in radios. He was a real nerd. He used to shut himself away in his shed at the bottom of the garden and speak to other nerds around the world. I used to sit in and listen to him when I was little. Never thought it would ever come in useful, though."

"If only he could see you now, eh?" Rajesh says, and Rachel glances up at him, unsure whether he's being sincere or mocking her.

It's just as they expect. Crackles and pops and nothing else but white noise. The bursts of static give them teasing, split-second moments of hope, but it doesn't sound like there's anyone out there.

"We look like the cast from one of those crappy end-of-the-world movies," Paul says, glancing around the room. "Just look at the state of us. Dirty clothes and unshaved faces."

"You think this is the end of the world then?" Stephen asks.

Paul looks across at him and shrugs. "Dunno. You tell me."

"I don't. It's not though, is it? Can't be."

"It is starting to feel that way," Matt says.

"Yeah, but that's only because our view is restricted. It's all gone to hell here, sure, but you can't tell me the same thing's going to be happening everywhere else."

"Rod said it was," Natalie reminds Stephen.

"Your mate Rod was full of shit," he answers quickly. "He told us he wasn't going back to the mainland either, if you remember. Soon changed his mind when things got shitty with Ruth this morning."

None of the Hazleton Adventure staff jump to the defense of their missing boss.

"I think Stephen's right. We've got a distorted view of things here," Rajesh says. "It's an unnatural environment. Our perspective's all skewed, and because we're confined, all of us are affected by everything that happens. There's no escape, no way out. I reckon that's made everything feel a thousand times worse than it is back home."

"I hope you're right," Matt says.

"Tell you what, I'll head home tomorrow, then I'll come back here and prove to you I was."

"Deal."

Another crackle of static comes from the radio. It's unexpectedly loud, abruptly silencing the conversation. "It's nothing," Rachel says, looking around and seeing six expectant faces staring back.

"Is this what it's usually like?" Paul asks. "I guess you don't get a lot of chatter out here."

"You'd be surprised," Natalie tells him. "Ruthie was a bit of a geek like Rachel's granddad. She had mates all over the place she used to talk to. You'd often find her in the back room talking to somebody somewhere on the radio. She and Stu liked the solitude of living out here together, but everybody needs someone to talk to sometimes, I guess."

Rachel's still playing with the controls. Matt's starting to think it's a pointless exercise. In some ways he thinks this is worse than if they didn't have the radio at all. At least then they could kid themselves that everything's all right elsewhere. This oppressive, never-ending silence seems only to confirm his worst suspicions.

Wait.

A voice. It's there just for a second, then it's gone.

"Hear that?" Rachel's eyes light up in the yellow-green glow from the radio display. She reverses the tuning, carefully working her way back through the frequencies to try to locate the signal again. After a few seconds, frustration kicks in. "Must have imagined it," she says, sounding dejected.

Matt's not so sure. "Well, if you imagined it, then I imagined it at the same time. There was definitely something there."

The harder Rachel forces herself to concentrate, the less control she seems to have. The sudden weight of expectation increases the pressure until her fingers feel swollen and numb, tips tingling with nerves. Her throat is dry. This job needs tiny adjustments and careful coordination, but with clammy hands and a racing heartbeat, right now that feels nigh on impossible. If there is a voice there, she thinks, she'll struggle to hear it over the noise of her racing pulse, which bangs and thumps like a drum solo in her head.

Got it.

Lost it.

Stay calm.

Got it again.

She finds the frequency and does everything she can to strengthen the signal. There's a little fading and washing, but she eventually locks onto the voice. It's male. British, by the sound of things.

Detached and unemotional. Outwardly friendly, but clearly controlling. It's one of those plummy, relaxed, but authoritative BBC voices designed to keep the population calm and reassured when the situation is clearly spiraling out of control.

"Sounds like one of those old public-service broadcasts," Ronan says from the corner. "*Protect and Survive*. Remember that? Survive a nuclear war by building a shelter from doors and covering it in cushions."

"Fuck me, is this for real?" Rajesh asks.

Matt's thinking, If I wasn't sure things were bad before, I am now.

The recorded voice is on a short loop. Same message, same five lines, over and over and over.

Remain calm.
Do not panic.
Take shelter.
Wait for further instructions.
The situation is under control.

There's silence in the room for the first few loops, then Natalie says what everyone's thinking. "Seriously? Are we supposed to believe this shit?"

"It's got to be good news, hasn't it?" Rachel looks at the other faces around her hopefully. "Can you not hear him? This situation is under control."

"Come on," Rajesh sighs, "really? It's just a recording. It's propaganda. Bullshit. I think you can take every line of that and turn it on its head. The situation is clearly *not* under control. Truth is, now I've heard that, I'm pretty much certain we're fucked."

FRIDAY

20

First light.

"I'm gone," Rajesh announces to whoever's awake enough to hear him. "I'm out of here."

"You really going to do this, Raj?" Natalie sits up quick, still half-asleep.

"Don't see that I have any choice. I'll go and see what's going on back home, then I'll find a way of getting back here to fetch you all."

"So what's your plan?" Matt asks, watching from the other side of the room. He's been awake for hours. "You do have a plan, don't you?"

"Of sorts. Get home and see how the land lies, then get hold of a decent-sized boat and get back here and get you lot."

"Where are you going to land?"

"Grimsby," Rajesh answers quickly. "I figure I'll have more chance if I head inshore up the Humber. I've done it a couple of times before."

"Makes sense."

"Glad you approve."

"I'm not being difficult," Matt says. "Just wondered what you'd got in mind, that's all."

"I know what I'm doing. Much as I want to get you lot home as quickly as I can, I'm not about to take any unnecessary chances."

"Good luck with that," Paul says. Matt looks around. He thought Paul was still asleep.

"Thanks for your support," Rajesh mumbles.

"I don't hold out much hope of you getting there and getting back, that's all."

"Well, maybe you should," Natalie tells Paul. "Because hope is just about all we've got left right now. We're running out of food and fuel, and half of us are dead. With our lord and master Rod having fucked off home without us, Raj is the only way we're going anywhere, remember? He's our last chance."

"Need any help?" Matt asks.

Raj shakes his head. "No, thanks. Like I said to your mate here yesterday, I work better on my own. I just need to grab a few things, get my kayak out from the stores, then get onto the water. Don't forget, this is what I do for a living."

Matt listens intently. As alien as this place still feels to him, he knows that it's a second home to Rajesh, Natalie, and the others. It's where these people live. And where many of them have died.

"You sure about the weather?" Natalie asks. "You're the one who's always telling us how it can change in seconds out there."

Rajesh smiles wryly as he looks out through the window, gazing up at the swirling white clouds overhead. "I know, I know. The wind's a bit unpredictable, but I should be okay. It was raining earlier, but it cleared up about an hour ago. There's a few clear patches overhead. Looks like the cloud's breaking up. I'll give it a go, anyway. I'll turn around and come back if I have to."

"I reckon I'd rather take my chances out there on the ocean than stay here," Paul says. "And I've never been in a bloody canoe."

Before he can talk himself out of it, and with the minimum of fuss, Rajesh is gone. He gives Natalie a bear hug (more for his benefit than hers), then lets himself out. She watches him from the door to the cottage as he sprints back to the main building. He disappears inside, then reappears a minute or so later with his waterproofs on, carrying various other odds and ends of equipment. He heads for the stores building, and Natalie pictures him having to work around the corpses to collect his kayak, paddle, and life jacket. She can't imagine how horrific it must be in there this morning.

She watches her friend until he's disappeared from view.

Rachel emerges from the bedroom a short while later. "Stuart's dead," she says casually. The news of his passing is met with a collective shrug of inevitability.

"It was only a matter of time," says Ronan, and he's right. There was never any chance of his recovering. Not having lost all that blood. Not with a carved-up body and a broken heart.

"I'm amazed he lasted as long as he did," Paul says, and as Rachel comes out, he goes into the back bedroom. He stands in the doorway watching Stuart's graying corpse like he expects it to come back to life and start attacking. They're not zombies, he keeps telling himself over and over and over, but he can't shake the feeling. He feels like he's stuck in a slasher movie, but in the films he remembers, it was easy to work out the rules and trace the killer. You knew where you were with Jason and Freddy. . . . Here on Skek the rules—if there even are any—feel like they're constantly changing. How can you avoid the killer when you don't know who it is? When it might even be you?

Something catches his eye.

On the floor on the far side of the bed is that damn girl. Louise is still unconscious, but she moves slightly as if she's trying to sub-liminally remind him, *Don't forget me. . . . I'm still here, I'm still watching you. . . .* He moves a little closer. It's hard to believe that this slight, deceptively fragile-looking creature is responsible for so much fear and death. He checks that the electrical flex is still tied tight around her ankle and traces its route back across the room. Rajesh did a good job. He wrapped it twice around the foot of the double bed, then plugged it into the wall and pushed the bed hard up against it. She's not going anywhere fast.

I could end all of this right now, he thinks. I could get a knife, or the bow and arrow, or a rock from outside , and I could kill this little bitch before she wakes up again. . . .

"Problem?" Rachel asks, startling him.

"Not as long as she stays like this."

"Leave her alone, Paul."

"What are you, her guardian angel? Her keeper?"

"No, I'm just not as quick to write people off as you are."

"You wouldn't say that if you'd seen what I'd seen."

"Doesn't make any difference. She's a sick kid. She's not going to harm anyone."

"She already has."

Rachel doesn't react. Paul waits a second longer, still standing over the girl, then he returns to the others.

He finds Natalie and Matt in the cramped kitchen. Matt's helped himself to a box of dry crackers from a half-empty cup-board and is stuffing them into his mouth, one after another.

"Can't believe you've got an appetite," Paul says.

"I haven't," Matt replies, spitting out crumbs, "but we need to eat." He offers the box around but both Natalie and Paul decline. "We need to keep our strength up."

"I couldn't eat a thing. Think I'd throw it straight back up again," Paul says.

Matt takes a swig from a plastic bottle of water. "Did you not hear me? I'm not hungry either, but we have to eat. We're working against the clock."

"What's that supposed to mean?" Natalie asks.

"We're running out of time, don't you think? Look around you, Nat. We need to be ready to move."

"You're starting to sound like a broken record. There's no way off the island without a boat, and until Rajesh comes back, there is no boat, remember?"

"I remember, but we have to make sure we're ready for whatever comes next. You don't really think that's it, do you? That those of us who've made it this far are all going to sit here in this frigging cottage happy as anything, just waiting for your mate to come back and save the day?"

"Don't mock me," Natalie says.

"I'm not. It's just that we're on a slippery slope here, or had you not noticed? The population numbers are getting lower, the stakes are getting higher. Chances are it'll be our necks on the line before long, and we need to be prepared. That's why I'm forcing myself to eat, and that's why I want you to eat something too."

She reluctantly does as he suggests. "This is just to stop you going on at me, right?" She struggles to force the first tasteless biscuit down.

"It's Rachel we need to watch," Paul says, taking Matt's advice and helping himself to food. "She's spending too much time fussing around that kid."

"Totally agree," says Stephen, standing in the doorway uninvited, virtually filling it. "She wrote me off without giving me chance to defend myself when Vanessa attacked me. She's a bloody liability, that one, always has been. Ronan only took her on because he fancies her. Practically told me as much, he did."

Natalie is appalled. "Fuck's sake, just listen to yourselves."

"You wouldn't say that if you knew her like we do," Paul says. "And like I said, she's inseparable from that kid."

"I don't know her as well as you do, but I do know she's got a kid back home, hasn't she? She was telling me about her when you lot first arrived here last week. Tracey, isn't it?"

"Stacey," Matt corrects her.

"Whatever. She's the only one of you who's got a child, isn't she?"

"So?" Paul asks, annoyed. "What's that got to do with anything?"

"So maybe she feels some kind of affinity for her, have you considered that? Maybe she's just looking out for a child who's been through an unimaginable trauma and who's sick?"

"She wouldn't think that if she'd seen the CCTV footage."

"No, maybe she wouldn't, but she hasn't seen it, and chances are she never will. Right now that little girl is virtually catatonic. If it makes Rachel feel better to fuss over her a little, so what? Believe me, if anything happens, I'll be the first in line to sort the kid out if she starts."

"You're not listening, are you?" Stephen says. "You're only seeing the parts of this you want to see. Since you found that girl and brought her back to the group, only two people have spent any decent length of time with her, Ruth and Rachel. And we all know what happened to Ruth. . . ."

"Three people, actually," Natalie corrects him. "Me too. I sat with her for a while when we first found her. Are you saying we're all Haters?"

"I'm not saying anything."

"Because you haven't got the balls to."

"No, because I genuinely don't know. I don't have to listen to this."

"Neither do I."

"It's important we do listen, though." Matt elbows his way into the increasingly fractious argument. "I like Rachel. I've always got on with her. Would it surprise you to know that she's talked to me about both of you two before now?"

"When?" Paul asks. "Fucking nerve."

"Back at work. Ages ago. Look, I'm not trying to cause more problems here, but I've heard her complaining about both you two. She didn't trust either of you. She said you were a letch, Stephen, and she thought Paul was full of shit."

"What's that got to do with anything?" Stephen's fuming now.

"Probably nothing," Matt answers quickly. "All I'm saying is we've got to put our opinions and assumptions to one side 'cause they don't count for much right now. Put it this way: I thought Ruth was pretty lovely until she tried to knife me yesterday."

"Good point, well made," says Natalie as Stephen storms off, muttering under his breath.

"So what's the answer?" Paul looks directly at Matt. "If you're so smart, what do we need to do to stay alive?"

Matt shrugs. "Logically we should all stay well away from each other, but I don't fancy that option. And it's hardly practical when this is the only habitable building we've got left."

"Maybe we should try and lose the rest of them," Paul says.

Natalie and Matt exchange glances.

"What?" Natalie asks.

"Well, I reckon the three of us should definitely stick together. We've done all right so far, haven't we? We've been through the same things and had pretty much the same reactions, so that makes me think we're on the same side."

"You're still assuming there are sides."

"And you're also assuming it's predetermined whether you're going to be a Hater or not," Matt adds. "How do you know? It might be down to something in the water or a wheat intolerance or the color of your eyes or the way you brush your hair in the morning. . . . We don't know if this is something you're born with, or something you catch."

"I get that, but whatever it is, the three of us have been okay together so far, yes?"

"So far."

"So I know I'm okay with you two, but I'm not so sure about everyone else. Maybe we should be thinking about being more proactive."

Natalie doesn't like where this is heading. "What do you mean? Barricade ourselves away again? Let them deal with each other, then come back when they've wiped each other out?"

"That's being passive, not proactive," Paul corrects her. "No, I'm talking about going a step further."

"Kill them before they kill us? Are you serious?"

Paul doesn't say much at first, then he reluctantly nods agreement. "Think about it. . . . If Rajesh doesn't come back for a while—if he comes back at all—and we're stuck in this situation, getting rid of the rest of them might be our only viable survival strategy."

"Christ's sake, just listen to yourself. You're just being stupid."

"No, stupid is doing nothing."

"Do you have any idea what you're saying?"

"Hang on, hang on." Matt's struggling to keep track of this increasingly surreal conversation. "You're talking about killing people before they kill you? Isn't that how Rod said the Haters behave? I don't want to rain on your parade or anything, Paul, but if you'd overheard Rachel telling Ronan that she thought she should probably kill you, me, and Nat because we might be a threat, you'd have her marked down as one of the enemy, wouldn't you?"

"Keep your bloody voice down."

"Why?" Matt asks, bemused. "Because you think they'll hear

us talking about lynching them and you're afraid of their reaction, or because you're worried they'll get in first? Come on. . . ."

"I just don't know who we can trust anymore."

"Let's keep things in perspective—we're talking about murder here. Cold-blooded, premeditated murder. I don't think you've got it in you. I don't think I could do it."

Paul looks straight at Matt. "If we're getting onto the subject of keeping things in perspective, let's remember which one of us has already killed, shall we?"

"That was different. I didn't mean for it to happen. It was self-defense, you know it was."

"Yeah, but judging from what we've heard and what you've just been saying, Ruth would probably have given the same reason for coming at you with the knife."

Natalie sighs. "Just ignore him, Matt."

Matt's expression has changed. He swallows hard. "It's okay . . . he might have a point. All along I've been thinking about these Haters and trying to imagine how it must feel to be one of them. I've been trying to work out what kind of emotions and thoughts must be running through someone's head to make them do the kind of things we've seen."

"And?" she presses impatiently.

"And now I'm standing here contemplating killing the rest of the people here before they can kill me, and I'm thinking, 'Is this how it begins? Have I got this all wrong? Am I a Hater? Are the three of us Haters? Are the others the ones who haven't changed?'"

"But it doesn't change anything," Natalie says. "It's still one side against the other. Us versus them."

"Now who's talking about sides?" Paul says.

Matt shakes his head. "Who's to say there even is any difference? Who's to say we're not all going out of our minds and manufacturing a problem that doesn't really exist?"

"I get all that. We are where we are. So for about the hundredth time of asking, what do we do now?"

"You tell us," Natalie says, frustrated. "Just let us know if you decide to go on a killing spree so we can get out of the way first."

"Have a go at me all you like, love, at least I'm trying."

"Trying? You're just talking, Paul. It's all you ever do from what I've seen. And for the record, I'm not your love, right?"

"Damn right you're not. Pity the bloke who ends up stuck with you and—"

"For Christ's sake, Paul, just stop," Matt snaps, uncharacteristically forceful. "As it happens, I don't think you're completely wrong this time. I say we do a final recce of the island and get together everything useful we can find, then barricade ourselves back in here and wait for Rajesh. First sign of trouble from anyone, and we deal with them. And by deal with them, I mean kill them."

Matt can't believe he's just said that out loud, but he knows it's the right thing to do.

The *only* thing to do.

21

"Do you not think we'd be better staying here?" Paul asks as he, Matt, Natalie, and Rachel strip the main building of anything left of value. "There's more space here than in the bungalow."

"I think we need less space, not more," Matt says. "The tighter the confines, the easier it'll be for us to keep track of who's doing what."

"Yeah, but the closer we are, the more chance there is of it spreading."

"It? *It?* Have you not been listening? This thing isn't an STD, you know."

"So what exactly is it?" Rachel asks.

The question floors Matt momentarily. "No idea," he's forced to admit.

Paul's at the far end of the main hall with only Frank's corpse for company. He's struggling to carry a couple of bulky duvets when his foot skids in a puddle of the dead man's blood, still not dry even after all this time. He loses his temper with himself when he almost falls. "Fuck this," he yells, and he throws the duvets across the room and kicks a chair with frustration. The noise fills the entire building.

Matt watches him. Natalie comes to check what the noise is and catches his eye. "He okay, d'you think?" she quietly asks.

"Shit scared, I reckon," Matt whispers back. "Too full of crap to admit it, though."

"What about you?"

"Me? Oh, no machismo here. I'm terrified."

He goes into the dorm where he and Paul slept and starts gathering up his own belongings. He doesn't have a lot, just a rucksack full of dirty clothes and his book. He looks for anything else that might be of use: a few odds and ends from the bathroom, a couple of pillows, someone's torch and alarm clock . . .

They carry what they can manage in relays, running the short distance between the base and the bungalow, eyes peeled even though they know there's no one else left here but them. It's ridiculous, he knows, but when he's outside, Matt feels like he's being watched. He feels exposed like he's in the crosshairs of a sniper's sights.

The island is cold and inhospitable this morning, but strangely beautiful too. For once the sky is deep blue and largely cloudless. Natalie hopes it's like this all the way over to the mainland. The calmer the water, the better Rajesh's chances of getting home, then getting back.

While Matt, Natalie, Rachel, and Paul are bringing useful stuff into the cottage, Stephen and Ronan are concentrating on getting unwanted stuff out. Stephen's doing 90 percent of the shifting, with Ronan doing more talking than heavy lifting. A pile of blood-soaked linen has been left in a heap in the front garden, and right now Stephen's struggling to manhandle Stuart's unwieldy corpse out of his former home. Ronan tells him what to do and how to do it, but does little to help.

"We've left it too late to shift him; we should have done this straightaway," Stephen complains as he drags the dead man's bulk down the hall. He's right—the cadaver has become rigid, arms and legs frozen into their final position. The stiffness in his joints makes Stuart feel peculiarly brittle, fragile almost, even though he's clearly not. When he becomes stuck, one foot hooked around a shoe rack, Stephen yanks the deadweight hard with frustration.

Ronan is appalled. "Have some respect, for crying out loud."

"Respect? Don't you get it, Ronan? Stuart's gone. This is just dead flesh. Useless and empty and really fucking heavy."

"Yes, but . . ."

"But nothing. Look, instead of standing there like a lemon and watching, why don't you do something to help?"

Ronan moves more furniture out of the way and holds open the door—anything but touch the body. Stephen continues to wrestle with Stuart, grunting with exertion and turning him this way and that to make his awkward shape fit through the narrow gap like it's a macabre puzzle piece.

Matt's trying to get in as Stephen's trying to get out. No matter how much death Matt's seen over the last few days, he still feels nauseous when Stephen roughly drags Stuart out into the open and cracks the back of his head against the concrete step.

Stephen looks up, unapologetic. "He's not bothered."

Matt puts down the stuff he's been carrying, and between the two of them they carry Stuart down the side of the cottage along a pathway marked out with more unnecessary picket fence. They place him respectfully in his small, square back garden plot and cover him up. Matt stands with his hands on his hips and looks around at the unremarkable patch of land, just the same as the rest of the island, but somehow elevated in importance because someone decided to park a prefabricated bungalow here. It's quite surreal. It makes Matt chuckle, and the distraction is welcome.

If short-lived.

Ronan has made a quick dash back to base to collect more of his things. He comes rushing back from the other building with his arms piled high with personal belongings. He has files and paperwork, and his laptop is slung across his back in the trendy hipster rucksack he always carries it in. Matt—around the front of the house again now—accepts it without question, because this is the Ronan he's always known: business first, everything else second.

Natalie, though, is far less forgiving. "What the fuck have you got all that for?"

Ronan's wrong-footed by the directness of her question. "This paperwork's important. I can't leave confidential business information just lying around, can I?"

"You can." She snatches one of his folders from him and empties it into the wind. With his arms still overloaded, all he can do is watch his papers fly away. She grabs his shoulder and spins him around to get to his rucksack. "Is that your laptop? What the hell do you want your laptop for?"

"I thought I might be able to get online."

She's having none of it. "You won't. We tried that already."

"I can't risk leaving this stuff unattended. There's information on this machine that could seriously damage my business if it was to get into the wrong hands."

"Do you think that really matters now? I mean, apart from the fact there's no one here but us and there's very little chance of anyone else turning up unannounced, do you think anyone actually cares?"

He can't help himself. "Of course it matters. Do you have any idea how hard I had to work to build the business up from scratch?"

"No, but I'm guessing you're going to have to work a hell of a lot harder just to stay alive from here on in."

"I can't leave all this data where anyone could—"

"I think you're missing the point, you stupid little man," she yells. "Don't you get it? Half of your staff are dead and the other half are stuck here with you and me with no way out. By all accounts, the rest of the world appears to be fucked. It's all over, mate."

"How do you know for sure? How do you know what's really going on in the rest of the world?"

She interrupts, "Right now, this island *is* the rest of the world, and these people are everyone that's in it. The sooner you get that through your thick, corporate skull, the better."

Before he can protest—and for once he's having real trouble trying to find something to say—Natalie wrenches the laptop bag off him and empties it onto the ground. He halfheartedly tries to stop her, but she's taller than him and far more confident, and she pushes him away. She takes his precious laptop and smashes it repeatedly against the corner of the bungalow. It buckles, cracks, and shatters. No longer a repository of vital business information, it's now a useless lump of scrap. She grinds bits of it into the ground with the heel of her boot.

"Try stealing any trade secrets off that." She pants with the effort of the unexpectedly therapeutic destruction.

Ronan looks broken, as if he's lost his best friend, not his computer. "Some of the information on that was irreplaceable," he whimpers.

He starts to bend down to pick stuff up, but Natalie grabs his collar lightning fast, picks him up, and slams him up against the wall of the bungalow. "Gavin, Frank, and Joy were irreplaceable, not this. Fuck your business, Ronan, and fuck you."

"Don't hurt me." He squirms. "Please don't . . ."

She realizes he thinks she might be about to turn, and the panic in his face makes her smile. She taunts him, almost enjoying it. "You're not worth the effort." She lets him go, then heads back toward the main building. Ronan picks himself back up and brushes himself down. His heart's thumping so hard he thinks it might explode. He grabs Matt for support.

"Did you see what she did? Did you see how she looked at me? We need to keep an eye on her. I thought she was going to kill me."

Matt shrugs him off. "Grow up, Ronan. From what I've seen of Natalie, if she'd wanted to kill you, she'd have done it already. Now pull yourself together and do something useful."

Paul, Matt, and Natalie are in the main building, carrying out one final check for anything of value they might have missed. They've taken all the food they can find, and pretty much anything else that wasn't bolted down.

Natalie looks around at their grim surroundings. All she can focus on is bodies and blood. The stench of death coats everything. "Even if we shifted the corpses out, I don't reckon it would make any difference. This place is a frigging health hazard. There's no way we could stay here."

"This island is a frigging health hazard," Matt says quickly, and he's pleased when he notices the corner of Natalie's lips turn upward: almost a smile. An almost-smile is as good as it gets today.

One last check of the dorms.

He realizes plenty of stuff is still left in here. He goes back out to speak to the others. "Who checked this dorm?"

"I think Ronan did," Paul replies. "Why?"

On cue, Ronan appears in the main doorway. "What's the problem?"

"You've left loads of gear in here."

"But that's their stuff." The way he looks around, focusing on Frank's corpse in particular, leaves Matt in no doubt that by *them* he means the dead. "It just didn't seem right. . . ."

"Do you think they care? Do you think poor old Frank's going to give a damn if we're stuck here and we've run out of fuel and food and you're wearing a dead man's coat to keep warm?"

"That's hardly the point."

"It's *exactly* the point. Things have changed, Ronan. Priorities are different. All that matters is staying safe until Rajesh gets back, and you can make that as easy or as difficult for yourself as you like. As far as I'm concerned, though, none of the dead need any of this stuff anymore, but I do."

With that, Matt returns to the dorm and starts turfing through his ex-colleagues' belongings. It hurts, but it's a necessity. He feels uncomfortable, uncharacteristically insensitive, but he makes himself do it all the same. It's a relief when Natalie and Paul and then, reluctantly, Ronan start helping.

22

The inside of the bungalow has begun to resemble a landfill. It looks like it belongs to a hoarder. It reminds Matt of a documentary series he watched on Channel 4 one time, something about people who were addicted to collecting crap. He remembers one old guy having to climb and crawl over a mountain of newspapers each night to squeeze through a gap at the top of the doorframe to get to his bed. He thinks that old fella would have felt perfectly at home here in Stuart and Ruth's place today. It doesn't look like Stuart and Ruth's place anymore. All traces of its recently deceased former owners are gone (all but a nasty dark patch of dried blood on the bedroom carpet), and Matt thinks that's probably for the best. Ruth was a Hater, her husband one of her victims. The couple's mutual demise is a terrifying snapshot of what this disease (condition, affliction, syndrome, predisposition, *whatever*) appears capable of.

Ronan's at the window again. He's been sitting staring at the same view for hours. "You okay, boss?" Stephen asks.

Ronan looks up after a few seconds. "Don't call me that."

"What?"

"Don't call me boss. It's not right. Not anymore."

What's he thinking? Matt wonders. He can't imagine any of them going back home and returning to their jobs, and yet equally he can't imagine Ronan without the office. He never talks much about his private life. Matt suspects it's because he doesn't have one.

Matt and Paul are separated from each other by a pile of unsorted clothing. It occasionally smells of the people who are no longer here. Paul's been dozing on and off, but even though he still has his head bowed, he's wide-awake now. Matt can see him messing with his hands in his lap. He's nervously picking at the skin around the nail on his right thumb, has been for ages. It looks sore. Red raw. It's bleeding now, but he keeps picking. He looks up, then looks down again fast. Matt wonders what he's thinking. Is he scared of me? Does he think I'm one of them? Is he one? Am I? Matt stands up and stretches. He's unsteady on his feet, and Paul flinches when Matt overbalances and unexpectedly moves toward him. "Just going to the toilet," Matt tells him so he doesn't panic and overreact.

The sun's on the verge of beginning its daily descent. Matt slips past Natalie, who's sitting close to another window, head buried deep in a novel she took from the shelf in the lounge as a distraction, desperately clinging to the last rays of light so she can keep reading. She acknowledges him with a grunt as he squeezes past.

"Maybe we should start up the generator?" he suggests.

"Good idea," Ronan agrees from the other side of the room.

"Bad idea." Natalie barely lifts her head from the page.

"Why? You won't be able to read much longer if we don't do something about the light."

She looks across at Ronan in disbelief, dangling the book from the bottom corner of the front cover as if it were contaminated. "You think I'm interested in this? I'm only reading to try and forget where I am. No, we should leave the generator off for a while longer. We know where we all are, and no one's going anywhere. We don't have the fuel to waste."

Ronan doesn't look impressed.

"You scared of the dark?" Stephen asks, and from the way Ronan squirms and the expression on his oily face, Stephen thinks he might have struck a nerve.

There's movement from the bedroom. It takes everyone by surprise, and there's a momentary wave of nervous concern before they realize it's nothing to worry about. It's just Rachel. She's been sleeping for a while—lucky cow—but the noise the others are making has woken her up. She has a post-sleep expression on her face—part disorientation, part nausea. She beats Matt to the bathroom. The bolt slides across, sounding like a gunshot.

Matt trips over Stephen's outstretched feet. There's no bloody room in this cramped cottage anymore, and the reducing light levels only add to the confusion. Matt wonders if he should risk tackling Natalie about the electrics again. He'd happily volunteer to run over and start the generator up, if for no other reason than to get out of here for a few precious minutes.

"I'm hungry," Paul says as he barges through to get to the kitchen, where he starts to ferret through the cupboards and haphazard piles of supplies left lying around. He finds something edible and dives in like a vulture.

Matt finally makes it to the toilet, swapping places with Rachel, who slinks back to the bedroom. Their voices are muffled, but he can hear the others talking through the closed bathroom door. He thinks he prefers the peace and quiet in here. Isolation. Four enclosed walls. A lock. A water supply. A seat. He'd happily spend the night here, if not the rest of his time on Skek.

"I found a candle," he hears Paul say.

"Fantastic. That'll make all the difference." Stephen sighs sarcastically.

"At least I'm trying, mate."

"What's the point? So we can watch each other go out of our minds?"

"Don't be an idiot."

"We can't just give up." Ronan's distinctive nasal voice is grating. Matt wishes his hands were free so he could put them over his ears.

"I never said anything about giving up," Stephen replies. "I'm just being realistic, that's all. Your problem, Ronan, is you've always been too busy strategizing and crystallizing and *blue-sky thinking* to realize what's actually going on right in front of your face."

"That's not true."

"Stephen's got a point," Paul says. "The business was pretty much powered by your bullshit."

"You ungrateful little shit. I took a chance on you and gave you a hell of an opportunity. I'm paying well over the odds for someone with your experience, doing the job you do."

"*Did.*"

"Is that you handing in your notice?"

"You seriously think there's a job to go back to?"

Ronan's flustered. "You can't quit. You're fired."

Natalie's joining in now. "Are you two for real? I can't believe this. How can you bicker about something so unimportant? Our lives are on the line here. Do you have any idea of the danger we're facing?"

"Maybe we're not facing any danger," Ronan says from out of nowhere, spoiling for a fight. "Maybe it really is just a construct, just something we've built up out of thin air and bullshit. Christ knows there's been enough of that flying around recently. There was nothing wrong when we left the mainland—nothing more than usual, anyway—but now we're all talking like it's the end of the world."

"Haven't we had this conversation already? You think the bodies on the boat were a fucking construct or whatever you want to call it? That's just a convenient excuse you're choosing to hide behind because you can't handle the truth."

Now Matt can hear several voices at once, all of them competing to be heard and none of them backing down. "You need to calm down," he hears Stephen say. "Just take a breath and—"

"And what?" Ronan screams. "You think because I'm losing my temper that I'm going to start killing people? Are you all completely out of your minds?"

"Take it easy, Ronan," Paul shouts back, and Matt holds his breath and waits for the inevitable explosion. He's trying to work out his exit strategy. It was only ever a matter of time before someone cracked under the pressure.

Is this it? Is this how it ends? Hiding in a toilet while my ex-colleagues go on the rampage?

He leans against the door, both to stop anyone from getting inside and also so he can listen and work out what's happening without risking going out there himself.

If I wait here long enough, they might all kill each other. . . . He imagines being the only one left alive on the island, alone but finally safe.

A crash of movement. A sudden desperate commotion—people trying to get out of the way. More noise as something—someone?— is knocked over.

"Back off, Paul," Matt hears Natalie plead.

"Tell this little fucker to stand down first."

"You can't talk to me like that," Ronan yells.

"I'll talk to you how I fucking well like."

Each voice is progressively louder than the last. No one's backing down.

Matt knows he can't stay in here indefinitely.

Heart thumping.

Pulse racing.

Deep breath.

He lets himself out of the bathroom and immediately dives in to separate Ronan and Paul. He drags Ronan one way, while Natalie pushes Paul in the other direction. "Get a grip, you moron," she tells him. He tries to push her away, but she's got a height advantage and she pins him against the wall. "He's not worth it."

"Get off me," Paul yells.

"No fucking chance."

Matt's blocking Ronan. He's fractionally calmer. He peers around Matt and Natalie to try to work out Paul's next move. "Leave him," Matt warns.

"You think I'd waste my energy?"

"I'm not interested. Just pull yourself together and calm down, you damn idiot. Don't you think we've got enough to worry about without—"

He stops talking when the tiny box of a house is filled with a different noise. It's coming from the bedroom.

Stephen and Rachel are grappling with each other in the doorway. Matt has no idea why they're fighting at first. Stephen looks like he's trying to get past, while Rachel's intent on stopping him from getting through.

Wait?

Is Stephen trying to stop Rachel getting out?

Through a momentary gap between them, Matt sees something that makes his blood run cold.

The kid Louise.

She's on her feet.

Wide-awake and alert.

He only sees her for a fraction of a second, but it's long enough. She stands perfectly still, glowering and breathing hard. Her entire frame, though deceptively slight, seems to rise and fall with each deep, juddering breath. She looks as bloodied and beaten as when they first found her, but her intent is clear. She's ready to fight. To *kill*.

Now the chaos makes sense. Stephen's trying to stop Louise from getting out, and Rachel's trying to stop him getting anywhere near Louise. He barges Rachel out of the way, but she's up and at him again almost immediately. Behind her, Louise crouches, then pounces, but the electrical flex is still tied around her ankle. She leaps up into the air at Stephen but crashes back down when the cord reaches its limit. She hits the floor hard, nose bloodied.

Natalie's in the hallway, ready to dive in and try to stop the fighting, but Matt grabs her arm and pulls her back. She reacts badly, spinning around and unloading on him instead, trying to get him off her. He dodges her flailing fists but wraps his arms around her torso and drags her toward the front of the cottage.

Louise is unsteady but back up on her feet, blood pouring from her busted nose. She sways ominously, and he can't tell if she's about to attack or collapse. His view is obscured and he's still trying to get both Natalie and himself a safe distance away, but a bottleneck is behind him now as Paul and Ronan fight with each other to get out of the cottage first. They've both got armfuls of stuff and are wedged in the narrow hallway. Paul needs Ronan to move so he can get past, but Ronan's overloaded and he's stuck.

Natalie can tell from the expression on Matt's face that their worst fears have been realized. She stops struggling and turns back around, just in time to see Stephen shove Rachel away, then punch her in the gut when she comes at him again. Winded, she staggers back. She almost falls over Louise, who's on the floor now, trying to chew through the electrical flex.

"He's got a gun," Natalie says, but no one's listening. She watches helpless as Stephen aims a flare gun at Rachel, then fires at her from point-blank range. The graying shadows of early evening that filled the bungalow instantly disappear in a haze of white-hot red-tinged light. The flare hits Rachel just below her breastbone, embedding deep in her flesh, and the force of the impact sends her tripping back. She claws at her already-burning clothes, trying to scratch out the bloom of incandescent flame that's rapidly consuming her. Her clothes shrivel and melt, fusing to her skin. Hair withers away to nothing.

Yet she continues to fight.

Is she a Hater too?

It's as if the pain and inevitability hasn't yet registered. What's left of Rachel knocks Stephen off his feet. He hits the bedroom door with the back of his head and collapses against it, slamming it shut. As it closes, Matt catches a glimpse of Louise springing into action amid the fire and fury.

She's free now. Unstoppable. She scrambles over Rachel's burning bones to get to Stephen, desperate to be the one who makes the kill.

The four who remain on the other side of the door stand motionless in the hallway, numbed by what they've just witnessed. The speed of it. The ferocity. The finality.

"We have to help them," Ronan says instinctively, nervously, but all the time he's backing farther and farther away.

"They're beyond help," Matt tells him.

The shattering of glass is like an alarm. As the bedroom window blows out with the unbearable heat and that part of the building is filled with fresh flame, Natalie springs back into life. "Get what you can and get out," she shouts. *"Now!"*

There's no time to argue, for once. Ronan, Matt, Paul, and Natalie move quickly and cooperatively to save as much of their supplies as possible. They form a human chain and dump everything they're able to rescue in a heap in front of the cottage, but they quickly realize more distance is required. Matt makes another frantic dash inside for more, but the cottage is rapidly filling with noxious smoke.

The heat is rising in intensity, climbing by the second. There's no way anyone's left alive in the bedroom.

He snatches up another rucksack. He doesn't care whom it belonged to or what's in it. There'll be time to worry about that later, he hopes. He notices that the wood paneling is beginning to bubble and blister. Wallpaper is starting to curl and burn. They've stacked up so much combustible stuff in this tiny little building that the fire is spreading with astonishing rapidity; the heat is so fierce that it scythes through the air like an invisible hand, igniting everything it touches, jumping from place to place. After dumping another load of gear out front, Matt tries to go back one final time, but doesn't make it farther than a couple of steps before Natalie grabs the collar of his jacket and pulls him back in the other direction. He stands in the middle of the garden with his hands on his knees, coughing his guts up, lungs full of smoke.

It's raining hard out here again, the morning's brightness long forgotten. Everything they've managed to salvage is ruined. The ground has been churned to mud. The four of them stand back in a ragged line, silent and numb, and watch the fire consume the entire building. It's unstoppable. Inevitable. "We're screwed," says Ronan, and as the roof of the bungalow collapses, sending a cascade of sparks and embers spiraling into the darkening sky, the others can't help but agree. Matt thinks the fire would be impressive to watch if the implications weren't so completely fucking terrifying.

"Now what?" asks Paul.

"Get the stuff we've got under cover, then find somewhere to spend the night."

"Two buildings left," he says. "Both full of corpses. Nice."

"I reckon we head for the stores this time," Natalie suggests. "The bodies there will be easier to move out into the open. What do you reckon, Matt?"

Matt's not listening. Instead, he walks around the edge of what's left of the bungalow, the fierce heat forcing him to keep his distance. He reaches the charred black hole in the wall at the back of the ruin where the bedroom window used to be. He can see straight through into the inferno inside. It's a pointless, cursory inspection that he's carrying out for his own benefit, but he covers his mouth and nose and tries to count the bodies. Despite the dancing flames and the heat haze and the smoke, he can still make out definite shapes in there. The outline of the frame of the double bed. What's left of a wardrobe. There's just a single corpse, its presence given away by its instantly recognizable form: sticklike limbs, the curve of the spine, the butterfly-shaped pelvis. Its size dictates that it has to be either Rachel or Stephen. It lies facedown, barely distinguishable in color from the burned carpet and charred floorboards. Wasted. Brittle and awkward.

"Matt, come on," Paul yells.

"Wait."

"Fuck's sake, mate, we need to get a move on."

But Matt's not about to be hurried. Natalie senses there's a problem. She drops the kit she's just picked up and heads over to where he's standing. The heat is ferocious here and she can feel her face beginning to prickle and burn. "What's the matter?"

"Only one body." He starts looking at the ground near his feet for footprints and clues. Natalie follows him as he walks farther from the ruin, eyes stinging from the smoke, struggling to see anything in the gloom.

"Matt, come on . . . ," she says, but he's not listening. "What difference does it make?"

He speeds up. He's seen something.

A shape is on the grass a little farther ahead, and he breaks into a slow run to reach it. It's another body. Badly burned, but not as far gone as the one trapped in the cottage. Enough flesh and bulk remain for him to make an easy identification. It's Rachel. "Jesus

Christ." He crouches down to inspect her corpse. He covers his mouth and nose. The smell is appalling. "Poor bitch."

And Rachel reacts.

Somehow, she's still alive.

She lifts one arm and reaches out for him. Barely any skin is left on the fingers that claw desperately at the air. Her badly burned torso has been cut to ribbons by broken glass, slashed as she made a frantic escape through the window. She manages to raise her head and look up, and Matt cowers away. Rachel's face is a grotesque caricature of the one he remembers: her features are exaggerated and contorted with pain, skin alternatively blackened then raw, large patches of hair burned away to bald. Her eyes, though, are clear and full of hate.

"Leave her," Natalie says.

Rachel tries to scream, but her insides are as fucked as her outsides. She lasts just a couple more seconds, then drops her head and takes her last scorched breath.

"Where is she?" Matt asks, looking around, frantic now.

"Who?"

"Who d'you think? That bloody kid Louise. She's not in the house."

Natalie peers in through the bedroom window, but she too can only see one other body. "Worry about it later. Right now we need to get safe and under cover."

"But we're never going to be safe while she's still alive."

"We'll have more chance in the stores than out in the open."

Natalie grabs his hand and the two of them sprint, slip, and slide through the rain toward the stores building, pausing only to scoop up as much kit as they can carry between them.

Ronan and Paul are waiting by the open door. "Get in," Natalie shouts at them. "Get inside now!"

Inside the building there's nothing but dark. Fortunately she knows her way around. With outstretched hands she feels along a shelf to the immediate right of the door for the torch Ruth always insisted they leave handy in case the generator failed. She finds it with little problem, but the weak yellow glow is barely noticeable. Paul steps out of the way when she pushes past him looking for lanterns, and he inadvertently treads on the body of one of his former workmates. He looks down and sees Joy's outstretched hand under his boot. That crack he just heard that felt like twigs snapping . . . that was her fingers. "Fuck," he says, his mouth salivating like he's about to throw up. "Fuck."

Natalie scans the room as best she can with the torch. "That's not right."

"What's the problem?" Matt asks, immediately concerned.

"Someone's already been in here."

"So what? It's not exactly been kept under lock and key, has it? It could have been any one of us."

"Yeah, but it wasn't just anyone. The place hasn't been trashed. Whoever was here has been methodical. They knew what they were looking for."

"What about Rajesh?" Paul suggests. "It has to have been him, doesn't it?"

"I guess," she says, agreeing because there's a space on the rack where his kayak is usually kept, and the life jackets, spraydecks, and other kit he needed have also been moved.

As their eyes become accustomed to the shadows in the stores, it becomes apparent that almost all of the floor space is taken up by the dead. Those left alive are having to tiptoe around the edges of the makeshift morgue. "What do we do?" Ronan asks nervously. "Can we move them up to one end?"

"Get them all outside," Matt says. "We need the space more than they do. Ronan, get the door and watch for the kid."

"What . . . ?" he stammers nervously.

"That bloody kid's still on the loose. Look out for her. She's an animal."

Matt bends down and puts his hands under Joy's armpits, then drags her corpse outside. She loses a boot and her bare heel carves an arclike groove in the mud around to the side of the building, where he unceremoniously dumps her.

When he gets back inside, Natalie's managed to locate a couple of battery-powered lanterns. They illuminate enough for him to see that the others are just standing there staring at him. He tries to move one of the children that washed up on the beach, but this corpse proves more difficult to shift. The child's rigid legs are entangled with the next body alongside it. Already panting with effort, Matt looks up at Paul. "Come on! Help me, for God's sake!"

Matt's sudden outburst kicks him into action. Paul takes the child's legs and helps carry him outside. Natalie puts down the lamp and starts to shift another of them. It doesn't take long. The prospect of being attacked by Louise keeps the three of them working at breakneck speed.

The teenage boy that Nils killed is next. They each afford him a little silent deference. Natalie still feels a pang of regret. They had nothing to do with any of the other deaths, but this one was different. The boy came to them looking for help, but they rounded on him and slit his throat before he had chance to speak.

First in, last out. Vanessa's is the final corpse they move. Matt takes her legs while Paul and Natalie take an arm each. Paul gags when he picks her up. Her split skull has emptied, the contents gluing it to the ground as they've dried, leaving a clump of hair behind. Her head feels unnaturally light.

Outside, the relative order of the improvised stores-building morgue has been abandoned. The bodies have been left in a haphazard, tangled pile with Vanessa dumped on top. Paul is momentarily distracted: although he's getting used to seeing corpses, the expressions on their faces are getting to him. It's hard to see them fully because of their position and the increasing shadows of dusk, but he can make out enough to still be able to recognize the people he used to work with who'll now never leave Skek. Colleagues. Memories. Friends (of a sort).

"Get a move on," Natalie tells him, with no room for sentimentality.

"What?"

"That kid's on the prowl. Get inside."

"One kid, four of us," he says, instinctively resorting to empty bullshit and bluster.

"Yeah, and there were a lot more of us when we first got here, remember?"

With that she's gone, disappearing into the stores building. Outside there's just Paul and the rest of Skek. The panic catches up with him fast and he follows her inside, convinced he'll feel Louise's tiny fingers ripping into his flesh at any moment.

Matt busies himself inside. This place has been left relatively untouched over the last few days because, despite appearing outwardly functional and useful, in reality it isn't. Over the last week there's been barely any call for any of the kit that's usually kept in here. Climbing tackle, kayaks and paddles, life jackets, other outdoor-activity equipment . . . none of it's been of any use in helping them stay alive. Food, water, and heat are all they've needed, and those things are now in increasingly short supply. The stores building is drafty and cold, and their meager pile of scavenged scraps looks woefully insufficient in the middle of the bloodstained floor space.

Paul's left the door open. He goes to shut it, but Matt tells him not to. "Don't. It's the only way in or out. We need to be able to see her if she comes."

"*When* she comes," Natalie corrects. "Did you see her? Killing us is all that matters to her now."

"But aren't we just letting her know exactly where we are?" Ronan argues.

"She probably already knows. And if she doesn't, it won't take a lot of working out. So the question is, would you rather have thirty seconds warning when we see her coming, or the three seconds we'd get if she comes in through a closed door?"

Ronan has no answer to that.

The slightest trace of light is still outside, but the brightest beacon by far is the burning bungalow. Flames continue to lick at the ruin, which is framed perfectly in the open double doorway. The concrete outer shell stands proud. Empty like a ghost.

The four of them sit huddled together in the miserable light, closer to each other than they've been in a while. Closer to each other than they want to be. Almost touching. This building's not particularly large, but because of its barnlike shape and vaulted roof, it feels bigger than it is. Voices and sounds echo in the space. It's disorienting. Frightening. Imagined monsters are all around them in the shadows the light doesn't reach.

Natalie's found a mallet that's been left alongside some camping and shelter-building kit. She holds on to it like it's the most precious thing she owns. It's the closest she has to a weapon after losing the bow and arrow in the bungalow fire. She didn't even think about it at the time because she was too busy focusing on staying alive. "So should we go and hunt her out, or do we wait for her to come to us?" she asks.

"I say we wait until morning then hunt," Matt says, a surprising calm certainty to his voice. No one argues. "We need to get rid of her. Eliminate the threat. Then once she's dealt with, we sit tight and wait for Rajesh to come back."

23

They all have weapons now. Still sitting in the same spot as they were hours earlier, Natalie clings to her mallet while Matt tightly grips a small knife he pocketed in the kitchen of the bungalow. It's more suited to peeling potatoes and chopping vegetables than self-defense, but it's better than nothing. Just. Ronan and Paul both hold on to hand axes they discovered among the equipment stashed away in here. Paul cradles his like a teddy bear. They're both asleep. "Ironic, isn't it?" Matt whispers to Natalie. "The two with the best weapons are the two least prepared to use them."

"I was thinking the exact same thing."

Ronan stirs, reacting to the mumbled noise of their conversation. Matt waits a few seconds until he's sure Ronan's settled, then speaks again. "Why the hell did you even have axes here anyway? There aren't any trees."

"I know, I know. I'm always telling Stuart he should get rid of them. He's supposed to be doing something about them next month when he . . ." She stops when she realizes she's talking about her friend as if he were still here, discussing a future none of them might have. "Sorry. Force of habit."

"If we'd got a boat, we could disappear right now and leave these two behind. What do you reckon?" Matt says, trying to redirect the conversation. "We could be gone before they wake up, imagine that."

"It's tempting. I reckon I'd do it too," she says almost without hesitation. "Think you could get us back?"

"Reckon so if you can get your hands on a compass. That's all I need."

She gets up and searches through a plastic tub to her left, then sits back down and hands him a compass. "Orienteering kit."

"You sure you haven't got a boat hidden in here too?"

"I wish. There are more kayaks, but it's not as easy as Raj made it sound."

"He didn't make it sound particularly easy. Anyway, you get me a boat, and I'll get you home."

"Promise?"

"Promise."

"And what do you think we'll find when we get there?"

Matt stops and considers her question. "I think it'll be as bad as we're expecting. Probably worse. Doesn't matter what the cause is, we've both seen how the panic spread here. Just imagine that ramped up by a factor of several hundred thousand."

"You're probably right. I'd like to think we're both wrong, but I know we're not."

"Seems we've got as low an opinion of the rest of society as each other. Good to know."

"And I thought I was the only one. . . ."

"Nope. You and me both. I'm just trying to have a little more faith in your mate Raj."

"He won't let us down."

"You sure?"

"As sure as I can be."

"I just hope Jen's all right. You know I used to—" Matt stops speaking abruptly.

It unnerves Natalie. She sits upright fast, and her sudden movement wakes the others.

"What's the problem?" Paul mumbles, still half-asleep.

"Shh . . ." Matt gets up.

"Matt, what is it?" Natalie's voice is a loud whisper.

"There's someone outside. . . ."

Ronan's on his feet with unprecedented speed, immediately awake and alert. His ax is still gripped tight in his clammy hands. He squints into the darkness, certain he saw something moving. "It's her. It must be."

"Stand your ground," Natalie says. "Don't go out there. Don't risk it."

"Stick together," Paul agrees, on his feet now too.

The longer Matt stares into the impenetrable blackness outside, the less he can see.

He takes another hesitant step forward, then stops.

She's here.

There's no doubt, no question. Her height gives her away. She stands in the doorway on the outer edge of the circle of light coming from the lamps and torches, illuminated enough to distinguish her outline, but protected by enough shadow to hide her intent.

Ronan cracks. He runs at her before any of the others can react. He's driven by a pent-up, hate-fueled fear the likes of which he's never before felt. Though she's been catatonic for days, he holds this evil little bitch solely responsible for the hell he's been put through— the hell that's claimed the lives of so many of his employees and destroyed his business and his world. He's vaguely aware of the others calling out after him, trying to stop him, but he's not interested in anything they have to say. He has to act. Finishing this is the only thing that matters now. She's taken everything he had. . . .

The girl comes at him just as quickly, arms outstretched almost like she's begging him for help. Is this how she claimed her earlier victims? Did she fool them into thinking she was innocent and vulnerable, then murder them in cold blood?

Ronan's nervousness and doubt are all gone.

He knows he has to kill her.

He swings the ax around and brings it down hard. It wedges deep into the side of her torso with a sickening thud. First blood to Ronan. The metal ax head chinks against her hip bone, and the child screams with a desperate raw noise that's sad enough to break any heart.

Any heart except Ronan's.

He's been through too much to care anymore. Only now that he's facing the killer one-on-one does he realize the full extent of how much he's lost since arriving on Skek.

She has to pay for what she's done.

He wrenches the ax free and swings it at her again. He misses and almost loses his footing in the mud. Panicking, he lifts the ax a third time and this time hits his mark. It thuds into her sternum. He lets go and she staggers away, the ax still wedged in her delicate chest. A choked cry. Gurgled breath. Arms flailing, grasping at nothing.

She takes three more steps back, then stumbles. Slight recovery. Overcompensates and overbalances. Ronan watches with his fists clenched, ready to strike again if he has to. Two more backwards steps and she's had it. No longer able to support her weight, her legs buckle and she drops in an dignified heap.

Ronan turns to face the others, who remain huddled close to each other, subconsciously seeking the security and warmth the small group provides. The relief he feels is palpable, invigorating. "It's over." He pants hard with effort, throat dry. "I did it. I killed her."

Matt breaks ranks and edges closer. The girl might not be dead yet, he thinks. She nearly is, sure, but while there's breath left in her body, she's still a deadly threat. He's wondering whether he should take matters into his own hands and finish her off or just let nature take its course. Her outstretched fingers are digging into the ground, clawing the mud. Involuntary or conscious movements? Just a death twitch? He steps around Ronan and stands over the kid with his hopelessly inadequate two-inch vegetable knife held ready in case she comes at him.

She doesn't.

All movement stops.

She's dead now. No question.

"I did it," Ronan says again. "Things will be all right now."

"I'm not sure things will ever be all right." Natalie notices Matt hasn't taken his eyes off the girl's body. "You okay, Matt?"

He looks up, face ashen. "Ronan, what the fuck have you done?"

"What's the problem?" Paul shouts, holding back, still keeping his distance. "Matt, mate, what's up?"

"It's not her."

"What?"

Matt clears his throat. He crouches down. Double-checks. "It's not her."

"What do you mean?" Ronan mumbles.

"What do you fucking think I mean?" Matt screams at him. "It's not Louise. It's Jayde Hazleton."

Natalie pushes past Ronan and drops to her knees. She knows—knew—Jayde better than any of the others did. She tries to hold herself together but lets out an involuntary sob. In a week of shocks and sideswipes and cruel twists and bitter blows, this is by far the worst. She can barely comprehend what's just happened. "Fuck, Ronan . . . you . . . *you killed Jayde.*"

Right now Ronan's struggling to process anything. Instead, he simply shuts down. He stands his ground and stares into the darkness at the far end of the stores building, refusing to look anywhere else. Because if he doesn't look, he thinks, he might be able to convince himself that this hasn't happened, that he hasn't done what they're saying he's done, that he hasn't just murdered the wrong kid. His leg starts to twitch. Nervous muscle spasms. The harder he tries to keep it still, the worse it gets. "But it can't be. She's not supposed to be here. They said she'd gone. You told me she'd gone."

"You fucking idiot," Paul says, edging closer and looking down into the wrong dead girl's face. "You complete fucking idiot."

Ronan's desperate now, reality finally sinking in. He can barely stay upright. He grabs hold of Paul's jacket, hanging on to him for support, and screams into his face, "It wasn't my fault. How was I to know? What the hell was I supposed to do?"

"Not kill the wrong fucking kid, that was what you were supposed to do," Paul yells back.

"I didn't know. I swear, I didn't know. I couldn't see properly. I thought it was her. . . ."

"You couldn't see properly? You didn't think it was worth checking before you did it?"

"It's not my fault." Ronan's sobbing now, still holding on until Paul pushes him away.

Ronan staggers back and trips over Jayde's feet. On his hands and knees now, only a couple of meters from the girl he's just hacked down, he vomits with nerves. He wipes his mouth on the back of his sleeve and uses a sturdy metal shelving rack to pull himself back up. A string of drool dribbles from his bottom lip.

Wait. He has a thought. A get-out clause.

"No one's going to know, are they? No one's coming here. No one's going to care when so much else has happened." His fight is beginning to return. "It doesn't matter, does it? We'll be okay."

"It doesn't matter? For Christ's sake, Ronan, wake up." Natalie glares at him, unable to believe what she's hearing. "You just killed an innocent child."

"No, *we* killed her," he answers quickly, shirking responsibility and blame. "We're all in this together."

"We've not been together from the start," Matt says.

"Yeah, and you're the cunt who put an ax in her chest," Paul adds, goading Ronan.

Natalie still can't take her eyes off Jayde's body. The teenager's glazed eyes gaze upward unblinking. It hurts like hell, and she'd give anything for Jayde to still be alive, but she knows that what's done is done and nothing anyone says or does will bring her back. To an extent, and it pains her to admit it, Ronan's right. The loss of life shouldn't be trivialized, but more important things are at stake here. "You're all missing something," she announces.

"What?"

"Louise is still alive."

"Shit. So it's back to plan A. We wait for her until morning, then get rid of her."

"Not necessarily. We've got another option now."

"You think?"

"Rod would never have left Jayde here on the island. Christ, he was bitter enough when he lost custody after his divorce. He's one of those desperate custody dads now, you know? Clinging on to every second of time the court said he could have with her. I know he wouldn't have let her out of his sight."

"So what are you saying?" Matt's worked it out already, but he wants to hear her say it.

"I'm saying that Rod must still be on the island too. He wouldn't have left without her."

"And if Rod's still here . . ."

"Then so is his boat. I know we're supposed to be waiting for Raj, but we might be able to get off this rock tonight."

"But we checked down by the jetty earlier," Paul says. "There was no boat down there."

Natalie's one step ahead of him as usual. "Think about it, though. He said he didn't intend going back to the mainland, but he'd have wanted to keep his options open, wouldn't he? He knows this island as well as any of us. Crafty bastard's hidden the boat somewhere, I'm sure he has. We just need to find out where."

"Ask him," Matt says. "He's here."

An approaching silhouette. Thundering footsteps and gasping breaths. Rod's distinctive shape appears in the doorway and he leans against the wooden frame, hopelessly unfit.

"Where is she?"

The corpse is concealed by the lack of light. He's standing just inches from his daughter's body, yet he remains completely unaware. Details are hard to distinguish in the gloom, and the circle of lamplight around the four huddled survivors makes everything beyond its reach appear darker still.

"We thought you'd gone." Natalie's panicking now, not sure what to say or how to say it. "We thought you'd gone back to the mainland."

He's not listening. "Where is she?" His voice fills the building, echoing off the walls and reverberating across the otherwise empty island.

Ronan cringes, thinking that the noise will bring the real killer out of hiding. He gestures for Rod to quiet down. Matt tries to call Ronan back, but he's not listening.

"Please, Rod, don't . . . ," Ronan whispers. "You don't under-stand. . . ."

"Where's my daughter? We were down by the beach. She heard you lot and saw the cottage on fire. She waited till I was asleep, then did a runner."

Ronan moves closer to Rod to head him off and, by default, reveals everything they were trying to keep hidden. Rod looks down and sees Jayde's lifeless face looking back up.

"Wait, please, we can explain. . . ." Ronan's voice dries up to nothing.

Rod crumbles. On all fours now, he reaches out for his dead daughter, brain struggling to process. The ax sticks up from her chest like someone's deliberately left it there for safekeeping. He touches the handle but can't bring himself to remove it. Instead he runs his outstretched fingers down Jayde's cheek—frozen but still warm—then looks up at Ronan. Rod appears unnaturally calm. No longer shouting. Voice barely even audible now. "Who did this?"

Neither by design or coordination, Paul, Matt, and Natalie have all moved back, implicating Ronan by default. For an endless moment no one speaks, but the insinuations are clear. Ronan makes eye contact with Rod, then almost immediately looks away again, unable to either hide his guilt or face the man whose innocent daughter he's just slaughtered. His silver tongue and gift of the gab were often a blessing in business, allowing him to spin his way out of trouble and hide his failings through a haze of corporate babble and bullshit. Here, though, in this place and at this moment, his words are his undoing. He can't help himself.

"Listen, Rod . . . you've got to understand . . . I didn't know it was her. *We* didn't know. We thought it was Louise."

"Shut up, Ronan." Natalie's still backing away. "Just leave it."

She reverses into Matt, who stands his ground despite her best efforts to shove him along.

Rod still hasn't budged.

"You have to believe me." Ronan's digging an ever bigger hole for himself and everyone else. "If we'd known it was Jayde, then—"

His nervous bullshit is abruptly truncated. Rod's up on his feet and at him with remarkable speed. He's older than Ronan and twice his size, but in a rush of adrenaline-charged surprise, Ronan manages to just about squirm out of his way.

Standing on the other side of the stores, Paul sees something that scares him more than anything else. He grabs Matt's jacket and pulls him closer. "He's got a gun. Rod's got a fucking shotgun!"

Rod steadies himself and swings the weapon around. Slung across his back, the shotgun was difficult to see at first. Now it's the only thing any of them are looking at. Natalie tries to sink even deeper into the shadows, but realizes Matt is gripping her arm. He squeezes tight. Too tight. For a split second the fear that he's about to change into one of those inhuman Hater creatures is more frightening than the prospect of Rod with a shotgun, but when she raises her torch and makes eye contact, she knows they're still on the same side. "We need to get out of here right now," Matt hisses. "We need to find that bloody boat."

Ronan rushes Rod and grabs the barrel of the shotgun, trying to wrestle it from his grip before he has a chance to take aim and fire. With them both distracted, Matt bundles Natalie out of the building and back into the night. Paul's still focused on the two men now grappling on the ground in front of him, and it's a couple more seconds before he realizes the others have gone. He follows without thought or hesitation. Thankfully Natalie's still carrying her torch, and he follows the unsteady circle of light that's now racing down the slope toward the beach. He shouts for them to wait, but his voice is lost in the incessant wind.

Matt looks back when he hears someone thundering after them. Natalie spins around too and shines the light into the gloom, terrified it's Louise. With his pathetic vegetable knife held out in front of him, Matt readies himself for an attack, which doesn't come.

"It's me," Paul says, and Matt relaxes slightly. "You fuckers, why didn't you wait?"

"We need to find the boat," Natalie answers, trying to keep them moving, not wanting to stand still.

"And were you going to tell me, or were you just planning on sailing off into the sunset together?"

"Grow up. We wouldn't have gone without you."

Paul's not so sure. "You might." He's suddenly spoiling for a pointless fight. "You've been like a pair of frigging lovebirds all bloody night in the stores. Cuddling up to each other and whispering. I heard you. I reckon you'd have—"

He's silenced by a gunshot. The three of them look back up the hill. The stores building they've escaped from is invisible, shrouded by darkness, but its approximate position can still be gauged by the location of what's left of the bungalow. A plume of dirty smoke continues to drift up into the night, colored deep orange and given definition by a blizzard of glowing embers fueled by the wind.

Paul swallows hard. "Fuck. Ronan. You think we should help him?"

Matt doesn't hesitate. "I think we're too late."

"Keep moving," Natalie says, and this time no one argues.

A couple of minutes later, all they can hear is the crashing of the waves on the beach. They're close to the jetty. Paul wastes no time in vocalizing his concerns. "We've already been down here. There's no boat."

"Yeah, but Rod said him and Jayde were down by the beach, remember?" Matt says. "And the boat has to be on the water or somewhere close, doesn't it? We can work our way around the entire bloody coastline if we have to."

"And that's your great plan, is it?"

"I never said anything about having a great plan, but it's just about all I've got right now."

Natalie's already down on the shingle. "Where you going?" Paul shouts after her.

"Anywhere but here. It's open season, in case you hadn't noticed. Nowhere to hide."

Matt sprints to catch up with her, struggling to match her pace. "Nat, wait."

She slows down, then turns back to face him. "We don't have time to wait."

"We need to think about this logically."

"Logically? Fuck's sake, since when did logic apply to anything that's happened here?"

He ignores her. "Are there any other jetties?"

"Just this one."

"Anywhere else where he could have moored the boat?"

"There are a couple of small coves, not far from where the ferry hit the rocks. Nothing north or west."

"You're absolutely sure?"

"Yes, of course I'm sure. Jesus. What, d'you think there's one I've forgotten or a secret one I'm just not going to tell you about?"

Matt walks away. He's frustrated, embarrassed, and scared. Just as he wants to stay hidden, the clouds overhead begin to break up, and just for a second the moon appears. The light reveals a tantalizing glimpse of their surroundings, for so long hidden in darkness.

Wait, he thinks. I remember this.

With his back to the water, the view here reminds him of first thing Monday morning. He stood alone here on the beach back then, waiting to go home, and played mind games—convincing himself he was the last man on Earth. He laughs to himself; he's a lot closer to assuming that unwanted mantle now. But he didn't want to be the sole survivor back then, and he definitely doesn't want to be now.

Matt recalls the blissful ignorance of his work colleagues and the staff of Hazleton Adventure back then. How could things have gone so wrong? He recalls those last few moments of precious normality before Vanessa died and before the ferry was wrecked and before the others were killed. . . . He thinks back to the ordinary, mundane world he lived in with Jen before he ever set foot on Skek, and he wishes more than anything else he was back there again.

He remembers Paul coming down to the beach to look for him that morning, when all he wanted was to be alone. Where is Paul? Matt looks around for him, then stops.

Matt looks up at the rocks that rise up in front of him. The sky's marginally lighter than the land, and he can make out the outline of the craggy headland. Beyond that, he can see the flat roof of the old weed-strewn army lookout.

"What's the matter?" Natalie's watching him staring into space.

"Just a thought." With that, he's gone. He heads back they way they just came. Natalie shouts after him again but he's not listening.

Matt climbs up off the beach, ever aware of the threats still hiding in the shadows on Skek, and feeling more exposed than ever. The waves masked his noise while he was down near the water, but now that he's moving away from the ocean again, every sound he makes seems to be disproportionately amplified. He feels like his every move can be heard for miles in all directions, like every step gives away his location to everyone and everything on the island with them.

"Matt, hold on," Natalie says, but he's not waiting for anyone. On his way up to the army lookout, he barges past Paul, and when Natalie catches up, Matt gestures for her to shine her torch inside.

"What's going on?" Paul asks.

Matt leans back against the ruin of a building, relieved.

Inside is the boat.

For what it's worth.

"It's a life raft," Natalie says. "It's a frigging inflatable life raft. Are you serious?"

"Is that it?" Paul asks. "We'll never get anywhere on that."

"Well, Rod and his kid did," Matt reminds them.

"You're telling me the two of them sailed back here on that thing?"

"That's exactly what happened. How else did they get here?"

"Reckon you can drive it?"

"You don't drive a boat, you idiot, but, yeah, I reckon I can. We just need to point it in the right direction. I've got a compass. Should be okay."

Paul remains seriously unimpressed by their discovery and finds it hard to mask his disquiet. Natalie leans in and shines the torch around the lookout as Matt climbs through the overgrown entrance around the back. The boat is short and squat nosed. It looks sturdy, but nowhere near big enough.

"We're going to struggle," Natalie says. "I reckon it'll probably sink with the three of us on board."

Matt doesn't say as much, but he has a sneaking suspicion she's right. He kicks and prods the boat's rubber walls. "It feels pretty decent, though."

He turns his attention to the outboard motor, but trips in the dark. Clothes are by his feet and sleeping bags too. Opened cans of food. A camping stove and an empty water bottle. He holds some of the detritus up to show the others.

"Christ, no wonder his kid did a runner if she was stuck hiding here with her old man," Paul says. "You can't blame her."

"Give it a rest," Natalie says. "Have a bit of respect."

"What, respect for the psycho we just left waving a bloody shotgun at Ronan?"

"No, respect for his teenage daughter who didn't deserve to die."

"Give me the torch," Matt says. She hands it over and watches as he checks the outboard over. He shines the light at his feet.

"What's wrong?" she asks, immediately concerned.

"No key."

"Rod had it. He mentioned it when he first turned up, remember? That morning in the mess hall?"

"I'll just go and ask him for it then, shall I?" Paul sarcastically suggests.

"You do that," she tells him.

Matt kicks the side of the dinghy in frustration, then leans back against the cold, damp wall of the lookout. "It's like the closer we are to going home, the farther away it seems to get."

"We've got other options though, right?" Paul says hopefully. "Rajesh will be back, won't he? And there were more kayaks and paddles in the stores."

"We could use the paddles with this, couldn't we?" Natalie gestures at the boat.

"Possibly . . ."

Natalie senses Matt's reluctance. "But?"

"But we really need to get that key. It'll take us half the time to get home if we've got the engine, and half the effort."

"So how do we do it?" Paul asks.

"We have to go and get it off him. There's no other option," Natalie says.

"He dies or we die."

"Looks that way. Can't imagine he's just going to hand it over."

That stark reality makes them all feel even more nervous.

"We're not all going to make it to the morning, are we?"

"Way things are going, we'll be lucky if any of us are left alive," Matt says.

"But I thought we were the good guys."

Natalie and Matt both look at Paul. His comment sounds remarkably innocent. Naïve. No trace of irony. "There are no good guys anymore," Matt tells him.

Natalie agrees. "It's survival of the fittest. Always has been, really. It's just that we're usually better at keeping the aggression in check. Usually."

Paul swallows hard, realization hitting home. He has something to say, but he's not sure how to say it. "So, are we the Haters? Think about it. The strongest survive. We all started on a level playing field. Most of us are dead, but the three of us are still alive. We saw others change, but who's to say we haven't changed too?"

Natalie chews over his words, knowing there must be some kind of logic buried in there somewhere.

Paul looks longingly at the boat. It's more than a stolen rubber dinghy tonight, it's a lifeline. It's just about all they have left. Their only chance to get home. Some of them, anyway.

"Regardless of who's what, I don't see that we have any choice," Matt says. "We have to find Rod, deal with him, get the key, then get the hell out of here."

With that Matt exits the lookout. He's nervous, terrified even, but he can't let it show. He has an image of home and Jen in his head and nothing else left but a gut full of Hate.

SATURDAY

24

This naturally limited landscape feels impossibly vast tonight, and Paul, Matt, and Natalie are exposed by the lack of landmarks: no trees to hide behind, barely any buildings left to take shelter within and regroup. They're vulnerable out here. Easy targets. Easy pickings.

A gorse bush is the best cover they have. They crouch down behind it together, boots squelching in the claggy, rain-soaked ground. "What do you reckon?" Paul asks.

The sun is loitering on the horizon, threatening to rise. Morning is fast approaching. Looking north along the length of the island they can see both the stores building and the main base, as well as the rubble-strewn gap where, until last night, Ruth and Stuart's bungalow stood. There's no sign of movement anywhere. No sign of Rod, and no sign of the Hater kid either.

"He'll still be in the stores," Natalie says.

"What makes you so sure?"

"Because that's where Jayde is."

Her logic is sound.

"Then let's get this done before it gets too light," Matt says.

Paul's not convinced. "Wait . . . Matt, hold on. . . ."

"Don't you get it? We don't have any choice. No point delaying it." Matt gets up and starts toward the stores.

"Matt's right." Natalie sounds almost disappointed, and she reluctantly follows. The fear of being left on his own outweighs the fear of being shot at by Rod, and Paul sets off too.

Matt slows again. "Hold back. Split up. Come at him from different angles."

Matt figures he'll make less noise on his own, and that the others will act as decoys and distract Rod long enough so Matt can mount his attack. Except he doesn't know if he can attack. He realizes just how much is at stake here, but he's still not sure he'll be able to go for Rod before Rod goes for him. He's always been happier on defense than attack. Perversely, the nagging doubt in his head gives him the slightest crumb of comfort to hold on to. I might not be a Hater after all. . . .

The layout of the building works to Matt's advantage. He's approaching from the rear. The entrance is at the other end, meaning he's well out of sight for now. He takes his time, edging quietly closer. Natalie's sweeping around the other side. Paul's nowhere near.

With his back against the wooden wall, Matt shuffles along the narrow gap between the building and the heaped bodies of his dead work colleagues and others that they dumped here last night. When he looks down and sees their expressionless faces looking up, he realizes again how quickly the darkness is being eaten away. The ice-blue light of morning is rapidly dissolving away the black, stealing any advantage and leaving him exposed.

He pauses a meter or so back from the front of the building, listening for Rod's movements. Little noise is coming from inside, but it's enough to let Matt know for sure that Rod's in there. Deep, heavy breaths. Occasional coughs. Muted sobs and sniffs.

But Matt can hear something else now.

It's not the others—they're too far back—and it's not coming from behind him or from inside the building, it's dead ahead.

He realizes what it is just before she appears.

It's Louise.

What's left of her, anyway.

The killer kid's ravaged appearance is ghastly, even in this pale and sickly light. She's virtually naked, sinewy and lithe, yet some shreds of clothing remain. Matt can't tell where her ragged trousers and T-shirt end and where she begins. Parts of the material have fused to her flesh, melted in the fire. The back of her head is bald and glistening, hair burned away, and her left eye is fluid filled and swollen like a rotten egg. Head to toe she's covered in blood and mud and shit and Christ knows what else. She stands her ground and sucks in deep, rattling lungfuls of cold air. She's half his size but has a hundred times his presence. She's completely fucking terrifying.

Matt knows that this little bitch is feeling no pain or fear. He knows that right now every fiber of her being is consumed with just one thought, one desire: to kill.

Despite her appalling physical state, she moves with astonishing athleticism and predatory speed. She suddenly bursts into life and sprints toward the open stores, and though Matt wants nothing more than to stay hidden in the shadows, he knows he can't. This kid has to die. Forget Rod. As long as Louise is alive, Matt's chances of getting off this damn island and back to Jen are next to nil. Before he can talk himself out of it he runs to intercept her. She catches sight of him almost instantly through her one good eye and changes course, veering toward him. She leaps to attack him as he dives to tackle her. He wraps his arms around her legs and squeezes as hard as he can.

"Help me," he screams to anyone who can hear him. "I've got her."

Louise thrashes in his grip. Writhing. Squirming. The weeping discharge from her burns makes her alternatively leathery and then smooth skin difficult to keep hold of. Her arms are free and she rips and punches at Matt's head and face, and it's all he can do to keep looking down and ignore the ferocious hurt. He keeps his eyes screwed shut for fear of their being scratched out by her frantic clawing. She bunny-kicks and flexes continually, managing to pull one leg free. She brings her right knee up hard and it cracks against Matt's chin. He bites down on his tongue and his mouth fills with a flood of warm, salty blood.

The pain is intense and he almost lets her go. Almost.

She just about slips his grip, but he catches her ankle as she kicks for freedom, hauling her back down again. She tries to stand up, and the inhuman strength in her deceptively immature frame is astonishing. She howls in frustration: a dry, hacking, rasping scream full of anger.

Full of *hate*.

Matt glances up at her, then buries his face once more as she unleashes hell on him.

Then she stops, distracted.

He's winded and hurt and he's unable to prevent her kicking free and getting up. Terrified that she's going to attack Natalie or Paul, Matt rolls over and reaches out for her but misses.

Gunshot.

Louise stops.

He looks up and now she's just standing there, swaying. Bottom jaw hanging loose. Half her face blown away.

Reload. Click. Fire.

The second shot hits her full in the chest and knocks her off her feet. She lands in the grass a couple of meters away, twitching. Juddering.

Reload. Click. One more shot.

Point-blank range. Side of the head.

All over now.

Matt picks himself up and staggers back, numb with shock and filled with pain. He looks over at the gunman, but doesn't see whom he expected.

Not Rod.

Ronan.

Natalie's at Matt's side now, helping him to stand. "You okay?" She holds him. Hugs him.

"Not Rod . . ."

"I can see that."

Ronan's standing over what's left of Louise, prodding at her corpse. When the barrel of the shotgun's cool enough to hold, he turns the weapon around and swings the stock at her again and again as if he were alternately swinging a golf club and then hammering a stake into the ground. He refuses to stop, only slowing his attack a minute or so later when he's too exhausted to keep fighting. Even now he continues to watch her, checking for movements or signs of life. Even from a distance it's clear to the others that Louise is dead. Her blood and body parts have been spread across a huge swath of grass.

Paul's right behind Matt and Natalie. "Has he lost his fucking mind?"

"I think we all have," Natalie says.

When he hears them talking, Ronan stops and turns around. Sweat soaked. Gasping for air. Grinning.

"Oh, fuck," Paul says under his breath.

Ronan walks toward them, casually swinging the shotgun back over his shoulder. "It's over. Done it. We're going to be okay now."

"And how d'you figure that out?" Natalie asks.

Ronan's still struggling to catch his breath. "She's dead . . . ," he says with his hands on his knees, panting, "and he's dead." He points into the stores.

Paul goes to investigate. Rod's body is lying next to Jayde's. He has a gaping, blood-soaked hole in his gut.

"What have you done, Ronan?"

"Exactly what I had to do," he answers without hesitation. "It was necessary. Unpleasant, but necessary. I know I can work with you three, but Rod and the girl had to go."

"So what happens now?"

Ronan shrugs. "We wait. Make ourselves as comfortable as we can and wait this out."

"And that's your great plan, is it?" Paul returns to the others. "Doesn't solve the fact that we've not got any food or fuel."

"I know, but we're safe here. Safer, anyway. And Rod's boat is somewhere. When the time's right and things have calmed down, we can go back for supplies. We can use this place as a base. Thing is, if everything really is as shitty as we think it is back home, why go back there?"

"Because it's home?" Matt says. "Because there are people there we give a damn about? People we're worried sick about?"

"Not me. Look, if there's one thing you know about me, it's that I've got a nose for business. I know a good deal when I see one, and right now this is the best option for all of us."

"For you, maybe," Paul sneers.

"No, Paul, for all of us." Ronan is uncharacteristically calm. "What have I told you about looking at the bigger picture and considering all possible outcomes?"

"Now is really not the time for your corporate bullshit."

Ronan's not impressed. He shakes his head and takes hold of the shotgun again. "Look, I'm not asking you, I'm telling you.

Did you not hear me? I said consider all the possible outcomes. If you don't do what I say, I'll kill you."

Paul's had years of Ronan's hyperbole. His default response setting kicks in. "Yeah, right."

But something about their boss's expression Matt doesn't like. He puts his hand on Paul's arm to get his attention. "Leave it, Paul."

"Thank you, Matthew," says Ronan. "The voice of reason, as always. See? That's how you do it. Take the emotion out of the situation and make your decision based on the black-and-white facts like our friend the accountant here. And the facts, if you take a few moments to look around you this morning, are that I've just killed two people, and I'll do it again if I have to. I've got a pocket full of shotgun shells and all the time in the world."

25

Ronan's switched back into boss mode with alarming ease. He's in the corner of the mess hall, sitting with his back to the wall where he can see all three of them. He's giving out his orders and gesticulating with the barrel of the shotgun. He's decided—not that it was much of a decision to make, really—that staying in this building is the best course now that the bungalow's gone. He's got them cleaning the place and collecting up the bodies. Paul walks over to where Matt's working.

"We need to get that shotgun off that prick. We should rush him. Maybe wait until he falls asleep. What d'you reckon?"

"I was thinking something similar. We just need to bide our time."

"We should do it now."

"And risk being shot? Come on, Paul, get a grip. You know Ronan, he's bound to trip himself up sooner or later."

"Then let's just hope it's sooner."

Ronan taps the barrel of the shotgun against a metal chair leg, and the ugly clanging fills the room as if he were ringing a bell, calling them to order. "Stop whispering. You're making me feel uneasy."

"*We're* making *you* feel uneasy?" Matt says, unable to help himself.

Ronan's flustered. Right on the edge. Barely holding himself together. When conversations don't go down the route he's expecting, he changes topic. "We need to do something to get rid of the stench in here. It's not healthy."

"There's a couple of bottles of bleach in the kitchen," Natalie says. "We could water it down and clean the floors. That'd be a start."

"Good idea. Matthew, take a couple of buckets and fill them with seawater."

Matt doesn't argue. He knows there's no point just yet. Natalie fetches a mop bucket and a plastic water carrier from the kitchen and hands them to him. "Thanks," he mumbles, making fleeting eye contact. "Keep Paul under control."

She nods.

"And don't try anything stupid," Ronan says. "Remember, play ball and we'll all get out of this okay and in one piece."

Matt takes the bucket and water carrier and leaves the building. It's a relief to be outside and on his own. He'd take his time, but he doesn't like the idea of leaving Natalie on her own with those two. He's half expecting Rod or Paul to crack and attack the other, leaving Natalie caught in the cross fire.

It's a beautiful day out here. The sun's out fully again. The sky is clear blue and cloudless, the breeze gentle and cool. It feels a world away from the madness they just about managed to survive through last night. A lifetime away.

Dark thoughts still occupy Matt's mind as he walks down toward the ocean. He's so preoccupied that he doesn't notice Rajesh until he steps right out in front of Paul.

26

Two others are here from the mainland with Rajesh. They're a couple: Niall and Marion. Both are archetypal bikers—all leather, tattoos, and hair. All the bad feelings and mistrust among the existing islanders is temporarily forgotten—old divisions erased by a new dividing line—as the new arrivals breeze into the mess hall with remarkable confidence. There's a moment of silent apprehension as they all size one another up, but it's over quickly. Natalie finds an unopened bottle of water from somewhere for them to share. Marion swings a heavy rucksack off her back. "We brought our own," she says in a hard and abrasive Scottish accent.

"She's just trying to help," Rajesh says, but he shuts up quick. It's a struggle for him to speak. His speech is slurred. Matt notices that one side of his face is bruised.

"We're just being neighborly," Marion says, sounding distinctly unneighborly.

"What happened out there?" Matt asks.

Rajesh glances up before answering, struggling to stay composed. "It's like we thought. You can't—"

"The whole world is fucked." Niall cuts right across Rajesh. "That's why we're here. Every fucker's killing every other fucker back home."

His accent is equally intense as Marion's, and that, along with his sheer physical size, combine to give him an intimidating presence. The other half's no better. Marion looks like she could match him word for word and pound for pound.

"You've seen the pile of bodies out front?" Matt says. "It's just as bad here."

"Oh, no, friend, it's a lot better here, believe me. There's none of those bastards here, for a start."

"How do you know for sure?" Ronan demands, still cradling the shotgun. "You don't know how many of those people we've killed. How many *I've* killed."

"You're right, I don't," Niall immediately replies. "It doesn't matter, though. I don't know if you killed one of them or the whole frigging lot. One thing I do know, though, is that you're no Hater, friend. They're all out of the woodwork now, battle lines well and truly drawn. You'd know if I was one of them, same way I know you're not."

"How?"

"Because we wouldn't be standing here chewing the cud like this for a start. We'd have fucking lynched each other."

"But I—"

"You're not Haters. None of you. That's why we're staying here. We're all on the same side. We're all in this shitstorm together."

Rajesh stares into space. Matt tries to read his expression, but he looks vague and unfocused, preoccupied. "Tell us what happened, Raj," Matt asks again, intentionally directing his question.

Rajesh reaches for the water Natalie provided and takes a large swig. He wipes his mouth on his sleeve. "Everything Niall's saying is right. It's as bad as we imagined. Worse, even. I made it to shore and . . . and it was just a bloodbath. They're everywhere. It's a full-scale war."

Niall takes over again. "I mean, the army's rounding them up and getting rid of them as best they can, but it's a fucking hard fight, I can tell you that much."

"It was when they started trying to round us up too, that's when we knew we had to get out," Marion adds. "Niall says we should head for the coast, reckoned they'd all be heading inland. He was right too."

"You don't wanna get yourself stuck as part of a big group," Niall continues. "That's when they hit you the hardest. You're like frigging sitting ducks when you're there in numbers."

"We can breathe easy here," adds Marion.

Rajesh waits for them to finish. "I'd just got back to land when these two found me. . . ."

"And it's a fucking good job we did too. Wouldn't have lasted ten minutes there on your own, lad," Niall says. "We were down visiting relatives when it all kicked off." He nods at Marion. "Her uncle had this boat. We'd got it all loaded up and ready, couple of weeks' worth of food at least, and we were waiting for her folks to show, but they never made it, did they love? We'd given up waiting and were just about to head out to sea when Marion spots this joker, paddling up the river Humber like he's back from a fucking day trip. Didn't take a genius to figure he'd come from somewhere worth checking out. Only too happy to show us the way here, weren't you, son?"

Rajesh nods and drinks more water. "If you say so."

"I do."

"If we hadn't stopped you, you'd have been dead by now," Marion adds.

"So here we all are. All friends together." Niall slaps Rajesh's shoulder with far more force than is necessary. "We've food and drink. Enough to keep us all fed and watered for a couple of weeks at least."

Ronan gets up. The shotgun is very visible, but neither Niall nor Marion seems particularly bothered. "I'm Ronan Heggarty. I'm in charge here."

"No, you're not," Niall says.

"Look, I don't know who you people are or where you've come from, but you need to understand that—"

Ronan's silenced by a vicious right hook from Marion, which knocks him out cold. "Understand that, love," she says as he collapses at her feet. She picks up the shotgun and hands it to Niall.

"Me and my Marion are calling the shots here." Niall looks at each of the group in turn. "Right. Who's hungry?"

Food.

They've barely eaten for days—hardly even thought about it—but now there's food on the table, it's all any of them can think about. Marion doles out goodies fetched from the boat, and they all dive in hungrily. It's like feeding time at the zoo.

27

Niall, with Ronan's shotgun slung over his shoulder, has had Natalie take him on a tour of the island. They've been gone almost an hour. While they've been away, Rajesh, Paul, Matt, and Ronan have been put to work finishing cleaning the interior of the main building and fetching the food and other supplies from the boat. Marion has them getting the place just as she wants it. "We have to do something about this, Matthew," Ronan says in a snatched moment between tasks. "We can't let them come here and take over like this."

"Why not?"

Ronan just looks at him, incredulous. "You're not serious?"

"I am. We've food and drink and a Hater-free island. I could think of worse places to be right now."

"And that's it? You're just going to roll over and let them take control?"

Matt sighs. "Ronan, I'm beat. I've got nothing left. I just want to rest awhile before I decide what to do next. There are two boats on the island, so we're not trapped like we thought. We have far more options now than we had this time yesterday. We just need to get our breath back and build up our strength. Bide our time."

Ronan's less than impressed. He marches off to the bathroom.

Rajesh has kept himself to himself since he got back here. Paul's mopping out the dorm where Ruth was killed, and he watches Rajesh as he works. He looks exhausted—both physically and mentally. Paul can only begin to imagine how much effort it took to kayak back to the mainland. A couple of times he's tried to engage him in conversation, but Rajesh has been far from forthcoming. For now he seems content to keep himself occupied with whatever jobs Niall and Marion find for him to do.

Paul catches hold of Ronan's arm as he walks back from the bathroom. "There's something going on here. Have you seen the way Rajesh is sucking up to the pair of them."

"It's not lost on me," Ronan quietly replies. "I know Natalie thinks highly of him, but right now I wouldn't trust him as far as I could spit. I think he'll sell us out soon as look at us."

"And have the place for him and his new mates, I reckon."

"I think you're probably right."

Marion appears, looking for him. "Everything all right, Ronan?"

"Everything's fine," he answers quickly—a little too quickly, perhaps—and he returns to cleaning tables and shifting chairs in the mess hall.

Niall and Natalie are back. Rajesh stops what he's doing and walks over to speak to Niall. "I've been thinking. We should burn the bodies."

"Why?"

"If we're serious about staying here, we're going to have to get rid of them. The sooner we do it the better. There's a real risk of disease if we don't. We should either burn them or bury them, and burning's the obvious solution. Quicker. Less effort."

"Okay."

"I'll help," Natalie says.

"The three of us'll do it," Niall tells them.

Natalie fetches a half-empty jerrican of fuel from next to the generator shed and carries it over to the pile of corpses they've left midway between the main building and the stores. Rajesh and Niall rearrange the dead into a vertical stack with spaces in between like human-shaped Jenga pieces. "It'll help the oxygen to flow," Rajesh explains. "We should start with these few, then bring the others across once the flames have got hold."

Niall steps back out of the way as Natalie douses the bodies with fuel. Rod, Jayde, Nils . . .

"These folks mean something to you two?" Niall asks.

"Most of them."

"Hurts, don't it?"

Natalie doesn't answer at first. Niall's glib words feel trivial, almost dismissive. "*Hurt* doesn't even begin to cover it."

"You're not the only ones who've had it tough, love. Marion's sister was the first we saw lose it. Nearly wiped out the whole damn family. We were lucky to get out alive."

"You feel lucky, do you?"

"Now I'm here, yes, I do, as it happens. I guarantee that whatever you've seen while you've been hiding away out here is nothing compared to what's gone on back home."

"You don't know what we've seen. What we've done."

"Aye, true enough. We'll compare notes later."

Niall takes a packet of cigarettes from his pocket and lights up. He lowers the glowing tip of his smoke close enough to a puddle of fuel for the fumes to catch, and the whole damn thing goes up with a roar. A wave of heat billows outward, and for a split second, all the oxygen seems to be sucked from the atmosphere. Natalie steps back and watches through the heat haze as her friends and ex-colleagues begin to burn. She feels unexpectedly angry that Niall started the fire and took away her control. She wanted to do it. It felt like the closest she was going to get to paying her respects.

She attempts to share her frustrations with Rajesh, but he's not interested. He's already on his way back inside.

Rajesh's demeanor has suddenly changed. Matt picks up on it, but Paul and Ronan are too busy sucking up to Marion to notice. Rajesh approaches Matt unexpectedly. It's the first time they've spoken properly since Rajesh returned. He seems agitated. Preoccupied. Nervous.

"What's the story with these two, Raj?" Matt whispers

"Not important."

"But can we trust them? Are they going to—"

"We don't have time for this. We're not hanging around."

"What?"

"I told you I'd get you off the island."

"I don't understand. . . ."

"The Haters know we're here. Or somewhere near here, anyway." Rajesh stops and checks to make sure Marion and Niall are still distracted. "These two are bad news, really fucking bad news. They're all sweetness and light until they've got what they want from you, then you're dead to them. They used me to get them here."

"Mate, you really need to slow down. You've been through hell and back to get here and I think you should—"

"Shut up and listen." Rajesh's tone and the look in his eye immediately silence Matt. "We were followed. They won't tell you because they're trying to keep you onside for now, but we only just got away. There was a boat full of Haters after us. They know we're out here. We only got away because some other poor fuckers turned up and distracted them, took the heat off us temporarily."

"What are you talking about?"

"They're not going to have any trouble finding us."

"You said even people who know where Skek is have trouble finding it. We'll be okay."

"No, no . . . you don't get it. *I want them to find us.* That was why I wanted to burn the bodies. It's a beacon. I came back with a decent boat like I promised. It has enough fuel to head north all the way up the coast right into the Scottish Highlands. Fewer people there, less chance of trouble. I've thought this through and planned it carefully. We're going to dump these two and leave. Don't treat me like a fucking idiot, Matt, just do exactly what I tell you if you want to get off Skek alive."

28

Less than an hour later the Haters arrive. Eight of them in a life-boat, slicing through the waves with power and ease and ominous intent. The plume of gray-brown smoke continues to rise straight upward into the clear sky from the body bonfire, pointing right to the heart of Skek like the YOU ARE HERE marker on a tourist map. Marion's on her way back to the boat with Matt to collect more supplies. She stops when she sees the other boat racing toward the shore.

"Fuck. *Fuck!*"

She starts to run back to base. Matt ducks behind the army turret and watches for a few seconds longer.

Long enough to see the Haters ride the surf, then jump over the side of the boat and drag it up onto the shore.

Long enough to see them crawling all over the boat Rajesh and the others arrived here in, looking for the escapees.

Long enough to see them look up at where Matt's standing and see the path to the base.

He turns and sprints for all he's worth, overtaking Marion in seconds, leaving her for dust. By the time he's back inside the main building, the fastest of the Haters are on her. One grabs her legs and drags her down. Two more savagely beat her. She tries to fight back but her resistance lasts just seconds. It's a brutal, bloody, and completely one-sided massacre.

Niall's seen it all. "What the fuck? How did they . . . ? How did they know?" He's panicking. Doesn't know what to do.

Ronan, on the other hand, has a newfound inner strength. The spineless prick has developed a backbone, just at the wrong moment. He reclaims his shotgun from where Niall stashed it, loads it, then heads for the door.

"Don't be frigging stupid," Paul shouts after him, but Ronan's never listened to anything Paul's told him, and he's not about to start now. He marches out there, bold as anything, ready to stand his ground.

For almost a minute it works.

The nearest Hater—a slender woman in her thirties, similar in strength and stature to Natalie, long hair whipping behind her as she runs—throws herself at him, and he fires and hits her square in the chest. The force of the shot plucks her from the air and she drops like a stone. She's dead before she hits the ground.

A lucky misfire hits the second Hater at waist height, clipping the stocky man on the right side of his pelvis and sending him spinning away. He's down, but not out. Seemingly oblivious of the searing pain that must be coursing through every nerve, fiber, and sinew of his body, he drags himself back up and marches on, slowed but not stopped.

Ronan tries to reload. Hands shaking now. The pack of Haters getting ever nearer.

The shells are in and his weapon is ready, but Ronan's luck has run out. The next Hater—the biggest, meanest fucker of all, clearly the leader of the pack—is already on top of him. He grabs the barrel of the shotgun, wrenches it from Ronan's grip, then throws it well out of reach. Ronan tries to scramble away, but the Hater hauls him back by the scruff of his neck and pulls him onto an unspeakably savage-looking machete the Hater's holding with such force that the blade enters between Ronan's shoulder blades like a hot knife through butter, then erupts out of the front of his gut, showering the ground with crimson.

Ronan sinks to his knees, momentarily tries to push the blade back out and stem the blood loss and hold in his innards, then falls forward and smacks facedown into the grass.

Seven Haters left, five Unchanged.

Unequal numbers. Grossly unfair odds.

"Head north," Rajesh tells Niall. "There are caves at the far end of the island. Places we can hide."

Niall doesn't need to be told twice. He pushes his way past them and out the door, then sprints away, using the buildings as cover.

"Caves?" Paul says, confused.

Rajesh grabs his jacket and pulls him close. "There are no fucking caves, you idiot. He's a diversion. Keep out of sight, let him draw them away, then get yourself down to the boat and wait for me. Get out of sight and don't do anything stupid."

No argument.

Matt checks what's happening outside. Natalie's looking out the same window. Two of the Haters have split off from the rest of the pack and are chasing after Niall. He won't last long. Sure, he might put up a decent fight when they reach him, but it'll only hold them up for seconds. Natalie knows they'll need far longer to get away from these savage, ruthless bastards. Five more are still heading straight for base.

"Go," Natalie tells them. "Get under cover. Right now!"

She moves toward the door. Rajesh tries to stop her. "Don't be stupid, Nat. I'm giving us a chance here, you'll get yourself killed."

She shrugs him off. "I know what I'm doing. No one knows

this island better than you and me now. I'll loop around and keep them tied up a while longer. Wait for me on the beach. See you down there."

Gone.

Matt presses himself flat against the wall, just able to see outside, and watches her running north after Niall with adrenaline-fueled athleticism. Another pair of bloodthirsty animallike Haters peel away and follow her.

Three left. Two hunting, one wounded.

"Get to the beach," Rajesh orders. "Now!"

"But—"

"Now!"

Rajesh grabs a bow and arrow and a hand ax, then bursts out into the sunlight and heads for the still-burning, human-fueled bonfire. Outwardly calm, inwardly terrified, he raises the bow, loads an arrow, then fires at the nearest of the three remaining Haters. It hits the man in the belly. He stumbles, clutching his wound, but keeps moving for as long as he can. He comes at Rajesh, who sidesteps the killer and pushes him face-first into the flames. His screams are undeniably satisfying.

Rajesh reloads and fires wildly at the next one, but this time his shot's poor and the arrow whistles over the shoulder of a stocky twentysomething with a ragged beard and bloodstained clothing. He doesn't have time to reload before the man's all over him.

The animalistic savagery of the Hater is spellbinding. He's completely consumed with destroying Rajesh. Poor bastard is dead in seconds, but the Hater just doesn't stop. He has his back to Paul and Matt, and with him distracted, they escape the main building and run to the stores. Paul's quick moving, but Matt's slower. He's stunned by what he sees. The Hater's using the ax on Rajesh now, swinging it down again and again and again on his corpse like he never wants to stop. Fountains of blood fly up from the body. Flesh shredded. Matt makes it as far as the stores building before the killer looks up.

Paul's on his hands and knees, crawling through the grass to where Ronan's shotgun landed. He grabs it, then scrambles over to his dead boss's body and fishes in his pockets for as many shells as he can find. Then, still staying low, he gets ready to head for the beach.

Too late.

The Hater Ronan shot and wounded is here now.

This one is far older than the one who killed Rajesh and is badly hurt but no less terrifying. He whistles to his mate and they converge on the buildings. Paul ducks down and lies flat.

Matt's pressed up against the side wall of the stores building now, watching the Haters' every move but not knowing what to do or where to go. The taller of the pair has a clear line of vision all the way along the path to the beach and enough power and speed to stop anyone from getting away. His wounded cohunter is sniffing around the main building, leaning against the outside wall to keep himself upright and take the pressure off his injury. Even with a hole in his side he still looks capable of killing with ease.

Between the two of them, they've got Matt and Paul penned in and trapped.

Natalie's nerves are threatening to get the better of her. This beautiful, rugged island she regularly calls home now feels alien and inhospitable. It's like she doesn't belong here anymore. Is that because the Haters have taken control? The meek shall inherit the earth, wasn't that what they used to say? Well, today the opposite has proved to be true. That old cliché turned out to be bullshit.

She glances back. Niall didn't last long. The Haters who killed him split up and now three of them are coming after her. She's like a fox being hunted by a pack of dogs for sport. And that's exactly what it feels like, she thinks. Sport. She can tell from the Haters' relentless ferocity that the chase and the kill is what those evil fuckers crave. It's what keeps them alive.

Can't keep running forever. Going to run out of land.

She has to change direction.

Can't go back. Have to go around.

She breaks right, heading for the spot where Vanessa met her untimely death last Monday—the cliffs overlooking the wreck of the *Heavenly Vision*. The drop appears out of nowhere—it would be so easy to keep running and go over—but she knows this place too well and sees the safety line and anticipates the fall. She changes direction again and starts running down the precariously narrow path that twists and winds down to the rocks and waves below. Tide's in. More water than land down there right now. But she knows this is her only option. She either keeps moving and gets to the boat with Paul and Matt and Rajesh, or she dies.

The path ahead is uneven. Greasy. Potholes and pockmarks. If she slows down, they'll get her and she's fucked. If she puts one foot in the wrong place and falls, then the means will be different but the result will be the same: game over. She knows she has no choice but to keep running downhill at full pelt.

Matt can't see Paul, but he can see both of the Haters. The older of the two is just a couple of meters away, standing over the body of one of his dead brethren. Matt quickly slips into the stores building and climbs the racking, realizing too late that he's completely weaponless, not that it makes a whole lot of difference. From what he's seen, it's the ferocity and tenacity of these creatures that gives them such clear superiority. Right now he thinks if he had an AK-47 and free aim, he'd still come off second best.

He's wedged himself into the narrow gap between the top of the racking and the slope of the pitched roof. He holds his breath and lies completely still on his belly, thinking that even his heartbeat might give him away. The metal shelving is barely holding his weight. It creaks and groans if he moves even a muscle. Right now the relative darkness in here is Matt's only defense.

The Hater enters the building.

He's right below Matt now, almost close enough to touch. He sniffs and snorts the air like an animal trying to catch the scent of its prey. "There's one of them in here, I'm sure there is," he shouts to his mate.

"Then find him and kill the fucker," Matt hears the wounded Hater yell back from outside. He sounds close. From his high vantage point, Matt sees him limp past the open door of the stores and continue around to the area where Matt, Paul, and Natalie dumped the rest of the corpses last night.

The Hater outside is no tracker, and he's struggling to focus through the pain, but he's certain another of the Unchanged is near. He sees footprints in the mud and patches of flattened grass. All he wants is to kill. It's an insatiable bloodlust. Almost vampiric. Right now he can't think about anything else.

The Hater has seen enough death and decay since *the change* to treat these unclean, unchanged bodies with dismissive disdain. It's of no interest to him who or what these people used to be: all that matters is making sure they're dead. A young lad has holes in his face like his cheeks have been skewered, and several other bodies that are ice white and swollen, still bloated by water even though it's clearly been several days since they died. He sees a woman—a Hater woman, no less—with an empty skull and busted bones. He grabs her hand and pulls her out of the way and uncovers the face of another man near the bottom of the pile. This corpse looks fresher than the rest. Newly killed? Then why was it buried so deep among the dead?

Wait. Still alive.

When the Hater sees Paul's terrified eyes flicker, he drags more empty bodies out of the way. His sole focus is getting at the pathetic Unchanged man cowering at the bottom of this gruesome mound, soaked with other people's gore. Panic is in the Unchanged's eyes because this time there truly is no way out. A couple of seconds from now he'll be dead and he knows it. The Hater is completely focused on the kill. It's the only thing that matters.

He picks up the final body and discards it casually, stripping Paul's cover away and leaving Paul supine and exposed.

And also revealing the shotgun.

Before the Hater realizes he's been tricked, Paul pulls the trigger and shoots him in the face from less than a meter away.

The Hater in the stores reacts to the shotgun noise. And so does Matt. He flinches involuntarily, and his sudden movement gives the game away. The fighter looks up and sees him looking down and immediately begins to haul himself up the racking to get at him. The metal shelves are already buckling under the weight of this huge bastard's boots, and when Matt tries to scramble farther out of the way, the whole unsteady structure starts to sway. The Hater grabs Matt's ankle and he tries to kick free, but he can feel himself being dragged down and knows he's about to die.

Only one thing for it.

Matt grips the top of the metal racking tight, then kicks his free foot against the roof of the building. The whole lot comes crashing down on top of the Hater, and Matt comes down hard on top of the racking. He lands with his spine bent back across a supporting strut, the force of impact knocking the wind from his lungs. For a couple of seconds all he can do is lie there staring up at the ceiling, struggling to breathe.

Beneath him, the injured Hater starts to stir. Groggy, he tries to move but is pinned down by the weight of the storage shelving and by Matt on top.

Matt feels a hand grab the scruff of his collar and pick him up. He tries to fight and protest, but he's being dragged backward through the chaos of the storeroom. Back out in the bright sunlight again, he braces himself for attack.

No attack. It's Paul.

"Move! *Now!*"

Together the two men run down to the beach, sprinting as fast as their tired, terrified legs will carry them. Up the rise and down toward the jetty. Matt slows down but Paul keeps running. "Paul, wait," Matt shouts to him. "Look."

The boat Rajesh arrived here in is a wreck. The Haters have gone to town on it to stop the Unchanged from using it to get away. The hull has been smashed. The vessel is full of water. Their precious supplies have been washed away.

Paul runs back toward Matt. "Rod's boat," he says breathlessly.

"What about the Haters' boat?"

"No time."

"But we need the key for Rod's boat."

"I've got it."

"What?"

"I took it from his corpse earlier."

"And were you going to tell me that or . . . ?"

"Didn't have chance. Things got a bit chaotic."

Explanations and reasons can wait. Right now getting off this rock is all that matters. Between them, the two men frantically manhandle the dinghy out of the lookout and carry it down to the water. Paul checks the detritus of Rod's makeshift camp and finds another box of shotgun shells, which he pockets. Matt checks his own jacket and realizes just how underprepared he is. He has the compass Natalie gave him and his useless mobile phone, nothing else. No food, no water. Nothing.

"We need to find Natalie," he says, scanning the horizon nervously.

"We don't have time."

"Bullshit. We're not leaving without her."

Then they hear her shouting at them.

She's running toward them from the far side of the beach, approaching from the headland to the east. But wait. She's not running now. She's limping. Hobbling. Struggling to keep moving. Matt races over to help. He puts his arm around her and supports her weight, then dumps her on the shingle near Rod's boat.

"What happened?"

"Tripped on the rocks. Hurt my ankle. Think it might be broken."

It looks badly swollen. He wonders how she managed to keep moving on it. Has to be adrenaline, he decides, because that's the only reason he thinks he's still functioning.

"Where are they?" he asks, looking around for the remaining Haters.

"Still following me," she tells him. "One fell. Two of them left."

"Matt, get a fucking move on," Paul shouts, sounding desperate. He's dragged the boat down closer to the edge of the surf. "Get this thing sorted and get us out of here."

Matt picks up the rope attached to the boat and starts to drag it out to sea, but stops suddenly. It's ice-cold, and the temperature saps the last dregs of energy he has. He's numb. Exhausted. He's staring out across the endless ocean, trying not to be intimidated by its size and ferocity.

Is there any point?

He's wondering whether they'll make it back, and what will be waiting for them if they get home.

He's wondering how three people are going to fit in a boat barely big enough for two.

He's thinking about Jen, wondering if she's safe, wondering if she's given up on him or whether she believes he's still coming back. Will she be waiting? Will she be one of *us* or one of *them*? Will the two of them be on the opposing sides of this improbable, impossible battle?

And he's thinking about all the people he'll be leaving behind here. All the people who died and their families and friends and how they'll never know what happened to their loved ones on Skek, and he's thinking that whatever happens from here on in, the life he left behind when he boarded the ferry to come here just over a week ago is gone forever now.

This morning he feels infinitesimally small, trapped between the Haters on one side and the vast ocean on the other. Completely powerless.

"What's your fucking problem?" Paul yells at him.

The shape of the bay amplifies the strength of the tide. A strong wave hits Matt, distracted by his thoughts, and knocks him back. He drops the rope and almost loses his footing. He scrambles around in the surf, desperate to keep hold of the boat, cursing himself for not thinking to fetch life jackets from the stores and wondering if he has time to go back.

"They're coming," Natalie shouts.

She gestures back along the coast in the direction from which she just came. Matt can clearly see two figures scrambling over the rocks to get to them.

Gunshots take them both by surprise. Matt looks across and sees that Paul's taking potshots at the hull of the lifeboat used by the Haters, peppering it full of holes. "So the fuckers can't follow us."

"Never mind that. Help me with Natalie."

Matt tries to get her to stand, but her injury is far worse than it originally looked. She almost certainly did more damage running along the beach to reach the boat. Now the downward slope and the shingle make it difficult for her to even stay upright. She's struggling to put any weight at all on her busted leg.

She stumbles, and both of them go down.

"I'm okay."

"You're not," Matt immediately replies. "But you will be. We need to do something. Maybe get a splint or something."

"You don't have time."

"*We* do."

"It's no good." She's white-faced with shock and sweating profusely now. "Leave me here."

"Christ, Nat, that's such a cliché." Matt manages a half smile. "We're not going anywhere without you. Paul, help me."

"I'm serious." Clearly she is.

"So am I. We're not leaving you here."

Matt drags her back up onto her feet again, but another couple of hops is all she manages. She wrestles herself from his grip and falls back to the ground. Clammy. Nauseous. Exhausted. "There's no point."

"Yes, there is."

"No, Matt. Think about this logically. The three of us were never all going to fit in the boat."

"We'll find a way."

"Listen to what she's saying," Paul says.

"I'm not leaving her behind."

"You don't have any choice."

"I have *all* the choice." Matt is seething with anger now. "Without me navigating, you won't get home, and I'm not going anywhere without Nat. She goes or none of us go."

Matt tries to haul her up to her feet one last time, but she's exhausted and unable to support her own weight. The two of them end up back on the ground, locked in an unexpected embrace, faces almost touching.

"I really appreciate what you're trying to do," Natalie whispers, "but it's okay. Honest, it's all right. We tried. Go home and find Jen."

Matt gets up and staggers back, eyes filled with tears of frustration. He runs back into the waves to fetch the boat, figuring it'll be easier getting the boat to Natalie than getting Natalie to the boat. The Haters are closing in from the east. Another one appears at the top of the rise near the concrete lookout.

"Leave it, Matt," Paul shouts.

Matt ignores him. "Fuck you."

When Matt next looks up, he sees that Paul's reloaded the shotgun. The Haters are close enough that they can almost see the hatred in their faces.

Paul looks over at the Haters, then looks at Matt, then down at Natalie. He shoots her twice in the chest at point-blank range.

She drops back and hits the sand. Dead on impact.

"You bastard. You absolute bastard . . ."

Matt goes for Paul, but Paul's one step ahead. He aims the shotgun at Matt. "Don't be an idiot. Get the engine started and get us home."

"You killed her. . . . You think I'm going anywhere with you?"

Paul's face is emotionless. He gives a nonchalant shrug. "Then stay here with them. Natalie was dead anyway, and you know it. Now if you want to get back to your missus, you need to shut the fuck up and get moving."

The first of the remaining Haters comes racing down the beach and charges at them. Paul shoots and hits him in the shoulder, but the killer's hate is such that he keeps coming, oblivious of the pain.

Matt knows that no matter what he thinks about Paul, he was

right about one thing: if Matt wants to have any chance of seeing Jen again, getting in the boat and getting back to the mainland is the only way it's ever going to happen.

He drags the dinghy deep enough into the sea so it floats, then preps the outboard motor. The water's so cold now it hurts. Each wave is higher than the last. It's up to his waist, and it takes his breath away.

Paul splashes through the water, then climbs on board. Matt struggles to get in after him, and Paul helps pull him up with his free left hand, still holding the shotgun in his right. They shuffle around in the limited space so that Paul has his back to the prow and Matt's next to the motor. Paul fishes the key from his pocket and hands it over.

The Haters are in the water now. Still coming at them with predatory speed, barely slowed by the waves or by Paul as he shoots and reloads, shoots and reloads.

The motor starts at the second time of asking. Noise and dirty fumes. Matt sits down and takes the tiller. He opens up the throttle, and the distance between the Haters and their prey finally begins to increase.

29

"You know where you're going?" Paul shouts over the engine noise.

"What?"

"The way home? Do you know the way home?"

"It's not like a drive back from the shops." Matt checks the compass Natalie gave him. He struggles to focus on the needle with all the spray and the unpredictable rolling of the boat. "I think I can do it."

"You're gonna have to do better than that."

"We left the southernmost tip of the island. We follow the coast west for a while, then keep sailing due west away from Skek until we hit home. That's as precise as I can be."

"Is that going to be good enough?"

"It should be. We've got a thousand miles of coastline to aim for. We'll get back to the UK, I just can't tell you where we'll end up, that's all. The Scottish Highlands is out of the question though."

"Doesn't matter. Just get us back."

Matt watches Paul visibly relax the farther they get from Skek. "She was never gonna make it."

"Who are you trying to convince, you or me?"

"I had to make a decision. You get that, don't you? The rules have changed now. She was dead already."

"You've always been full of shit, Paul. No amount of spin will convince me otherwise."

"Sticks and stones, mate, sticks and stones."

Paul shuffles to get comfortable, but keeps the shotgun aimed directly at Matt at all times. Matt thinks, You wouldn't do it, but then remembers Paul already has. Matt knows that Paul needs him for now, but things will inevitably change if they make it home. Matt thinks he'll split from Paul the first chance he gets. Much as Matt hates to accept it, though, right now he feels like he needs the additional manpower.

Time is without measure this morning. Neither of the men has a watch, and their phones haven't been charged all week—reduced to useless blocks of metal, plastic, and glass. Paul tried to conserve some charge in his phone for the long-delayed journey home, but it's waterlogged and the screen is cracked and he knows it's ruined. Matt's has fared slightly better in it's overly protective rubber case, but all the protection in the world's no good when you're out of power. They might have been on the water for ten minutes, it might have been ten hours. Their disorientation is complete, and for a while Matt starts to wonder if they're the ones who've died. The longer they're out here, the more it begins to feel like they're stuck in a gloriously bizarre *Twilight Zone* episode; like the rest of the world has been erased so all that's left is him and Paul and judgment day. There's nothing but water for as far as they can see in every direction, and now the clouds are closing in, the bright sun of this morning long forgotten. The light is dull gray and the temperature low. Matt can barely feel his feet. Shock or hypothermia? He's not sure which it is, but he's feeling increasingly detached from reality. There's nothing to lock onto as a point of reference or scale out here. The plastic compass he grips tight in his water-wrinkled hand is the only thing he has any faith in anymore.

Paul is virtually lying down opposite him, shriveled and shrunken to protect himself from the cold. "We nearly there?" he asks for what must be the hundredth time, like a frustrated kid in the back of his parents' car. "You sure we're going the right way?"

"We're heading west."

"Yeah, but is that the right way? Wouldn't be surprised if you'd deliberately sent us the wrong way just to make a point."

"You think I'd choose this on purpose? Being stuck out here in the middle of nowhere with you?"

Up ahead, the clouds are interrupted by a smudge of black. Within minutes the stain has spread across much of the sky. It's too dark for storm clouds, Matt thinks, and it seems to be rising up, not across. Paul notices Matt's expression and cranes his neck to try to see what it is he's watching. "Land?" he asks hopefully.

"Don't think so."

Matt's forced to take evasive action when the prow of an enormous ship cuts through the water dead ahead. He opens the throttle as much as he dares and banks hard to port.

"Jesus, be careful," Paul says, holding on as the side of the boat dips and then bounces through the bow wave.

When they're far enough away to be safe, Matt corrects his course. They're now sailing alongside an immense cruise ship, and it's clear it'll take an age to reach the end of its considerable length. It dwarfs the *Heavenly Vision*, but appears to be equally lifeless. It's stuck in the water, going nowhere fast. The top decks are burned out. Oily smoke belches out through broken windows.

"Where the hell did that come from?"

"From Hull, I think," Matt says, giving Paul an intentionally literal answer.

"How come you didn't see it? Frigging hell, you could have got us both killed."

"I didn't see it because of the mist, and I didn't hear it because its engines aren't running. If you'd shut up long enough to listen, you'd have realized that."

"Watch your mouth," Paul snaps quickly, then he shuts up and takes in the silence. The massive liner is a ghost ship, that much is clear. The dinghy is insignificant in its wake, an ant trying to escape an elephant's foot. As they watch, a lone figure hangs out of a cabin window. It's a Hater, so desperate to kill that it has no concerns for its own safety. The monster drops down into the water from a ridiculous height and swims after them, but its rabid tenacity is no match for the relative speed of the boat's engine.

Paul watches the evil creature floundering in the ice-cold murk. He thinks it won't last long, and though it's not particularly a threat, its relentless ire is terrifying. It sacrificed itself to try to kill the two of them. He says nothing to Matt, but his nervousness is increasing the closer they get to home.

30

Land eventually appears on the horizon. The miserable weather makes the distance hard to estimate, so there's little time to assess and make plans before they've reached the shore. Matt cuts the outboard, letting the waves carry them the last few meters home. Other than for the lapping of the water, the world is deafeningly silent.

Drifting closer now, and they can see they've definitely made it back to the UK. That much is certain, but exactly where they are is as yet unknown. It's a run-down seaside town: all lifeless promenade lights and boarded-up buildings. From out here it looks as dead as the island they left behind.

"We must look so conspicuous," Matt says. "Look at the state of us. I've been wearing the same clothes since Monday. I look like I've aged twenty-five years in a week. I look like a damn ghost."

"You think anybody cares? You'll have plenty of chance to tidy yourself up before you get back home to her indoors. Now shut up and concentrate on finding us somewhere safe to land."

But Matt can't shut up. His stomach's churning with nerves and his chattering becomes incessant. "What if we're wrong?"

"What about?"

"Everything. All the trouble. The Haters . . . what if none of it happened like we were told. We made a lot of assumptions and filled in lots of blanks while we were away."

"So?"

"All that killing . . . everything we did on Skek."

"You think we're going to be in trouble?"

"Maybe."

"Bullshit."

"How can you be so casual about it after what you did to Natalie? We were on the same side, for crying out loud."

That clearly stings. "Don't push me, mate." Paul tightens his grip on the shotgun again. "All I needed you for was to get me home. Your usefulness is about to run out, so don't give me an excuse to do the same to you."

"You didn't seem to need much of an excuse from where I was standing."

"We all had a hand in what happened back there before the Haters turned up. I did what I had to do. It was Natalie or one of us. Deal with it."

But Matt's not sure he can.

The waves beneath the boat feel increasingly angry as they near the shore. The closer they get, the harder Matt's finding it to keep the dinghy under control. He's struggling to stay focused, not least because the scene that greets them is leaving him in no doubt that the mainland they've returned to this morning is a very different place to that which they left just over a week ago. It reminds him of the opening scene from *Saving Private Ryan*. He's guessing that Paul's thinking something similar because he's quiet too, stunned into submission. He's on his knees looking out over the front of the boat, staring at a scene of almost surreal devastation.

The first easily discernible thing Matt notices is a family car sticking out of the sand, nose down. It's completely wrecked, and completely out of place. It's like the driver had lost control and driven up and over the sea defenses at speed, then plummeted down hard. The doors are hanging open like broken wings, and clearly it's been like this for several days because seaweed and sand drifts are everywhere. It looks as if it were being sucked down into the beach at marginal speed, steadily sinking inch by inch.

But that's just the beginning.

Much of the rest of the beach for as far as they can see in either direction is littered with debris. The boat washes up on a narrow slice of shingle. Paul's out quickly, but Matt waits a second longer, wondering if he should stow the dinghy somewhere or maybe just turn around and head back out to sea. No point, he decides. We're not going anywhere.

Paul's already reached the upturned car, trying to work out how and why it was left like this. A dead woman is in the driver's seat, her body white and swollen, hair still wet. She's anchored in position by her safety belt, hanging upside down. Matt taps Paul's shoulder, startling him, and gestures farther along the long stretch of grubby yellow-gray sand to another body. What's left of one. Its sex is impossible to distinguish because everything identifiable has been burned away. It's completely black, charred to the bone. Wisps of smoke still curl up from brittle limbs. Its arms are clutched tight across its empty chest, and its legs both finish at the knee. Nearby a fresh crater is in the sand. Matt crouches down to inspect it and finds twisted shards of metal mixed with the pebbles and seashells. Way over to his right are several sets of tire tracks—deep grooves and vicious scars. Two realities appear to have collided in this place: family bucket-and-spade holidays meets all-out war. "What the hell's happened to the world?" he asks. His question goes unanswered. Other than the waves, the gusting wind, and the constant cawing of scavenging seagulls, it's ominously quiet. "Have you noticed? It sounds as empty as the island."

Paul checks the horizon behind them, then looks inland, scanning left to right and back again. He's looking for signs of life but sees nothing. A gull is sitting on the chest of another corpse, pecking at its flesh. "It's got to give you some confidence though, hasn't it?"

"What has?"

"All this? Everything we went through on Skek? We survived, mate. The world went to hell, and we survived. Means we're made of tougher stuff than most."

"Or that we were lucky."

"Bullshit. No luck involved. Bring on the Haters."

"You've got to be kidding me."

But he clearly isn't.

Paul's arrogance is astonishing. Matt thinks he'd leave him here on the beach, but being in the company of this deluded prick is marginally preferable to being on his own. He tries to walk on, but Paul stops him.

"You've got to start being more positive about this. It's survival of the fittest, and it looks like we're among the fittest left, you and me. The whys and wherefores aren't important."

"You reckon?"

"Absolutely. Look back at Skek . . . all those people, and we're the only ones who made it home alive. A boat full of Haters and we got away. We're fighters, mate, you and me. We're *survivors*. We've earned our stripes and there's nobody going to take that away from us now. Anyone gets in our way and we'll fucking kill them."

"But you saw them . . . you saw how vicious those bastards are, how driven?"

"Yeah, but they still go down when you fire a frigging shotgun at them."

Paul marches on, unafraid. But when he reaches the high gray-stone seawall, he stops.

"What's the matter?" Matt asks, immediately concerned.

"Listen. Can you hear it?"

Matt can't hear anything. "Hear what?"

He strains, not sure what he's supposed to be listening for, but then it starts to become clear. A faint noise in the distance that's difficult to pick out. Voices. Machinery. Artillery? It sounds like a far-off battle. "Two sides fighting. One of them must be friendly. More people like us."

Paul pushes him forward.

A quick scramble up a steep set of steps set into the stone wall and they're off the beach and on land proper. After climbing up and over a grassy embankment, they cross an open patch of sandy scrubland. They pause at the highest point and take their first proper look at civilization in over a week.

Matt's not sure what he was expecting to see, but it wasn't this.

Over to their left, something resembling normality. It's a small town. The streets appear ghostly quiet, but it's otherwise unremarkable. Over to their right, a typically British holiday park has been almost completely razed to the ground. Instead of line after line of virtually identical caravans and holiday homes, there are now equally spaced rectangular black burn marks and buckled metal skeletons. A fire has swept through the park unchecked, destroying plot after plot. "Why didn't anyone put it out?" Matt asks. Parts of the sprawling site are still on fire. Was that a fairground? A helter-skelter? A high board next to a swimming pool? Even now a pall of black smoke hangs heavy in the sky overhead like a bad memory that refuses to fade.

They keep moving. Down another set of steps, and now they're walking along a raised footpath, separated by metal railings and wire mesh from an ordinary-looking suburban street. Ordinary, that is, save for the ominous hole in the row of houses directly opposite. A detached house has half-collapsed, leaving an obvious gap like a missing front tooth. Where the garage and bedroom above used to be is an enormous pile of masonry. Matt's distracted by what's left of the upstairs bathroom. A toilet hangs precariously, suspended in midair like a trophy mounted on a hunter's wall.

"Keep going," Paul says, and he climbs over the railings and jumps down to street level. He hits the ground with a heavy thud, then gestures for Matt to follow.

Matt takes his time lowering himself down. "We should keep out of sight. Just until we know what's what."

Paul has no such concerns. He's strolling down the middle of the street, taking in the sights as if it were just another Saturday afternoon in any old seaside town, still buoyed with questionable confidence. "What do you reckon the crosses are for?" His voice echoes off the empty walls.

"What crosses?"

Paul points the end of the shotgun at an uneven cross that has been daubed in white emulsion on the front door of an apartment block. He touches it and checks his fingertips to see if it's dry.

"Looks like the plague," Matt says.

"The plague?"

"Remember your history lessons? Didn't they used to mark houses like this where there was infection? The Black Death, wasn't it?"

"So d'you think they've found infection in every one of the houses in this street?"

Matt takes a step back and looks. Paul's right. Just about every house has been marked with a cross.

"Don't know."

"Let's have a look then, shall we?"

Before Matt can stop him, Paul's already trying the door of another house nearby. It's ajar, and he cautiously pushes it farther open, then sticks his head through the gap. "Hello. Anyone home?"

Nothing.

"Leave it, Paul. It's not worth it. Let's keep going."

"There's no one in here. You can feel it. It's as cold inside as it is out here."

He's right, but it doesn't sway Matt. "We should keep moving." His unease is rapidly mounting.

"Don't be such a fucking wimp. There's no one here."

He's almost right.

They find a body in the lounge. The middle-aged man is wearing only a vest, boxer shorts, and a brutal-looking gunshot wound to the face. His jaw has been blown away, leaving his mouth an impossibly wide-gaping maw. What's left of his throat is a vicious-looking, dried-up hole.

They swiftly check the rest of the house, looking for clues but finding nothing. They change into dry, reasonably well-fitting clothes they take from upstairs, then attack the kitchen. The cupboards are fairly well stocked and they waste no time. "Didn't realize how hungry I was." Matt stuffs his face with whatever he can lay his hands on. "I'm starving."

There's water too, but the gas supply has been cut. Paul's visibly disappointed. He stands there with the kettle he's just filled, trying to light the hob. "Bloody hell," he complains, like everything that happened has been forgotten and this is the most important thing in the world. "I haven't had a decent cuppa since Tuesday."

A short time later they're interrupted by something happening outside.

Paul rushes to an upstairs window at the back of the house and leans out, craning his neck. From here he can see between the homes on the street that backs onto this one. Unlike the road he and Matt walked down to get here, though, this one is swarming with activity.

"Haters?" Matt asks, anxiously watching over Paul's shoulder.

"Don't think so."

"How can you tell?"

"Because they're running, not fighting."

He's right. Matt goes to another window to try to get a better view. A mass of people are being herded down the street. They move quickly and quietly, arms loaded up with bags and boxes—clothes, food, and possessions. An evacuation? A mass exodus? Matt can't tell, but from the expressions on the few faces he can make out from this distance, these people look completely fucking terrified.

And now he can see why.

There are far fewer of them—maybe only half as many, perhaps even less—but Haters are hunting this crowd of people down. They move with the familiar ferocity and intent, and seeing them immediately takes Matt back to Skek and fills him with the same helpless terror he felt when the pack of Haters landed on the island. The steely determination scares him most, that he knows they won't give up, no matter what. He knows that if he were the only Unchanged man left alive and a hundred of them were on his trail, they'd kill one another to be the one to kill him.

The fastest Haters quickly reach the slowest Unchanged, and both Matt and Paul are glad that the worst of what's happening down at street level is now obscured from view.

The noise outside increases as the killing continues, and now they can hear gunfire too. It's not the dull staccato crack of a shotgun like the one Paul still clings onto; this is the noise of far more deadly weapons. Machine guns and pistols.

From up here, they can't tell who's firing and who's being shot at.

There are noises at the front of the house they're hiding in. Paul goes to see what's happening, and Matt follows, concerned Paul will do something stupid and advertise they're here. He finds that Paul's only made it as far as the top of the stairs. He can see down to the front door from here. Light and dark outside. Flickering shadows. The street out front is now full of movement too. Matt tiptoes through the empty upstairs rooms and presses himself against the wall next to a bedroom window. He can only see a fraction of what's happening outside, but it's more than enough to be able to work out what's going on. He watches as a number of crazed Haters corner a young woman and set upon her like a pack of fighting dogs. They tear her limb from limb. He's thankful he can't properly make out what they're doing, but the copious amount of blood now running down the gutter leaves little to the imagination.

He and Paul stand together in absolute silence as the carnage continues below.

"We can't stay here," Paul announces.

"Well, we can't leave. Not yet."

"We have to."

"And go where? Are you fucking crazy? Take one step outside and we'll end up dead."

"You think we'll have any better chance waiting here? Come on, get a grip."

The roar of a heavy engine arrives quickly and stops abruptly. Shouted orders. A loud thump, a second of silence, then the belly-rumbling thud of a devastating explosion nearby, close enough to shake the bones of this house and make cascades of plaster dust rain down from the bedroom ceiling.

Outside, the Haters are sent running for cover.

A tank is in the street in front of the house. It trundles slowly forward, then stops again and fires a shell at another large group of Haters. The sick bastards are so preoccupied attacking more Unchanged that they don't realize the strike is coming until the shell hits them. A corner of a house is obliterated, and though the precariously balanced remains of the building hold steady at first, another strike brings the whole damn lot crashing down. Those people not killed by the first hit are wiped out by the falling debris from the second. The mangled bodies of Haters and Unchanged alike are everywhere, shredded. Indistinguishable from one another in death.

The front door bursts open downstairs and a man rushes inside, looking for cover. Paul and Matt edge out onto the landing and look down. Whoever he is, he looks fucking terrified. He's covered in dust and breathing hard. For the moment all he's interested in is escaping what's happening outside, and he doesn't see them watching. Soldiers in the street are advancing in a wave, firing indiscriminately at anyone who shows any sign of being about to attack.

Paul looks at Matt, and Matt looks at Paul. Neither of them dare speak, but their panicked expressions both ask the same unanswerable question: *Unchanged or Hater? Us or them?*

The man downstairs can hear them now.

Paul runs for cover and shuts himself inside a wardrobe with louver doors like a kid playing hide-and-seek for impossibly high stakes. He pushes himself back against the wall inside the closet and drags clothing along the rail, wrapping long coats and dresses around himself so he can't be seen. Only his eyes remain uncovered. Through the gap he can see the entire length of the landing.

Matt's gone in the opposite direction. He's in the bathroom at the other end of the house, wedged into a narrow gap between the toilet and the wall, hiding behind the half-closed door and watching through the crack. He can see the intruder from here. The way his behavior has changed now he knows he's not alone in the house is terrifying. There's no question which side he's on because all thoughts of his own safety have been forgotten now that he senses the prospect of an Unchanged kill.

He's a Hater.

He creeps upstairs, the noise of his movements camouflaged by the continuing chaos of the fighting outside, then pauses at the top of the landing. Matt's so scared he doesn't even allow himself to blink. He knows that one mistake is all it'll take. He doesn't swallow. Barely even breathes.

The Hater pushes the bathroom door and looks inside. Empty bath. Empty shower. Wash basin opposite. It's only seconds, but it feels as if he were standing there forever. Matt's struggling to stay still, his already narrow hiding space reduced still farther as the door is pushed closer to the wall. He has all his weight on one foot. Body twisted and contorted.

And then he flinches.

The Hater hears him and reaches for the door, but Paul reacts first.

He bursts out of the wardrobe, sprints the length of the short landing, then shoves the Hater in the small of his back and sends him flying forward. He hits his head on the sink with a nauseating crack and staggers back. While he's off-balance, Paul pushes him into the bath.

"Move!" Paul grabs Matt's shoulder and drags him downstairs.

"Wait. . . . Don't . . ."

But Paul's not listening. He bursts out of the front door at full pelt with Matt in tow and runs straight into a group of black-suited, face-masked, machine-gun-wielding soldiers coming the other way. Both he and Matt immediately raise their hands in submission, but it's a futile gesture.

"Fucking sort them out," one of the soldiers yells, and two of them grab one man each and drag them away. They're shoved up against the nearest wall, machine guns in their faces. Matt tries to protest, to explain, to plead, but no one's listening. He takes the butt of a weapon to the gut for his troubles.

The Hater comes staggering out of the house, looking for his prey. Four more soldiers turn on him and unload their guns, hitting him with enough bullets to bring down twenty men.

"They're clear, Sarge. They have to be," the soldier pushing Matt's face against the brickwork shouts to his commanding officer, voice muffled by his mask.

"Check 'em," the sergeant shouts back.

"But, Sarge, if they haven't gone for us, then—"

"Fucking check them! Now!"

"Sir."

Matt is turned around and pushed against the wall again, arms pinned behind him. His neck and shoulders are held as another faceless trooper pricks his skin with some kind of needle-sharp sensor, then checks a small, tabletlike machine. Matt can only move his eyes, but he's aware of enough rough movement to his immediate right to know that the exact same thing is happening to Paul. They're both held for what feels like forever but in reality is just a few seconds.

"Clear," the soldier checking Paul shouts.

Another wait. Is something wrong?

"And this one," the soldier in front of Matt confirms. The grip on his neck is relaxed, but several guns still remain trained on him.

The sergeant steps forward—face hidden, indeterminable intent—and barks out more orders. "Get 'em out of here. Get 'em on one of the buses if they ain't already gone."

The soldiers march Matt and Paul down a short alleyway and across a desolate-looking street, then push them toward a retail park. An empty horseshoe of familiar high-street stores around a large car park, which is is half-full of people left waiting.

People like Paul and Matt.

The Unchanged.

Temporary two-meter-tall metal barriers have been wrapped

around the car park. Is it to keep the crowds in or keep the Haters out? Matt can't tell which. He and Paul are herded into the midst of the masses. Matt realizes Paul's somehow still clinging to his precious shotgun. Strange how no one protests, Matt thinks. Strange that no one cares.

"What the fuck's going on?" Paul demands, though he knows Matt doesn't have any answers.

More soldiers are here, corralling the public. A young woman—who looks as terrified as Matt feels—offers an explanation. "They're shipping us out to Lincoln. It's the closest camp."

"Camp? What the hell?"

She doesn't reply, the movement of the crowd carrying her away before she has chance.

The sounds of more gunfire and mortar rounds come from the area Paul and Matt have just escaped. Then a more familiar noise as a convoy of three beaten-up coaches races down the road and pulls up near the entrance to the car park. Metal grilles are welded over windows.

More through luck than judgment, Paul and Matt are near to where the coaches stop. The crowd surges, and they're carried toward the first of the transports. Paul catches Matt's eye as they're separated by the surge, Matt involuntarily moving ahead. "Just get on the bus."

"Stay close, mate," Paul shouts back, desperately trying to keep up.

Between twenty and thirty soldiers form an outward facing funnel at the door of each bus, giving the public some protection as they pile forward. Matt manages to slip through and get on board. But Paul is pushed farther back and struggles to get anywhere close.

Haters.

Paul glances back over his shoulder and sees a massive pack of them approaching. They sprint toward the retail park en masse, breaking through the military's first line of defense with arrogant ease. The fastest few start climbing up and over the barriers and are brought down by machine-gun fire. It's a testament to how volatile and dangerous this nightmare situation is that the soldiers fire without any consideration for the safety of the public they've been sent here to protect, and as many civilians as Haters are mown down. It seems the amount of collateral damage is unimportant today. No cost is too great. All that matters is destroying the attacking enemy.

Paul's struggling to move in any direction now. The panicking crowd is tightly packed around him, so close he can barely breathe, and he's finding it hard to keep his feet on the ground. The thought of being trampled to death is marginally less terrifying than the idea of being torn apart by Haters. His view is obscured—all he can see are people as desperate as he is clamoring for the same safety he himself craves.

He doesn't see the Hater who drags down one of the soldiers defending the retail park. She's still firing as he attacks her, finger stuck on the trigger, bullets spraying wildly in all directions.

The soldier inadvertently wipes out a swath of troops and civilians before her life is brutally ended. Almost everyone to Paul's immediate left is killed, and for a second he just stands there numb, alone and exposed, soaked with blood spray. The tank they saw earlier is here now, and it fires a shell at the biggest group of Haters. It explodes with a deafening noise, which temporarily silences everything else.

Paul is surrounded by corpses, standing like a lone tree in an otherwise fallen forest. His eyes sting with smoke and grit and his ears are ringing with muted sounds and a high-pitch whistling. He's still motionless. Stunned.

". . . fucking idiot, move!"

Someone's shouting at him, but he can barely make out the person through the chaos.

"Paul, *move!*"

It's Matt. He reaches out for him and pulls him up onto the bus just as it starts to pull away. Matt drags him deeper into the impossibly overcrowded vehicle, and when the driver banks around a corner at speed, the two of them are thrown over to one side. They fall down two steps midway down the length of the vehicle, holding on to each other for support. A storage hatch is down here. Matt pulls the door open and they cram themselves inside and block it behind them. Pushed up tight against each other. Unable to move.

The rest of the bus is filled with deafening noise.

Wave after wave of Haters attack.

31

The speed of the bus increases and the ferocity of the attacks eventually subsides. Now the only noise Matt and Paul can hear is the god-awful din from their fellow passengers: the terrified, the injured, the dying. It's virtually pitch-black down here. Sensory deprivation. Not being able to see makes what's happening outside all the more terrifying.

"I need to move," Paul says.

"What?"

"Got a cramp in my leg. Need to fucking move."

"Tough. There's no room." Matt feels Paul push against him. The barrel of the shotgun presses against Matt's gut. "Mind that damn gun!"

"Open the door, Matt."

"I can't."

"Open the bloody door!"

Paul tries himself, but it won't budge. The stairwell outside is packed with people. That's the only explanation.

"I've got to get out of here," he whines. "Please, mate, get me out of here. I can't stand it. I can't—"

Paul's voice is silenced when the coach veers hard over to the right. It mounts the curb, then collides with something, then topples over and skids to an abrupt halt on its side. Paul smacks his head against the side of the vehicle and is knocked out cold. Pinned beneath his dead weight, all Matt can do is listen and wait.

The coach is rocked as another wave of Hater attacks begins.

Countless footsteps. Hammering on metal walls. Glass being smashed. Doors being wrenched open.

Soon all Matt can hear are the helpless screams as another cold-blooded massacre unfolds.

32

When Paul wakes up, Matt has his hand over his mouth. "Shh . . . not a sound."

Disorientated and claustrophobic, he still tries to fight. Matt increases the pressure.

"Shut up, calm down. They're still out there."

It's several hours before it's quiet for long enough for them to risk moving.

The door is wedged shut by three dead people. Lying supine, it takes both Matt and Paul pushing together to shift them. A middle-aged woman is taking up most of the space. Once he gets a hand through, Matt is able to push her onto her side, then over onto another body, so there's room enough to get the door open. He crawls over Paul to get out first, but stops moving again and listens when he's barely halfway.

Not a sound.

Dead.

The two men scramble out from their hiding place, climbing up and over bodies. The coach is lying on its side, its interior rotated through ninety degrees. Seats jut out from the wall at right angles to the ground. Matt uses them to haul himself up, then gazes around to try to get his bearings.

"Fuck."

They've both seen a hell of a lot of terrible things in the last week, but nothing like this. The interior of the coach is like the bloodbath on the *Heavenly Vision* multiplied by a factor of several thousand. At least on the wreck of the ferry the individual bodies were discernible. Here it's impossible to tell where one ends and the next begins. This is butchery on an unprecedented scale. This is fucking terrifying.

"We need to find some cover," Matt says. "Can't risk being out in the open."

He walks along the side of the coach in the space between the seats and the roof, crunching glass beneath his boots. Fortunately the exit is open. He stands on the blood-soaked driver's chair, then reaches up and grabs a handrail. He hauls himself up out of the chaos, then lies flat on the upturned side of the beached vehicle. He ducks his head back inside and looks for Paul. He's several steps behind. Eyes wide with fear. Clinging to the shotgun like his life depends on it.

"Quick," Matt hisses. "Move."

The coach was ambushed on a stretch of narrow country lane, miles from anywhere. Low hedges are on either side of the tarmac, and open countryside beyond in all directions. They couldn't be more exposed here.

Matt helps Paul up and out.

"We're fucked," Paul says. "We're completely fucked."

"We're still breathing, aren't we?"

"Yeah, but for how much longer?"

Matt climbs down onto the road, ready to run.

"Where you going?" Paul shouts after him, sounding desperate.

"Somewhere. *Anywhere.*"

"It's not safe. We should stay here."

"And how's that gonna help?"

"We might run into more of them out there."

"We probably will. We're okay at the moment though."

Matt looks around. Everything's clear. Too clear for his liking. He stares out across the fields and imagines swarms of Haters converging on them from all directions.

Paul's just behind him now, half-crouching in the road like he doesn't want to be seen. "Come on, mate, get back inside. Please."

"Why? You expect me to sit in there and just wait for them to find us?"

"They're gonna find us anyway."

"Maybe. So we can either sit and wait for them to kill us, or we can die trying to get away. We could look for a car. Try and get to Lincoln if that's where the bus was heading."

"I can't see any cars. Can you?"

"Not here, no. Look farther than the end of your nose, for crying out loud. There's a whole bloody world out there."

"Yeah, a whole bloody world full of *them.*"

"Fine. You stay here." With that, Matt's gone. He starts jogging down the road, conserving his energy so he doesn't run out of steam, but moving fast enough not to get caught napping.

He glances back. Paul's following. *No surprise.*

Going around a meandering, S-shaped bend in the road, Matt stops sharp and doubles back when he sees a lone figure up ahead. A disheveled-looking man is leaning up against a tree as if he's taking a pee. When, after a few seconds, the man hasn't moved,

Matt does. He takes a few more tentative steps forward, then relaxes when he realizes the man's dead. He's been impaled against the trunk. His torso has been pierced with a sports javelin, snatched from a local school playing field perhaps, and used as a basic, but incredibly effective, weapon. It's been bent and buckled and has snapped just where it sticks out of his back, presumably so the javelin's owner could find some other victim and make maximum use of the weapon: two spikes, two kills.

"Fucking hell," Paul says, breathless, almost sounding like he admires the Hater's handiwork.

Now that they've stopped again, once he's checked there's no one else (still living) around, Matt snatches a couple of seconds to try to get his bearings. It doesn't matter where they are, he decides, because neither of them know the area and they have no idea where they're going next. But through the brittle-branched trees up ahead, Matt spies red-gray roof tiles. "What do you reckon?" he asks, though in all honesty he's little interest in his reluctant companion's opinion anymore. He starts running again before Paul has a chance to answer.

The house they choose to hide in is small and unassuming. It's the second home along on a new development that'll now never be finished or fully occupied. Some look like they were lived in, but many of the homes here are just shells. Some are only half-built. The roads and pavements haven't yet been laid. Pretty much everything is covered in a fine layer of gray dust.

This one was a show home. It's immaculately decorated inside, finished to an artificially high standard. Most important, it's unlived-in. No one's been here for a long time, it seems. Matt hopes no one else will come here for a while longer yet.

He leaves Paul in the house and checks out some of the other homes in the development and the rest of the construction site because he's quickly realized that the downside of the model hideout they've chosen is that the cupboards are completely bare. He climbs over fences and skulks across unturfed back gardens to avoid being out on the road and being seen. For a heart-stopping second he thinks his number's up when he sees a woman leaning against a patio door watching him, but when he realizes just how much her revealing negligee is actually revealing, he knows he's safe. She's drenched with blood from the waist down. She's died propped upright, trying to get out. Christ, was she in the middle of sex when her other half killed her? The level of callous violence on display here is startling. Such speed and intense brutality. The Haters kill first, then think about it later.

He checks the dead woman's house, figuring the presence of a corpse is a reasonable indication the place is safe. A little food is in the kitchen. It's not much, but it'll do for tonight and maybe the morning. He finds a few other bits and pieces from the garage that might prove useful, stuffs them into a couple of bags he finds, and takes it all back. It makes him feel surprisingly vulnerable and ineffective, transporting the bulk of his impromptu end-of-the-world survival kit in a supermarket carrier bag. The irony that it has BAG FOR LIFE printed on the side is not lost on him.

Still, if he's struggling to adjust, his companion is acting like a complete fucking amateur. Matt stops outside the house they're hiding in and watches him. He's sitting in the window of the kitchen–dining room in plain view. Anyone could have seen him.

Paul sees him and lets him back inside. They drink and eat as best they can, but neither of them has any appetite. The nerves are unbearable. "This was just the kind of place Jen wanted us to buy," Matt says, thinking out loud. Paul just grunts. When the food's finished, Matt goes through the rest of the slim pickings he found. He has a Stanley knife and a few chisels they can use as weapons.

"Fat lot of good they'll do you against those bastards," Paul says. "I reckon even if we both had Uzis and they were bare-handed, the odds would still be against us."

As Matt's emptying his pockets, he realizes he's still carrying his mobile phone. "Old habits die hard."

"What?"

"My phone. Almost forgot I had it."

Paul grunts again and moves closer to the window again, peeking out at the world from behind a long curtain.

Instinctively, Matt tries to turn the phone on. Despite still being wrapped in the overprotective cover Jen bought for him, the screen is chipped. The damage annoys him more than it should. Without thinking, he starts working out how long he's got left on his current contract before he can get an upgrade. He quickly realizes how pointless a thought that is. It's three or four months, he reckons, something like that, but the reality is that right now he's doubtful he'll even be alive when his contract's up.

The screen lights up and the phone turns on.

Shit.

Matt's amazed. He knows he can't have long, but a few seconds of charge is a few seconds longer than he'd ever expected. He puts the phone on the kitchen counter and watches it cycle through all its usual checks, ready for it to suddenly switch off and die as he thinks it inevitably will.

But it doesn't.

Barely any battery left. The faintest flicker of signal strength . . . it doesn't matter. He knows what he has to do.

His recent missed-call list is the same name again and again and again: *Jen, Jen, Jen, Jen, Jen, Jen, Jen, Jen* . . . He calls her back on their landline number before the inevitable deluge of voice mails and text messages can arrive.

The wait for connection is never ending. The impossibly empty-sounding silence can only be seconds but feels like hours. Then a click. Then it starts ringing.

Paul can tell from Matt's reaction that something's happening. "You got through?" he asks, as surprised as Matt. The world's so quiet that the noise from the phone seems to fill the entire house. Matt angrily gestures at Paul to shut up.

"Hello . . . ?"

"Jen? Jen, is that you?"

Nothing for a moment. "Matt? I thought you were—"

Dead.

He holds the phone in his hand and stares at its blank screen, every last residual scrap of charge now used up. He studies his reflection in the tempered glass, struggling to recognize the ragged man who's staring back at him, and struggling even more to absorb that he's just spoken to Jen. She's alive. She's at home. She sounds okay.

Unless she's one of them.

Paul clears his dry throat. He next speaks with even more uncertainty than usual. "So what are you going to do?"

"What do you think? I'm going home."

"When?"

"Soon as I can."

"It's got to be at least a hundred miles if we are near Lincoln. Might be even farther than that."

"So?"

"So you've seen what it's like out there. It's fucking madness. You'll never make it. It's suicide."

"Yeah, but Jen's there and she's alive. What else can I do? I have to try."

"When?"

"I need to rest first. Early tomorrow, I guess. Maybe later to-night."

"How?"

"However I can. I'll walk there if I have to."

33

The day melts away. Exhaustion overtakes nerves. Paul snatches a little fitful sleep on a king-size bed in an overfussy master bedroom. Matt dozes under a single bed in the kid's room next door, hidden by a duvet draped down over the edge. He feels safer underneath than on top, less exposed.

It's as if they're suffering from jet lag: everything's on a delay so that the afternoon feels like the evening and the evening feels like night. They both manage to get enough sleep to take the edge off their exhaustion, but anxiety prevents either of them from crashing out fully.

The power's still on here, but the lights in the house remain switched off. Being seen is too great a risk. As the night wears on, they hunker down together right in the middle of the building, all exits covered. Matt watches through a narrow gap in the curtains as shadows swallow up the land. He can see little, but he senses them out there. The Haters. Swarms of them everywhere. At the moment he thinks they're safe here, but he knows it won't take much to bring them sniffing around.

Every once in a while he hears a car outside. Now and then he gets to the window in time to see someone racing away through the inky blackness. He still thinks that's his best bet, getting hold of a vehicle somehow. No one's going to be able to tell which side I'm on when I'm driving past at a hundred miles an hour, he thinks.

He focuses on transport because now that he knows Jen's alive, staying here is most definitely no longer an option. He has to get home.

Nothing to be gained from putting it off.

He returns to the kitchen and gets ready to leave. The noise he's making soon attracts Paul. "You all right, Matt?" He sounds anxious.

Matt's busy and doesn't immediately reply.

"What are you doing, mate?"

"What's it look like I'm doing?"

Paul watches Matt collecting up the few sparse supplies hoarded from the construction site earlier. "It looks like you're going."

"Correct."

"But you can't."

"I already told you. I'm going home. Jen needs me."

"But you can't." Paul starts to stammer. "It's too dangerous out there. *Really* fucking dangerous. You're taking too much of a risk going at night."

"I think my chances might be better after dark. If they can't see me, how will they know I'm not like them?"

"You can't go." Paul takes him by surprise. "It's suicide."

"What's it to you?"

"I just don't think you should do it, that's all. We're a team, mate. We got through all this so far because we stuck together. You should stay here with me."

"A team? Seriously? You've never given a shit about anyone but yourself. You're a passenger. You use people."

"Come on . . . that's a bit harsh."

Matt's speechless. "Are you serious? Have you already forgotten what you did to Natalie? Or was that just her taking one for the team?"

"That was different."

"How?"

"She was injured. She wouldn't have made it. None of us would have made it if we'd tried to take her."

"She still had a chance. At least she did until you pulled the trigger."

"I had to make a choice. It was her or us."

"Whatever. Justify it to yourself however you want, it doesn't make any difference."

Paul's floundering, doing what he can not to lose his temper. "Just wait until morning, okay? Things might look different in the morning."

"Were you not listening to me? The dark's a help, not a hindrance."

Paul's on the back foot. "I just can't see any sense in you throwing your life away for the sake of waiting a few hours, that's all."

"And I don't see how things will be any different tomorrow."

Matt's found a small rucksack from somewhere. He starts filling it with the stuff he can't fit in his pockets.

"You can't take all that. What am I going to do?"

Matt looks at Paul in disbelief. "You'll have to find some more stuff, won't you. You'll have to do what I did and get off your backside and get on with it."

"Yeah, but it's not that easy, is it?"

"It's not that difficult either. Put it this way: it's no more difficult than anything else we've had to do since the world went to hell."

Job done. Bag packed. Ready to leave. Matt goes to swing it onto his back, but Paul gets up from his seat quickly and snatches it from him.

"What the hell are you doing?"

"You're not going anywhere." Paul throws the bag across the room and grabs the shotgun, which he's left propped up against the side of a kitchen unit. He aims it at Matt.

"Fuck you, Paul," Matt says, unfazed. "You really think that thing's going to work? It got soaked in the boat on the way over here, remember?"

"Yeah, so did your phone. That worked."

"My phone's got a waterproof cover. The shotgun hasn't."

"Are you prepared to take the risk?" A panicked glint is in Paul's eyes.

"So let me get this straight." Matt watches the other man's every movement in the low light. "You don't want me to go, so you're going to kill me if I try to leave? That's some seriously screwed-up logic."

Paul looks like he's ready to shoot, and Matt thinks he might just do it. "Try me," Paul goads. "Come on . . . fucking try me."

But Matt's already stared death in the face more than enough times in the last twenty-four hours. "Go on then, pull the trigger."

"What?"

"You heard me, big man. Pull the trigger. Let's get it over with. Let's see how far you get without me. You still don't get it, do you? We've got through this so far precisely because we *haven't* attacked first. To survive now we're going to need brains and stealth, and I don't reckon you've got either. Just look at you. First sign of a problem and you try and fight. You just don't think things through."

Paul shuffles and tightens his finger on the trigger, but he still doesn't fire. He swallows hard and adjusts his position again. "Don't make me kill you."

"And that's the most ironic thing of all, you won't kill me. You *can't*. You're no Hater. Neither of us are. You're full of shit. All noise and no action. Long as I've known you, you've always been the same. Come on, Paul, shoot me and see how long you make it on your own. I don't think it'll be long, if I'm honest. I reckon that a gunshot will be heard for miles around, and I know they might take their time finding out exactly where you are, but the Haters *will* find you. And next time I won't be here to bail you out."

"I don't need you to bail me out."

"Then bloody well shoot me!" Matt shouts.

The sound of his voice makes Paul uncomfortable. "Don't be stupid . . . and keep your frigging voice down."

"Maybe I'll keep shouting? Let them know where you're hiding?"

Paul's running out of options. He lowers the shotgun slightly and changes tack. "Okay, okay. I'll come with you."

Matt laughs. "No thanks. First off, I don't need you to come with me, and second, I don't want you to. You're a liability. I'll be better off on my own."

"We need each other, you said so yourself."

"You weren't listening. I said you need me. You, Paul O'Keefe, are the very last thing I need."

"You'll be dead in hours. . . ."

"Then I won't suffer long."

Ignoring the shotgun, Matt picks his rucksack off the floor and swings it onto his back. He zips up his jacket and makes for the door.

Paul blocks his way through. "I told you, you're staying here."

Matt's patience is wearing thin. "Get out of my way." He shoves Paul to one side. Paul comes back at him but Matt just sidesteps.

Furious, frustrated, and frightened, Paul panics and shoots.

The force of the shot and the recoil catch him off guard. Neither of them were expecting the gun to fire. He misses Matt and blasts a hole in the recently plastered kitchen wall. Rubble and dust rain down onto the marble-effect floor tiles.

"You dumb bastard. Which part of keeping quiet don't you understand? Have you got a death wish?"

Paul lifts the shotgun again. Matt senses the mounting desperation and fear that's rapidly consuming this obnoxious little prick. Matt knows time's running out. The shotgun blast might as well have been a starting pistol. The Haters will be here before long.

Paul feels it too. "Look, mate, I'm sorry. I didn't mean anything by it. I freaked out . . . it won't happen again."

"Damn right it won't."

He edges Matt toward the door. "We need to go. They'll be here soon. They'll fucking kill us."

Matt stops and stands his ground, then pushes Paul back into the kitchen. "I told you, you're not coming with me."

"But, Matt . . ."

"But nothing."

"Let me come. Please. I don't want to be on my own. . . ."

Matt shrugs him off, but Paul grabs his jacket and won't let go.

All out of options, Matt swings his fist and catches Paul on the side of the head, so hard that he feels several knuckles crack on impact. He shakes his hand, worried he might have broken a finger or two, never mind what he's done to Paul's face.

Doesn't matter. He's quiet at last. It's had the desired effect. Paul's out cold in a heap on the kitchen floor.

34

When Paul comes around minutes later, he can't move. His arms and legs are bound to a metal-framed kitchen chair with plastic cable ties, right in the middle of the show-home kitchen floor. The light's on. He tries to talk but his mouth is full of wadding, packed so tight it makes him gag. He tries to spit it out, but tape is over his mouth.

He's stuck.

Captive.

Can't move a fucking muscle.

Matt's at the window, gazing out into the darkness, waiting for the inevitable. He knows he doesn't have long now; they've been on their way here since the gunshot, and the light will just help them get here faster. He hears Paul struggling as he regains consciousness, and Matt turns around to face him. "Won't be long. I think they're close."

At the mention of the Haters, Paul struggles even more. He fights to escape his binds but he's not going anywhere. He rocks from side to side on the chair, then overbalances and tips over. He hits the deck hard and his head cracks against the floor. He screams out, his pain clearly audible despite the wadding.

"I've never much liked you, Paul." Matt's calm as anything. "You've always been out for yourself, and that's never sat well with me. You're a bully and a bullshitter. Worst of all, you're selfish. You always get what you want, and you don't care who gets hurt in the process. You're a nasty little man, Paul."

Paul looks up at him with tearstained eyes. He desperately tries to speak—straining to reason, to beg, to plead—but it just comes out as a muffled, unintelligible noise.

"What was it you said last night?" Matt knows full well there's no way Paul can answer. "Remember? When we were talking about getting the key to the outboard motor off Rod? You said it was him or us. You said something about how one of us would be dead by morning. What an arrogant, misguided idiot you are. Well, let's see which of us is still around when the sun comes up tomorrow, eh?"

He rips the tape from Paul's mouth. Paul spits out the wadding, then spits out venom. "You'll be dead too, you cunt!"

"Shh . . . ," Matt whispers. "Calm down. Seriously, the more noise you make, the quicker they're going to find you."

Paul's demeanor immediately changes. "I'm sorry, Matt. . . . I just got scared. It was just nerves talking, I swear. . . ."

Matt looks at him for a moment longer, then makes for the door.

"Matt, don't!" Paul screams at him. "Don't go. Please . . ."

"Good luck, Paul."

"Take me with you. Please, Matt. Please come back. . . ."

But Matt's not listening anymore. He's had enough. Paul keeps shouting, and Matt just keeps walking.

Fuck, but it's dangerous as hell out here tonight. Matt feels like he's walking blindfolded through a minefield. The Haters are everywhere. He can hear them . . . almost feel them. He waits near the edge of the housing development in the gap between two unfinished buildings and presses himself tight against a wall, blending into the darkness as they swarm ever closer. One of them almost brushes against him, too focused on getting to the useless fuckup still screaming blue murder in the lit-up house nearby to notice Matt hiding out here in the shadows. Matt holds his breath until he's sure the Hater is well out of earshot.

The way ahead looks clear now. As clear as it's going to be tonight.

The air is filled with Paul's strangled cries as the Haters kick down the door of the house, then pile inside and attack. The sound has little impact on Matt. He feels nothing for the man he left behind. He has more important things to think about.

He's going home to Jen.

Paul's on his own now.

Fuck him.